Also by Julia Thomas

The English Boys

D1007996

PENHALE
WOOD

A MYSTERY

JULIA
THOMAS

MIDNIGHT INK
WOODBURY, MINNESOTA
MIDNIGHT
INK

FIRST EDITION
First Printing, 2017

Book format by Bob Gaul
Cover design by Kevin R. Brown

Midnight Ink, an imprint of Llewellyn Worldwide Ltd.

Library of Congress Cataloging-in-Publication Data
Names: Thomas, Julia, author.
Title: Penhale wood / Julia Thomas.
Description: First edition. | Woodbury, Minnesota: Midnight Ink, [2017]
Identifiers: LCCN 2017006569 (print) | LCCN 2017010850 (ebook) | ISBN
   9780738752501 (alk. paper) | ISBN 9780738752846
Subjects: LCSH: Murder—Investigation—Fiction. | GSAFD: Mystery fiction.
Classification: LCC PS3620.H6286 P46 2017 (print) | LCC PS3620.H6286 (ebook)
   | DDC 813/.6—dc23
LC record available at https://lccn.loc.gov/2017006569

Midnight Ink
Llewellyn Worldwide Ltd.
2143 Wooddale Drive
Woodbury, MN 55125-2989
www.midnightinkbooks.com

Printed in the United States of America

To Caitlin and Heather, with love

ONE

DETECTIVE CHIEF INSPECTOR ROBERT McIntyre stared out the foggy window as his train pulled into Paddington Station, trying to ignore the bustle of passengers around him. It was a few days before Christmas, and he was looking forward to seeing his brother, although anything would have been a break after the brutal murder case he'd been working on for the past nine weeks. An attractive, thirty-eight-year-old mother of two who ran a local estate agent's had been found stabbed to death in her car in mid-October. The woman's ex-husband, who admitted to a bitter custody dispute involving their two children, had been the prime suspect due to lack of an alibi on the night in question. Nothing was found, however, and the case stalled for lack of evidence.

Just a week earlier, however, McIntyre had gotten a break when an anonymous tip led him to a construction worker in Falmouth who had bragged to a mate that he'd killed her because she hadn't responded to his advances. The man had followed her for some weeks trying to ask her out, and murdered her when she'd threatened to call the police. The case finally ended with the man's confession and an arrest, causing the entire Truro Police force to heave a collective sigh of relief. Murder in small communities could be devastating, particularly those that went unsolved, and McIntyre had seen his share of those. But for now, he could relax and think about the holiday and put it all behind him.

It had been a long, tiring journey. He sat up and rubbed his neck, which was stiff and sore from spending five hours in the same position. He'd been trying to concentrate on a book—Alison's book—though he'd been unable to get past the first chapter. They'd been living together for ten years when she left, right after completing her novel. In spite of the reviews, he found it inaccessible. She'd had a side to her that was cold and even calculating, he supposed, in order to walk out on him without a word.

Hours earlier, he'd stumbled onto her novel at a bookshop and purchased it on impulse, though most of the trip had been spent staring at her photograph on the inside back cover. In it, she wore an Aran Isles sweater, her blonde hair falling below her shoulders. The photo had been taken in Robin Hood's Bay two summers ago, outside her favorite hotel. He knew because he'd taken it himself. It had been a perfect week, walking along the sea and talking in pubs. He'd bought her a heather-colored shawl and she hadn't taken it off the entire time. Even afterwards, she'd worn it often, and when it wasn't being worn, she draped it over an armchair in their bedroom.

He should have known the relationship was over when she put it away. Two months after she moved out, he discovered the shawl in a bottom drawer. For a while, he draped it over the chair again, but it didn't feel right. He folded it again and put it away, hoping one day she would reappear and claim it.

This was the first time in a decade he'd spent a Christmas without her, and he missed her. He missed being part of a couple, as well. They had always looked forward to a week in London at the holidays, taking in a play and ice skating at Somerset House. He was focused on his work the rest of the year, and left her alone too much. Every few days, he unloaded his troubles with peers over a pint, and she amused herself decorating his house and setting up a study in which she could write. She soon joined a poetry club and was gone two nights a week, reading her verses aloud to small crowds. Before long, she took to inviting fledgling poets to their house for long nights of drinking wine and discussing Eliot and Yeats. He grew tired of the constant influx of visitors, not to mention the dent in his wine bill.

Eventually, Alison decided to write a novel. He'd encouraged her in the beginning, but after a few months, he began to have his doubts. It was a long and arduous process, and she withdrew from him more each passing day. One evening, when he'd come home after work, she was gone. He never knew what had gone wrong, and she didn't return his calls. A friend at the station located her a couple of weeks later at a rented house in Lincolnshire, but he didn't try to contact her. There was simply no point.

The train shuddered to a stop. McIntyre stood, anxious to stretch his limbs. He put the book on the seat and proceeded to tug on his coat. People jostled him as they moved forward to collect their belongings.

"Excuse me," a young woman said behind him, tapping him on the shoulder. Her cheeks were scarlet, as if she'd been standing outside in the cold rather than suffering piped-in heat in a stuffy railway car.

He glanced back, certain that he had not cut in front of her. "Yes?"

"Is that yours?" She gestured toward his vacant seat, at Alison's book.

McIntyre hesitated for a moment. "No. No, it isn't."

"But it's the Alison Kendall book."

"Someone must have left it," he said, shrugging.

She reached down and retrieved it from the seat. "I'll take it, then. I've been wanting to read it myself."

"By all means." He wouldn't be able to get through Christmas if he read it now. It was too depressing. He'd get another copy later, when the holidays were over.

Somewhere behind them a man coughed, and McIntyre realized they were holding up the line. He moved forward, ready to get his luggage and hoping to forget about Alison altogether. After pulling down his bag, he made his way down to Platform One and then to the crowded taxi rank. No one spoke. Most of his fellow passengers were reading the paper or sending texts, the queue moving forward every few moments when the taxi marshals settled another passenger in a cab. The cold air was bracing but welcome after the train, and McIntyre shuffled forward with the others, waiting his turn.

In previous years, they had arrived in London loaded with packages for his nieces and nephew. That was one of the things he'd loved about Alison: she had adopted his brother's family as her own. David had recently mentioned that she hadn't forgotten any of the children's birthdays during the past year, sending cards from Lincolnshire with packets of treats. He was pleased about that. She'd always seemed to love them as much as he had. Sighing, he allowed himself at last to be ushered into a cab.

"Harrods, please," he told the driver. "Basil Street entrance."

He hadn't been able to bring himself to buy presents alone in Truro, but neither would he show up at the door without gifts for the children. The driver plunged into the heavy afternoon traffic, going through Bayswater and then south on Kensington Church Road. Normally, McIntyre enjoyed looking at London decorated for Christmas, but today, the city seemed monochromatic and dull. The streets were wet from melted snow, which was still falling only to dissolve under the tires of passing vehicles. Corner shops were full of frantic people buying curries and tea, trying to get home before dark. The temperature had dropped below freezing, and he could almost see his breath inside the cab.

He suddenly longed for sunshine and warmth. It had been too long since he'd had a proper holiday. DS Dugan, who was not only a good colleague but something of a friend, had put a guide to Greece on his desk the week before, and in spite of himself, he'd read in detail about Athens and the islands. He'd never thought about going to Greece, but now the warm climate was appealing. He could listen to folk music and eat squid or octopus or whatever it was they ate. It wasn't perfect, but it might take his mind off Alison and murder.

He paid the fare and then brushed shoulders with a man leaving Harrods who wanted his cab, righting his wheeled case on the pavement before opening the door to the building. Inside, he checked his bag in the left luggage department and consulted the map. The enormity of the place was dispiriting after the long trip. He almost wished he'd stopped for a Scotch before tackling the job. After a few minutes of searching, he located the toy department on the fourth floor. Instead of jostling amongst the crowd to get to the miniature railways and dolls, he went to a counter and picked up two bears, one dressed as a gardener, the other as a sailor. Children loved bears, didn't they? Weren't his nephew and nieces' rooms littered with the things?

Suddenly, he felt someone watching him, and looked up. It was a small girl with dark hair and brown eyes, wearing a navy blue coat and a red-and-white knit cap. She looked familiar, though he wasn't certain why. His nieces and nephew were blond, almost Nordic-looking, like their mother. They were uncomplicated, happy-looking children, unlike this witch-eyed girl.

"What about these?" he asked, holding up the bears for her inspection. "Would they make a good present?"

The girl neither answered nor moved. A moment later, her mother took her by the shoulders, guiding her away. She was right. One couldn't be too careful these days. Children were stolen from more innocent places than this. Then it struck him why the girl looked so familiar. She bore a strong likeness to the young child who had been murdered near Truro last December.

It came flooding back to him, the sight of three-year-old Sophie Flynn lodged between a rotting log and the riverbank along Penhale Wood, her arms and legs bent at unnatural angles. Her dark, matted hair covered her face, an image that had nearly made him ill when he'd seen it. Her skin had a waxy, pallid cast after drifting in the Tresillian for more than twelve hours, and there had been bruises along her neck where it had been broken. It wasn't a typical case, and he hadn't seen anything like it before. He would never forget that image as long as he lived.

It had been a peculiar case, in fact. No clear motive for the killing had been discovered, and the suspect had vanished. He wondered what society was coming to. It seemed that so many more children were being abducted than he remembered in the early years of his career. Cases like that made him want to quit police work altogether. Sometimes he reminded himself it wasn't too late to take up another profession, such as a cook or a postman; anything that had nothing to do with the rising crime in Britain.

He looked down at the two bears in his hands, wondering if his nieces would like them. The twins, Annabelle and Lisette, were five years old, and his nephew, Peter, was seven. In the next year or two, they would be too old for things like stuffed bears, and then he would have to think of real presents.

As he stood there, exhausted, the little girl came back and stopped in front of him. She was a beautiful child, and her solemn eyes immobilized him. She pointed to the sailor bear, touching it with her finger. Then she turned and ran to find her mother.

"Thank you," he called after her, staring as her mother escorted her away.

He bought a cashmere scarf for his brother and a box of chocolates for David's wife, Susan. Laden with packages, including three ridiculously large bears, he collected his suitcase and made his way onto the street. In spite of the crowd, he managed to get a taxi right away.

"Holland Park," he told the driver.

The traffic was fierce. He sat back and pushed the packages onto the seat, staring at the buildings they passed. People struggled with bags and umbrellas along the wet pavement, darting in and out of shops. Obviously he wasn't the only one to leave Christmas to the last minute.

When the cab pulled up in front of his brother's house, he saw that none of the lights were on. With a sigh, he paid the driver and collected his things. Climbing the steps to the front door, he wondered why David hadn't rung. He stood there for a moment before remembering he had a key from last summer, when he'd stayed in the house while his brother's family were on holiday.

He unlocked the door and deposited everything on the floor, turning on a lamp. Pulling his mobile phone from his coat pocket, he cursed as he found it was set to silent. He must have turned off the ringer in the bookshop while trying to decide whether or not to buy Alison's book. He remembered thinking it must have been a dull day in Truro for Dugan to keep from pestering him all the way to London.

There were four new messages. He shrugged out of his coat, hung it over the back of a chair, and walked into the kitchen to put on a kettle for tea.

"Rob, is your phone off?" The first call was from David. "I can't believe it. Give me a ring."

He turned on the tap and filled the kettle, the fire from the stove giving the white, sterile room a sudden glow.

The next message was from Dugan. "Hey, boss. Miller took down a ten-man drug ring stationed in an old warehouse in Trennick Lane. Can you hear the celebrating? We're two for two. Now it *will* be a happy Christmas."

McIntyre rummaged in a cupboard for a mug as he listened to a protracted round of cheers from his team. He was too tired to care that he'd missed it.

The third call was David again. "Rob, Susan's mother has taken ill, so we've brought the kids to Gloucestershire to look after her for a couple of days. Hope to be back by Christmas. Stay out of the Laphroaig, old man. We'll party when I get back, all right? Ring me."

"Ah, Scotch," McIntyre said aloud, turning off the kettle. He held the phone to his ear as he went to examine the contents of his brother's drinks table.

The phone beeped through a fourth message. He stopped when he heard the sound of Alison's voice. "Hello, Rob. I know it's been a while since we've spoken, but I thought … Well, never mind. I'm off to London for a couple of days to take care of some business. I'll ring you soon."

In other words, he thought: don't phone her back. Frowning, he broke the seal on his brother's best bottle of Scotch and poured the drink. Then he sat on the long sofa without turning on a lamp. He would ring David later when he wasn't so tired.

He was suddenly irritable. He had no desire to do anything without Alison. If he'd gotten the message while still in Cornwall, he would have been able to go to work, but here, he was in no mood for solitary exploring. It wasn't worth it to make the five-hour trip back only to return a day or two later. No, it made sense to stay in London. Gifts had been purchased, friends and family were busy with holiday plans, and even a drug bust had been managed without him. He was left to sit in the house for a few days and wonder why Alison had rung. Had the holidays made her sentimental, or had she realized that she'd packed his favorite volume on steam engines among her books and just wanted to return it?

He took a drink and set the glass on a table, then kicked off his shoes and lay back on Susan's perfect sofa. He closed his eyes, wondering why Alison had called.

Sometime later, McIntyre awoke with a start in the darkened room, realizing there had been a knock at the door. Scratching the stubble on his chin, he looked at his watch. It was almost eleven. He stood, barking his shin on a table as he made his way to the door, hoping David and Susan had changed their minds and come home. He would welcome the chaos of children and family and friends coming and going. It would keep him occupied and get him through the holiday.

Instead, he opened the door to find a strange woman on the other side, holding a large duffel bag. She looked at him as though they knew one another.

"Inspector McIntyre, I need to speak to you."

He stood, blinking, trying to remember where he'd seen that face before.

TWO

McIntyre stared at the woman standing outside the door, wondering why she seemed familiar. She was at least thirty, from the lines in her face, yet she had a girlish appearance in her clothes and manner. She had striking looks: straight, dark hair, strong cheekbones, and dark, brooding eyes. Even in the dim light, he could see her scuffed boots and an ancient Gap sweatshirt hanging loosely under her coat, like hand-me-downs she hadn't quite grown into.

"I'm not sure if you remember me," she said. "I'm Iris Flynn."

He suddenly remembered. She was the woman whose daughter's face had haunted him for more than a year. No one should have to lose a child like that, and he still itched to find the killer. DCI Miller had talked with the Flynns the night Sophie had gone missing, but McIntyre was present early the following morning when the call had come in. He and Dugan had been among the first to view the crime scene, and he'd gone to the house to inform the Flynns that a body matching the description of their daughter had been discovered several miles away in the Tresillian River. He hated telling people that their loved ones had been found dead, to watch the look on their faces as they went from hope to fear to complete terror in a matter of seconds. Iris Flynn had been no exception.

The suspect was known to the victim's family. In fact, she'd been working as a nanny for them and living with them prior to the child's death. The woman had disappeared with the child a year ago, and in spite of a vigorous police investigation, no trace of her had ever been found. There were no photos of the suspect to give to the local newspapers, no eyewitnesses to the crime, and no known motives in the case. A jogger had chanced upon the child's body the following morning and called the police. The station was flooded with crank calls and false leads for weeks, none of which had led to a single clue to the suspect's whereabouts. In fact, there was some thought that the young woman had herself been a victim, but no information had come in to confirm or deny that theory. The only explanation they had, which came from Iris Flynn's five-year-old daughter who was present when her sister was taken, seemed to repudiate it.

McIntyre's gut feeling was that the suspect had killed the child and fled, but he'd never been able to prove it. After a few months, he'd shelved the case and moved on. Occasionally, the police failed to solve a crime. It was unfortunate, but they couldn't expect to have a perfect success rate. It wasn't possible. He would have preferred to forget the case, but here stood Iris Flynn on the doorstep of his brother's house as a reminder that the Devon and Cornwall Constabulary, himself in particular, had let down two grieving parents while a murderer went free.

"I remember, yes," he said. In spite of the fact that Iris was the last person he wanted to see, he realized he was leaving her standing in the cold night air. "Come in."

She walked through the doorway and he could see that she was shivering. He glanced around, but there was no cab on the street. She must have walked some distance to reach him, although he could not imagine why. Her hair was pulled back in a knot, and she wore no gloves on her raw, red hands.

"This way," he said, leading her to the kitchen. He glanced at the clock on the wall. It was past eleven. Ordinarily, it was too late for tea, but there was no doubt she needed to be warmed or she would develop hypothermia. He was sorry that David and Susan weren't home. He would have preferred to relinquish her into his sister-in-law's care, and then later he could have tried to find out what was going on. She put her bag on the floor next to the table and sat down in a chair.

"How did you find me?" he asked. "This isn't my house."

"Someone in your office gave me this address."

"Who?" he asked, irritated. Dugan wouldn't give out personal information to a complete stranger, he knew. He would stake his life on it, but others in his department might have thought it a good joke.

"Some woman," she said, looking up at him. Her gaze made him uncomfortable. "I told them I was your sister."

For once, he regretted being so private about his personal life. No one would have known he only had a brother.

"There are official channels one must go through if you're looking for information about the case, Mrs. Flynn," he said. "You would have been assisted by another qualified detective."

"I don't want another detective."

"I don't understand," he said, narrowing his eyes. "You were in Truro today?"

"No, I called from the airport when I arrived in London." She brushed her bangs back from her eyes. "I'm sorry. I'm exhausted. It's been a long trip. I borrowed money from my sister and flew all the way from Sydney to speak to you."

"What's happened?" he asked. "Do you have a lead on the case?"

"No," she answered, pulling her coat about her. "That's why I'm here. I'm going to help you find the woman who killed my daughter."

McIntyre took down two mugs and measured the tea. He gave her a sidelong glance and then opened a drawer for spoons. "Where are you staying?"

"Nowhere, yet."

"Do you have any family in London?"

"No."

"Any friends? Acquaintances?"

"No."

Of course she didn't. She and her Australian husband were transients. Nick Flynn had worked at various jobs, none of them for very long, and the previous year, the family had arrived in Truro from what he could only imagine was a rather unstable stay in the United States. McIntyre had been to their rented cottage once during the brief investigation, and had been staggered by the odd, camplike appearance of the place. None of the children had beds. They had shared a cramped room where two hammocks hung from the ceiling for the three-year-old and five-year-old, and the baby slept on a stack of quilts in the corner. There weren't many personal things, apart from a few items of clothing that were strewn about the floor.

It was rustic, but Iris Flynn hadn't been ashamed of it, as any other woman he'd known would have been. He'd gone back once only to find they had vacated the premises. The door of the cottage had stood open and almost nothing had been taken with them. They were peculiar people.

"Here," McIntyre said, handing her a mug of tea.

He waited for Iris to say something, but she drank the tea in silence. It seemed clear that her only plan had been to get to him. Now that she was here, he wondered what she expected him to do. He had a sudden fear that she would become weepy and maudlin. Although he was good at the technical part of his job, dealing with the public could be challenging, in spite of how well he understood their pain. But she didn't move, her eyes half closed in exhaustion.

"I don't think we should talk anymore tonight," he said.

"We haven't made a plan, yet."

"We'll talk about it tomorrow. You need some sleep."

McIntyre stood, trying to decide what to do. Her eyes had closed and yet she was still holding the hot mug, too tired to even drink from it. His choices were either take her to a hotel or put her in a cab, neither of which was a good idea. By the looks of her, she didn't have the money for a decent hotel, and if he put her in a cab, she probably wouldn't have any idea where she could find an affordable place to stay. He would have to let her spend the night. He couldn't very well put her in David and Susan's room, and he always stayed in the guest room, which left one of the children's bedrooms. He was too tall himself to fit into one of the children's beds. Lifting the mug out of her hands, he set it on the counter.

"You'd better stay here for the night."

He led her up the flight of stairs to the twins' domain, thinking it more comfortable than his nephew's. As soon as he opened the door, he realized his mistake. The pink and lavender room, decorated with Hello Kitty and shelves of dolls, would only remind her of the daughter she'd lost. Iris paused in the doorway, but it was too late. She looked around the room, the rucksack over her shoulder, her coat tucked under her arm.

"Get some rest," he said. "We'll talk in the morning."

She nodded. Even in the doorway, she looked lost in the maze of books and toys. She walked over to the nearest of the two beds and put her coat on the edge as he left the room.

McIntyre went to bed but couldn't sleep. He stared at the ceiling for a couple of hours before sitting up and looking at the clock. It was half past two. He thought of Alison's book and almost wished he hadn't left it behind. In the last months, she'd been secretive about the manuscript. He decided to buy it again, wondering if he would be able to concentrate on the story or if he would scan the pages for clues to their relationship.

He had driven Alison away. Though he'd read some of her writing, and even made the occasional encouraging remark, he hadn't believed that she would finish a book, let alone get it published. Or perhaps that had been his hope, for as long as she was struggling to write, she was dependent upon him. Now she'd found a way to make a life on her own. He shouldn't have taken her for granted. He should have gone after her instead of letting her go without a fight. That idea had never occurred to him before, and he wasn't certain what he would have done if it had.

The Flynn case was just one more failure. It was unsettling having the dead girl's mother on the other side of the house. Though he knew he should resist the impulse, he got out of bed and went to check on her. He walked down the dim but familiar hall to his nieces' room. The room was not as dark as the hallway, but it took a moment for his eyes to adjust. She was not in either bed. His heart skipped a beat, his professional side imagining all sorts of things, when suddenly he spotted her on the floor. It took a second to realize that she'd lain there on purpose, avoiding beds that were finer than any she had owned herself, or in which her children slept. Her coat was pulled over her body, and she was using the duffle as a pillow. He wondered if he should move her, and then decided it would mortify them both. He closed the door, more certain than ever that it would be difficult, if not impossible, to get to sleep.

At eight o'clock the next morning, he took out his mobile phone and called the station. Someone had some explaining to do.

"Miller," a rough, familiar voice answered. Ed Miller's office was next to his own, and although he didn't consider him a friend, they talked through cases together from time to time.

"It's McIntyre. I need a favor."

"What sort of favor?" Miller asked. At the moment, he was none too happy about manning the Detective Division during Christmas with a skeletal staff.

"Do you remember the Flynn case? The kidnapping last year?"

"Of course."

"Well, the mother has tracked me down," McIntyre said. "She showed up here in the middle of the night and wants me to solve the case. Some wanker gave her my brother's address in London."

"I don't see what I can do," Miller answered. "You'll have to get rid of her somehow."

"Could you just find out if anything new has made its way into the file?"

"Like I have the time."

"I need something to discourage her with when she wakes up."

"She slept over?" Miller asked, laughing.

"Just get the information, would you?"

"I'll look into it and ring you back."

McIntyre shoved his phone back in his pocket and waited. Suddenly, his brother's house felt stifling. He might have managed if he'd been alone, listening to music, watching sport on the television, perhaps cooking a meal on his own. He resented Iris Flynn ruining his holiday plans and making him think about a dead-end case when there was nothing he could do about it. He paced around the kitchen, and then grabbed his coat and went outside, lighting a cigarette as he waited. He'd tried to quit a couple of times but hadn't managed to do it so far. The air was cold, but there was no wind. He tossed the half-smoked cigarette down onto the snowy step and crushed it with his boot before going back inside.

His mobile finally rang. Instead of Miller, it was Dugan.

"Boss?" Alex said. "Can't believe you're working on holiday. I thought you were taking a few days off."

"I've got the Flynn woman here. She showed up at the door last night."

"There in London? I thought they left the country."

"Just tell me there's nothing new going on with the case," McIntyre said, interrupting him.

Dugan hesitated for a moment. "Well, you never spoke to the woman connected to the Jennings murder. Remember that one, sir? She phoned in a tip on the Flynn case three or four months ago."

"You mean—"

"Yes, sir. The psychic."

"Bloody hell."

"She helped crack that case. And she says she knows the location of the nanny, Karen Peterson."

"Knows the location, or thinks she knows the location?"

"Thinks she knows, I suppose. She's using her ESP or whatever, from what I understand."

"Christ." McIntyre balled his fist and stuck it into his pocket. "Is this psychic local?"

"No. She's in Hampshire."

He tried to collect himself. "Is that it?"

17

"Yes, sir. Do you want me to do anything? About the psychic, I mean?"

"No. I'll be in touch later."

He tossed his phone onto the counter. A psychic was not a legitimate lead, no matter what Dugan thought. He was skeptical about how helpful she'd actually been in the Jennings case, anyway. Trying to deal with her now would be a nuisance, and there was no way that she could shed any light on the situation after all this time.

What did the Flynn woman want anyway? he wondered. Cases never got solved a year later, not in these sort of circumstances. She was wasting his time. As far as he was concerned, she should turn around and go straight back where she came from.

He loaded his mug into the dishwasher and then went in to look at the news. It was the same old, rehashed stories: the economy was sluggish and people weren't spending as much on Christmas as usual; the price of petrol was rising; the Christmas tree in Trafalgar Square.

"Every year since 1947, a tree is donated to the people of London from Norway in gratitude for Britain's support in World War II," the presenter explained. "The tree is typically a Norwegian spruce, fifty to sixty years old. Carol singers come from every corner ... "

McIntyre switched off the television, looking around the room. If he'd been on his own, he would have headed to the nearest bookshop. Instead, he wandered into his brother's study and looked at the books before selecting one on German architecture. Sinking into a deep armchair, he flipped the pages, unable to concentrate on the book in his hands.

Sophie Flynn had been, by all accounts, a happy child, too young to know that her parents were little more than gypsies. She'd gone willingly with a trusted adult and, over the course of the next two hours, was brutally murdered and thrown into an icy river. She deserved justice, of that he was certain. He just didn't know how to get it. Iris Flynn was asking the impossible.

It was almost noon before she finally awoke. She came downstairs with her dark hair pulled back, wearing the same clothes as she had the day before. She wore no makeup on her pale face. He resisted the impulse to ask how she'd slept, offering her coffee instead.

"Would tea be all right?" she asked.

"Of course. I have hot water at the ready." McIntyre filled the teapot and then brought it back to the table and placed it in front of her. He watched as she picked it up and poured herself a cup.

"I've wasted half the day," she said.

"You were exhausted from the long flight." He watched as she lifted the cup to her lips. "So, you've come all the way from Australia? What about your husband?"

"He stayed behind to start a new job."

"And your girls?" If he remembered correctly, they would be two and six years old now, and both looked like the sister who had been killed. He could still picture their terrified faces when he'd arrived at their door.

"My sister is keeping them while I sort this out."

"I rang the station. There are no major leads."

"Something's happened," she argued. "They just don't know about it."

"It's hard to do this without my files, but the suspect's name is Karen Peterson, is that correct?"

"Yes."

"Tell me again how you met her, where you were; any details you can remember." He took a pen and notepad from his pocket, flipping the page to a clean sheet. He'd humor her for a few minutes. It was the least he could do after she'd come all that way.

19

"I've told you already."

"There's always something more," he insisted. "Try to remember. Was there anything unusual about her? Did she have any odd habits? Something you used to wonder about?"

Iris glanced up at him. "I used to wonder where she went when she left the house. We'd been neighbors in Oregon. Nick had always wanted to go there. He found us a small house not far from the coast, where he could spend time on the water. Karen lived next door. She didn't work. She lived with her boyfriend, but she said he was abusing her. Shouting at her, knocking her about. She would come over and drink tea and play with the girls. I was lonely, too, since Nick was gone a lot. Apart from getting groceries, I never saw her leave her house."

"What about after you brought her with you to Truro?"

"She started going out every day. She liked to take walks. I didn't care. I always thought she'd eventually go off on her own and meet somebody."

"How old is she?"

"Twenty-five, I think. She looked young."

"Did she have any odd quirks? Tapping her fingers, or anything?"

Iris paused, thinking. "Well, she was fussy. The carton of milk always had to be on the right side of the fridge, not the left. The cheeses were ordered by color: yellow to white." She looked at McIntyre. "I know it's strange, but honestly, it didn't matter to me. She was reliable and quiet. That's all we cared about."

"It sounds as if she had some OCD tendencies." He made a few notations. "Put us in her shoes for a minute. She's being bullied by a boyfriend in America. Did she ask to come to England with you, or was it your idea?"

"Nick got tired of Oregon, and I talked him into coming back to Cornwall to be near my brother," she replied. "I thought he could get Nick a job. Karen kept saying, 'I wish I could come with you.' I finally said, 'Why don't you?' She told me her boyfriend would never let her. But on the day we left, she showed up with a suitcase and said 'I'm coming with you.' She agreed to help with the girls. That's all I know."

"How long had you been in Oregon?"

"Around a year and a half, I think," she said.

"And before that?"

"South Africa."

"You get around."

"It's Nick. The world is too small for him."

McIntyre closed the notebook and walked over to the window. The glass was covered in frost, but he could make out the chairs in the garden, dusted with snow.

After a moment, she looked up at him and frowned. "Wait. You said there weren't any major leads."

"That's correct."

"What about minor leads?"

"Mrs. Flynn—"

"Inspector McIntyre, are there any minor leads?"

"There was something," he admitted. Mentally, he cursed Dugan for telling him about it. "But it won't come to anything."

"What is it?" She leaned forward as she spoke, and he knew it was wrong to encourage her.

"There was a psychic … "

She met his gaze. "A psychic."

"That's why I didn't want to tell you."

"And she thinks she knows where to find Karen?"

He sighed. "She helped crack a big case last year, but we believe it was just coincidence. Nevertheless, we'll still check into her story."

"Who's 'we'?"

"Well, I'll check into it when I get back."

"We have to find Karen, Inspector. And if it takes a psychic to do it, then fine." Iris stood. "I'll get my things."

"I beg your pardon?"

"Aren't we going back to Truro? I assume that's where this psychic is located."

"As a matter of fact, she's in Hampshire."

"Then we'd better go."

"Look, you can't just go barging into a case like this. Things have to be handled a certain way. I doubt she could tell us anything we can use, anyway."

"It can't hurt," she argued.

"Let's get lunch. We'll talk about it." McIntyre still felt he owed Iris Flynn something for coming all that way, but he knew the case was as cold and dead as her three-year-old daughter. As disturbed as he was about it, there was nothing he could do but give her a proper meal and then send her on her way.

She grabbed her coat and pulled it on. He couldn't help noticing her neck, which was bare. Reaching up to the hooks where his brother's family hung their coats, he pulled down a woolen scarf as bright as the panicles of a flame tree. He held it out to her, watching as she wound the bit of scarlet about her throat. She reminded him of a house sparrow, finding her way back to London after a brutal winter. It was painful to watch her suffering, and the sooner he could be shed of her, the better.

THREE

"Here's a place," Iris suggested. She struggled to keep up with McIntyre, who had decided to walk the streets of Holland Park to find a café rather than taking a taxi to a known destination. She was freezing in her corduroy coat, even with her hands thrust into the pockets and the collar turned up. As they walked, she tightened her grip on the mobile phone in her pocket. There were still a few days until Saturday, when she could phone Nick. When they were apart, which was often, she always rang him on Saturday. It was the one thing she could hold on to. He wasn't happy that she'd come back to fight a losing battle, but one of the good things about him was that he didn't hold a grudge. He'd had to let her go. She was falling apart right in front of his eyes. She'd been depressed for a solid year and had reached her breaking point.

"Not there," McIntyre answered. "It's wheat germ and yoghurt. Let's have real food."

"That is real food," she argued, though she would tolerate any-thing if it meant he would sit and listen to her and tell her what they should do next. As she suspected, he led her into a pub on the next street, ordering a pint almost as soon as they were in the door.

"What will you drink?" he asked.

"Water," she answered.

"She'll have water," McIntyre said to the man behind the bar, raising his brow as if she might infect him with her healthy habits. Iris unbuttoned her coat and studied him. Robert McIntyre wasn't a big man, but he was wiry and strong. He had a serious face, with short, sandy hair and blue-gray eyes that reminded her of the sea on a stormy day. When he concentrated, one eye squinted shut more than the other. There was a cleft in his chin that no doubt caught the eye of nearly every woman who laid eyes on him. Iris was not one of those women.

McIntyre lifted his glass as soon as it was set in front of him. He ordered steak and kidney pie for both of them, and Iris didn't bother to tell him she didn't eat meat. She would have to force herself to eat something to regain her equilibrium, anyway. The long trip had made her feel worse than she realized.

"You should ring this woman, the psychic," she said, taking off her coat and draping it on the back of her chair. "We could go to see her today."

"That's not how it works." McIntyre lifted his glass and then set it down again. "I need to do some research first. Besides, it's doubtful she can give us any real information. These tossers like to see their name in print, that's all."

"It's something," Iris insisted. "We have to talk to her."

"What more can you tell me about this Peterson woman?" he asked, changing the subject. "Do you know anything about her background? Had she ever mentioned suffering a miscarriage or losing a child?"

"No," Iris replied. "She never said anything like that. But we know she took Sophie. She's capable of hurting another child."

"I'm not a psychiatrist," he argued, "but I doubt she would. If she is responsible for your daughter's death, and that's still a big 'if,' she's had a near miss. It might have even been an accident and she got scared and ran. She's probably gone back to America and put it all behind her."

"As you say, you're not a psychiatrist," Iris said. "Maybe we should speak to one. Karen Peterson took my children from my home. She left Charlotte and India on a rocky riverbank at night and disappeared with Sophie. She killed her, Inspector. She killed my child and she's getting away with murder."

"You act as if the police haven't done anything," he said, bristling. "My men have sifted through hundreds of leads, the majority of them phoned in by cranks. Nothing has turned up. Nothing. And this clairvoyant business is just another way to get attention from the press."

"But you said she solved a crime last year."

"Coincidence. Every now and then, even a psychic gets lucky."

Their food arrived at the table, and McIntyre picked up his fork and began to eat. Iris waited, watching him. He wanted to get rid of her, she knew. It wasn't personal. No one would want to help her, not after all this time. In about fifteen minutes, he would pack her into a cab and send her back to Heathrow unless she could somehow convince him otherwise.

"Let me ask you something," she said. "What were you going to do today if I weren't here?"

"I don't see how that's relevant."

"You're sitting in an empty house, right? Are you waiting for someone?"

"It's my brother's house, but he and his family had to go out of town."

"So you have at least one whole day when you're not expected at the office, and your personal plans are on hold," she said. "What could be the harm of checking out one good lead?"

"It's not a good lead. It's a bad lead."

"I'll take anything I can get."

He sighed. "Mrs. Flynn—"

"I need to know Karen can't hurt anyone again. Please, make a few calls. If it doesn't work out, I'll leave."

He sighed and threw his napkin onto the table. "I'll see what I can find out."

Iris nodded, relieved. As he took out his mobile and stepped outside, she looked around the half empty pub. Couples sat across from each other, talking in low voices, having an ordinary meal on an ordinary day. She couldn't imagine what that felt like. Nothing about her life had been ordinary, and what little she'd managed to cobble together had fallen apart.

After several minutes, McIntyre returned to the table. "All right. Dugan's spoken to the psychic. She can see us first thing in the morning. If we hurry, we can make the 4:05. Does that suit?"

"Of course," she replied, relieved. "Thank you for arranging to see her."

"Let's go by the house and get our things. We'll have to spend the night."

McIntyre paid the bill and she followed him outside, where he hailed a cab. She wished Nick were there. He'd taken a job with his father's company, fishing up and down the eastern coastline of Australia if he managed to stick with it. She hoped he did. They certainly needed the money. For the last year, they had been staying with Nick's parents, and the Flynns had been neither sympathetic nor sentimental about Sophie, leaving Iris isolated in her grief. Death was a part of life, they reasoned. Lots of people lost children. Thoughts like that had driven Iris to the edge.

Sophie's death had changed her, and she would never be the same. Nick had withdrawn, shutting out his grief, and seemed all but oblivious to hers. He'd been different when they met, charming and witty with a sense of adventure that bordered on dangerous. Danger attracted Iris. She'd been twenty years old when she met him, visiting her older sister, Sarah, in Sydney. It was her first trip abroad, and everything from the long flight from London to the hot climate had appealed to her. The first time she saw the Flynns' property, she thought it wild and romantic. The house and outbuildings had seemed airy rather than sparse and desolate, as she felt about them now. It was no place to raise her children, and certainly no place to recover from the worst tragedy a mother could endure.

Charlotte was still suffering, too. Even at six, she was old enough to understand what had happened. She remembered going without meals, enduring frantic scenes in police stations, and crying herself to sleep at night, hungry and exhausted and afraid. She hadn't merely been inconvenienced for a few dreadful weeks. Little sisters could be taken, Charlotte knew: taken directly from your arms and murdered.

Of course, Iris felt guilty. She hadn't given any of them the attention they deserved. Her only hope was to find Sophie's killer. Until she did, she couldn't put any of their lives back together.

After getting their things, he locked the house and they took a taxi to Waterloo Station, where McIntyre purchased tickets and led her into a crowded waiting room. People perched on suitcases and sprawled in the narrow aisles. McIntyre was studying the sign announcing which train was boarding next, and Iris realized she didn't feel well. She felt her cheeks with the back of her fingers, knowing she was flushed not from the exertion but from fever. A kiosk, yards away, would take a few minutes to reach, but she had to have an aspirin.

"I'll be right back," she said.

"Wait!" he protested, but she didn't stop, stepping around piles of coats and limbs stretched out in every direction.

After standing in a long queue, she purchased the aspirin and hurried back to McIntyre. He stood at the crowded threshold of the departure gate with dozens of people trying to board their train, holding out a hand to her. She took hold of it and was pulled toward him against the tide of coat-clad bodies and fussing children. He didn't let go until they'd passed through to the railway platform and he'd guided her to the train.

"I thought I was going without you," he said as they found their seats.

Leaning back, she clutched the bottle of aspirin in her fist.

"Are you all right?" he asked, sitting down beside her.

"I have a headache," she said. "This will fix it."

Iris stood and went to the washroom and splashed water on her face before swallowing one of the tablets. She looked at herself in the mirror, almost not recognizing the woman she saw there. She would never be free of the guilt she felt over Sophie's death. It was her fault, and she had no one to blame but herself. She'd personally handed her daughter over to the woman who had killed her, and no amount of grieving would help her get over it.

Going back to her seat, she fixed her gaze on the passing countryside, trying to shut off her mind, if only for a short time. Nick didn't dwell on the past. He'd been just as crushed as she had, but eventually accepted the situation. He'd said they didn't really have any choice, but something in her constitution prevented her from moving on. She closed her eyes, concentrating on the train rumbling along the tracks.

Sometime later, she sat up and noticed McIntyre jotting notes on his pad. She raised a shoulder, trying to flex it without disturbing him, but he stopped writing when he noticed her movement.

"You're probably sick to death of traveling," he remarked.

"It doesn't matter," she said. "We'll be there soon."

Turning back to the window, she thought of Charlotte and India. They were staying with Sarah, who lived with her husband and their young son, Charlie, and daughter, Tess, in an enormous house with a sunny garden. It was the safest place she could have left them. She and Sarah hadn't been close, and Iris always thought her sister judged her for the directions her life had taken, but nevertheless, she trusted her. Now she'd compounded her humiliation by borrowing money she would never be able to repay for a plane ticket to London. Coming back to England had to mean more than just forcing McIntyre into a cursory reexamination of the case. If they didn't give up, they would find Karen. She knew it. And she wouldn't go back until they did.

Eventually, Portsmouth came into view. McIntyre got a taxi when they arrived and helped her inside. He was silent as they drove through the town, which suited her mood. They passed churches and old buildings, getting the occasional glimpse of the sea. The taxi rattled through the center of town until it came to a stop in Craneswater Gate, in front of a large Victorian house with two-story bow windows flanking the front door and mock Tudor beams stretching to the roof. A beribboned wreath hung on the door, reminding her of the season.

"What day is it?" she asked McIntyre as they got out of the cab and walked up to the door.

"The twenty-third," he answered.

It was impossible to judge his mood. He'd been less argumentative since they'd left London, but she didn't know him well enough to judge whether that was a good sign.

"Wait here. I'll make the arrangements."

Iris listened as he registered them into rooms. She insisted on paying for her own, but it would be her last night in a good hotel. She had to conserve what little money she had left to help in the search. Afterward, she followed him up a wide staircase to the second floor.

"This is your room," he said, unlocking one of the doors. "Do you want to rest a while?"

"I'll unpack," she answered.

After he closed her door, she threw her duffel on the ground and pulled out a notebook. She didn't care where she slept. Nothing mattered until she got what she'd come for. Since Sophie's death, she'd been making her own case notes, though she had already given McIntyre most of the pertinent facts. She'd created a timeline of the case, and every clue she could recall from the investigation. She went over the notes, line by line, trying to jog her memory.

The day Sophie had gone missing, Iris had bought her a pair of shoes. Red patent leather, Mary Jane straps. She'd spent nearly thirty pounds, an unimaginable amount of money. Iris had never spent more than five pounds on any article of shoes or clothing the girls owned since they were born. In fact, most everything they possessed had been trawled from charity sales. Nick did not have a job and, as usual, they didn't have that kind of money to throw around. Normally she wouldn't have even thought of buying a pair of expensive shoes, particularly for a child. The problem was that she'd been given a bag of clothes from a neighbor with four children that contained a pair of almost-new leather shoes just the right size for Charlotte. India was eighteen months old, too young to care, but Sophie had seen Charlotte's and wanted a pair, too.

Iris had taken one look at Sophie's runny nose dribbling down to her lip, which, before she could react, Sophie had wiped with her sleeve. Her children would have runny noses and old shoes most of their lives, and in a rare flash of anger, she couldn't stand it. She realized later that if she had sat down and let the moment pass, her daughter would be alive today. Alive, though wearing ugly, broken shoes. However, it was one of those days when she didn't sit down and let the moment pass. She'd given in, and as expected, Nick had been irritated.

"What's this, then?" Nick asked when she'd come home from her shopping. They had only been in Truro for a few weeks, renting a house from an old acquaintance of her brother's who had given them a break on rent. Iris was relieved to be back in England. She'd grown sick of America. She hated trying to figure out the money, and she wanted recognizable food and the familiar countryside of home. Not least, she'd held out hope that if they settled in Cornwall, Nick could find some kind of employment that he liked and they could have a semblance of stability.

"Just shoes. Sophie's had worn holes in them."

"For free, I hope." He lay on the sofa with his feet up, with his hands folded across his chest. Karen had returned from a walk and was sitting on the floor scribbling in a journal.

Iris hesitated, shifting India to her other hip while setting the bag on the table. She never lied to Nick about anything because he was usually even-tempered, even blasé, about most things, but mostly because she wasn't the sort of person to lie. "No, actually. This time they weren't."

He held up one of the shoes. "What's a new pair like this cost? Twelve, fifteen pounds?"

"Twenty-nine."

"Jesus, Iris! Fuck me!" he shouted. "D'ya think we're made of money?"

"Not in front of the children, please," she said, turning around to put India on the floor. Her cheeks burned. The truth was, she wasn't as concerned about the children hearing his occasional foul language as she was about Karen hearing it. That was the problem with having someone live in; they could be such a bloody nuisance.

Karen was still drawing in her journal, tracing leaves and jotting drawings of signs she'd seen in the village. She was an odd girl, quiet but self-contained, which Iris had appreciated, but she had no desire for her to witness what was certain to be a bitter argument.

Now that Nick had lost his temper, Karen suddenly stood, offering to take the girls for a walk. It was cold outside; not the best time to take three children under the age of six into the elements, but Iris had relented, if only for the opportunity to fight with Nick in peace. Karen pulled on her red coat with the toggle buttons and looped her handbag over her shoulder. Later, Iris would wonder why she hadn't thought it odd that Karen had taken her handbag to get a few minutes of fresh air, but she had other things on her mind. An hour after they'd departed, she and Nick began to wonder what was taking them so long. Iris hadn't been alarmed at first. Karen was a dawdler, anyway. Eventually, they decided to go after them.

"I'll walk down to the shops and you can go to the river," Nick had said. Unlike Cadgwith, where she'd grown up, Truro was an inland city situated on a river, and in fair weather, it was a good walk.

Iris nodded. Nick would probably find them, and he could be the one who gave Karen a tongue-lashing. She hated conflict in any form. That's what husbands were for, anyway. Though her nerves were thrumming, she hadn't begun to panic. A short jog toward the Truro River would get a rush of blood to her head and she would go back refreshed and put everyone to bed.

After walking for a while, Iris was sorry she hadn't brought a torch. Hands shoved deep into her pockets, she walked along the stony bank. It was difficult to hear anything above the rise and fall of the tide and the ever-present wind. She stopped next to a toy boat which lay upturned on the wet rocks. Of course Karen wouldn't have come here, she thought, especially in the dark. Iris shivered, hunching her shoulders against the cold and listening to the sound of her own ragged breathing. She hadn't gained any weight since India was born, but there was no doubt she was out of shape. She turned as she heard a sound.

"Karen?" she shouted in frustration, looking to the left and right, trying to locate the sound. After a moment, she thought she must have imagined it. She turned around to go back to the house. No one in their right mind would walk with children along the riverbank in the dark. Then she heard something again, and this time she knew it was Charlotte.

"Mummy!"

Iris ran forward in the dark, tripping on a rusty bicycle in the sand. A protruding piece of metal cut her ankle, making blood run into her shoe. She didn't stop. A few steps later, she found them, Charlotte and India, huddled in the cleft of a large rock. India was red-faced. Iris had no idea how long she had been squalling, her small body wracked with sobs. Iris scooped her up in one motion, holding her to her breast and wiping her nose with her bare hand.

"Where's Sophie?" she demanded.

"I don't know," Charlotte answered.

She was crying, too, but Iris was too desperate to deal with it. She grabbed Charlotte's arm and shook her in pure fear. They were standing less than twenty yards from the river. The thought of her three-year-old floating face down was more than she could bear.

"Where's Karen?"

Shivering, Charlotte pointed up the slope of the bank toward town as she tried to control her crying.

"Did she go alone?" Iris screamed.

"No. With Sophie."

Iris took a deep breath and let go of her daughter's arm. She pulled Charlotte closer and rocked India, who wouldn't stop screeching. "Sophie's not in the water?"

"No. Karen took her up there." The five-year-old lost her inner struggle and began to sob.

"Why?" Iris shouted. "I don't understand. Why did she leave you?"

Charlotte couldn't answer. Iris was beside herself, wondering if Sophie had been hurt. Why else would Karen have left the others in such a vulnerable position? Her heart was hammering so hard she thought it would burst.

She would never forget the last time she saw Sophie. She'd plopped a knit cap on her head none too gently, a misshapen one she'd made herself, and taken a final glance at the little red shoes. They were never recovered after Sophie's body was found. As far as Iris was concerned, Karen had kept them, a trophy from her grisly crime. If it was the last thing she would ever do, she would find Karen Peterson and make her pay for killing her daughter.

————

An hour later, there was a light rap on the door, and Iris closed her notebook and got up to answer it. McIntyre looked about at her hotel room, jingling his keys in his pocket, forcing her back into the present with a jolt.

"I hate to be shut up like this," he said. "Fancy a walk?"

Iris nodded. Some fresh air would do her good. "Only if we can go down to the docks."

"Where else can you go in Portsmouth?"

She pulled on her coat and followed him down the stairs and out to the street, where he debated for a moment before turning left.

"Are you from Cornwall originally?" he asked when they'd walked far enough to smell the sea air and hear the gulls shrieking by the bay.

"I grew up on the southern coast," she said. "What about you?"

"Truro. Never got away from it."

"I liked Truro, especially when I was growing up. We'd go there sometimes to visit the markets. I think it's what inspired my brother to move there and go into the antiques business."

"How long did you live there before … " He trailed off, unable to say the words.

"Before Sophie died? Only a few weeks."

They wandered down toward the quay, and Iris found herself staring at a tall, forbidding structure that looked like an alien craft. It seemed out of place among the boats and ships.

"What is it?" she asked.

"It's the Spinnaker Tower. You can go up in it and see for miles in every direction." He walked up to the ticket stand and plunked pound notes onto the counter.

"That's not necessary," she said.

"Might as well."

"We're not on holiday. You don't have to give me the obligatory tour."

"I've never been up here before," he said, ignoring the remark.

Iris sighed and followed him to the tower. No one else had bought tickets, leaving them to stand in empty silence in the glass-enclosed lift. It was several minutes before the doors shut and it began to move.

"Must not be the busy time of year," she said. She grasped the rail tightly as the lift rose.

"Don't look down," McIntyre cautioned. "Look over there, at the sea."

To her left, she watched the ferries gliding in and out of port like a choreographed ballet. Behind them, the city took on a glow as the sun began to set. Lights began to come on in the homes and businesses along the coast.

"That's the Isle of Wight," he said, pointing in the distance.

"Have you been there?" she asked.

"Our family spent a few summers there when I was a boy. We rented a cottage in Ventnor and I spent most of my time fishing on the beach." He sighed. "Of course, you love it at the time, and then hardly ever think of it again."

She tried to conjure happy childhood memories, but nothing particular came to mind.

Gripping the rail, she thought of her children. What memories would they have to look back on? Moving from place to place, country to country, without roots, without belongings, without friends? Didn't she owe them more than that? Perhaps they would be better off staying with Sarah in the end, Iris thought. She hadn't given them a real home. In fact, she hadn't even been able to keep them all alive.

Suddenly, it was hard to breathe. She put a hand on her chest, turning away from McIntyre so he wouldn't notice. It might have been jet lag, or it might be something more serious. She wasn't certain.

The pulleys gave a lurch, and Iris realized to her relief that they were finally going down.

"Where would you like to go now?" McIntyre asked when they stepped out of the lift.

Back in time, she almost answered.

When she didn't respond, he tightened his lips, as if to prevent his thoughts from escaping, and turned back in the direction of the hotel.

FOUR

THE FOLLOWING MORNING, ROB McIntyre found himself sitting uncomfortably close to Iris Flynn on a psychic's sofa. She wasn't his responsibility, he knew, but every time he thought of getting Miller or anyone else from the station to deal with her, he thought of how he would feel if he were in her shoes. He would tear buildings apart brick by brick and ruin other people's holidays and wreak complete and utter chaos if it had been his child who'd been killed. He couldn't blame her, but he resented the situation all the same.

He had been given the case because it was his turn. He had no special expertise with child abductions, but it was clear that Iris Flynn believed he was ordained to see the thing through. It wouldn't end well, of course. Sophie Flynn had already been murdered. People never realized how unsatisfying the end of an investigation was, even if it culminated in an arrest. There would still be questions, dozens of them, frustrating the families of the victims for the rest of their lives. What could they have done differently? Why hadn't someone phoned in a tip earlier? How much had the child

38

suffered? McIntyre knew that Iris Flynn, like all parents of murdered children, longed for justice and closure to the worst chapter of their lives. The trouble was, they never got it. Fifteen years from now, he thought, she'll still wake up some mornings having forgotten, and the memory will come flooding back, stabbing her heart as if it has all just happened again. There was no relief from the pain. He knew it. The police force knew it. Every parent who had gone through the pain knew it, too. Only the naïve, frustrated, newly bereaved parents believed they would live to see an end to their suffering. He dreaded the moment she would be through with him, for by then every scale would have fallen from her eyes and she would blame him. It was all there was left to do.

The fact that they were there to see a psychic was another source of irritation for McIntyre. He did not believe in telepathic ability, or extrasensory perception, or aliens, or anything that deviated from the normal life he'd lived for forty years. Every inspector in the country had heard of the Jennings case, though many remained skeptics, as did he. In that circumstance, a young girl of nine had been lured into an unmarked van parked near a playground and murdered. Searches to find the killer were fruitless. The parents had been frantic, coming to the police station on a daily basis. They talked to the newspapers, complicating the search and causing dozens of false leads to arise all around the country. Weeks after the crime, the psychic had come forward with information about the location of the child's body. When this was found to be correct, the woman herself was arrested, until it was proven that she'd contacted the police many times about various crimes over the past several years. With no motive and a good alibi, she'd been released from police custody. Nevertheless, McIntyre still found it suspicious.

He looked about the room and at the woman who owned it. Vanessa Foley looked far more ordinary that he expected. She wore a silk blouse over a pair of linen trousers and neat makeup on her aging face. Her only jewelry a pair of diamond earrings. Her home was cluttered with odd bits of china in Welsh dressers and there were Staffordshire dogs on the mantle. Not one pair, but three. McIntyre had half expected to see boiling potions of catmint and wolfberries or hex symbols on the walls; instead, it was an ordinary home.

Spread out on a table in front of them were newspaper articles with Sophie Flynn's photograph prominently displayed. He noticed that Iris refused to look at them, and he didn't blame her. He didn't want to look at them, either.

"Mrs. Foley," he said. "What can you tell us about the disappearance of Karen Peterson?"

"I've already given my statement to the police, Inspector McIntyre."

"I understand. However, I'm looking at the case again and would like to hear from you personally what information you might have."

"I contacted the department weeks ago. I'm afraid my information may no longer be relevant."

"We get a great number of tips. It's a large task to sift through them all."

"I'm sure it is." She lifted a pot from a silver tray. "Tea, anyone?"

"Yes, thank you," Iris said. He hadn't given her name to Mrs. Foley and was pleased that she hadn't volunteered it, either.

"Tea, Inspector?"

McIntyre nodded. It annoyed him how no one was ever forthcoming with information. It had to be coaxed from witnesses every time. He watched as the Foley woman made a show of pouring the tea and Iris poured milk into hers, stirring in two cubes of sugar. He drank his black, inwardly cursing.

"Please continue, Mrs. Foley," he said at last, trying to exercise some restraint. His blood pressure was rising by the moment.

"I saw her," she said, setting the teapot on the table next to a tray. "I saw the woman who killed the Flynns' child."

"What do you mean, you saw her? Through some sort of vision?" he asked, trying to expedite her story.

"In a manner of speaking."

"Can you be more specific?"

"Some people can look at an item belonging to the victim of a crime and conjure them up, or their location," Vanessa Foley said. "That is called 'remote viewing.'"

"What does that mean?" Iris asked.

"It means that one person, a 'receiver' if you will, sees through paranormal experience what the victim saw, after meditating on an article of clothing or some possession belonging to the victim. However, I receive information about an object or event through means other than the five senses."

"In other words," McIntyre said, "through psychic visions."

"That's correct. I saw an event that made me realize I was viewing the murderer of the Flynn child."

"Can you relate it to us, please?" he asked.

"There were two people in a small room," she said. "At least one was a woman. Brown hair, dark eyes. She was looking at newspaper articles about the murder."

"How do you know she was the murderer?"

"The woman was reveling in what she read in the newspaper. 'Listen to this,' she said. 'It's so grisly.' She was speaking as though she knew nothing of the case, but her tone, her appearance, everything about her convinced me that she was the murderer."

"How could you know a location to give to the police? Did you get a vision of her outside, standing near a sign that read 'Woolton' or some other location?"

"Cynicism is as unbecoming as sarcasm, Inspector," Mrs. Foley answered. "You don't have to believe me. I merely felt it my duty to tell what I know."

"I'm sorry. It's a little farfetched, I'm sure you realize."

She gave a thin smile. "I'm afraid I do. The woman was indoors at the time I saw her, but I have maps, Inspector McIntyre. I meditated over maps of the country and was drawn to the area where the murderer could be found."

"And what area is that?" he asked.

"She's in London. At least she was a while back. Near St. Pancras, I believe."

"Are there any distinguishing features you can give me?"

"Of the woman? Only that she wore dark colors. If you have a photograph of her, you should show it around there."

He didn't mention that there were not enough constables at his disposal to show a photograph around St. Pancras, even if he had a photograph of Karen Peterson to show.

"How old was she?"

"I would put her in her mid-twenties."

"How long was her hair? Could you describe it?"

"Not long. Below shoulder length, I'd say. Of course, that was weeks ago, as I said. You shouldn't have waited so long, Inspector."

"Would you be willing to let an officer make a sketch from your description?"

She paused for a moment. "I suppose that would be all right."

"Are you certain you can remember her face?" McIntyre couldn't get over how much Mrs. Foley reminded him of his mother, from her teapot to her pale linen suit. Nothing about her made him think her a psychic.

"Oh, I would know that face anywhere. I was tempted at the time to go to London and walk the streets until I found her myself. However, I'm not as young as I used to be. It's not an easy proposition for someone of my age to wander about London in this weather. I'm sure you understand." She put her teacup on the table and looked at Iris.

"And you can't describe the second person at all?" he asked.

"I'm afraid not. It's as if I'm seeing her through the second person's eyes. That person is invisible to me."

McIntyre cleared his throat. "I'll see if we can get a sketch artist out here today, if that's all right."

Mrs. Foley sat up straight in her wing chair and looked at Iris. "You're her. You're the mother."

"Yes," Iris admitted.

The woman leaned forward and grasped her by the wrists. Iris started, then sat still as a mummy, waiting for whatever would come.

"She's there," Vanessa Foley said after a moment. "She's still in London. There's a cat. Not an ordinary cat, either. Something most unusual."

Iris nodded. McIntyre couldn't tell if she believed that nonsense or not. At length, Mrs. Foley released her and Iris sat back in her chair.

"We should go," he said, disconcerted. He stood. "Thank you for your cooperation."

"You'll find her," the psychic said, looking at Iris.

"Someone will call 'round to make a sketch, and I'll have them fax it to me. Then Mrs. Flynn can determine if it's the same woman."

43

"It's the same woman, all right." The psychic pointed to the table. "She was looking directly at the child's photo in the newspaper."

"Thank you, Mrs. Foley." McIntyre guided Iris Flynn out of the door. She'd hardly spoken a word.

"It's not her," Iris said once they were outside and the door was shut behind her. "It's not Karen Peterson."

"Why not?" he asked, though he was inclined to agree.

"Karen's hair was short."

"Hair's the easiest thing in the world to change. You can grow it, dye it, or get a wig."

They fell silent as they walked. It was only a few short blocks to the hotel, and McIntyre had no desire to be shut up in a cab. The frigid air whipped about their coats as they fell in step with one another. He wasn't sure what to think of Vanessa Foley. The woman had seemed genuine enough, if one disregarded her claim to interpreting or channeling paranormal visions. He didn't believe in clairvoyance. It wasn't possible to see into the lives of others miles away, to know their thoughts and secret behaviors. If it were, he would be out of a job.

"Her description was too vague," Iris said, breaking into his thoughts.

"That's her stock-in-trade," McIntyre agreed. "Get too specific and you're easily proven wrong."

"I know you don't believe her, but the dark hair part is right, and the newspaper bit troubles me."

"I'm sorry you had to see it there."

"That's not what I mean. It's what she said about her gloating over the newspaper. It sounds like something Karen would have done."

"Look," McIntyre said, stopping in the middle of the empty street. "Not only was the description too vague, but it doesn't give us a single fact to go on. And St. Pancras! My God, if you can find a busier part of

London, I'd like to see it. There's so much foot traffic in that area. You have students at the University of London and the Royal Academy of Dramatic Art. You have the British Library, and in Bloomsbury, the British Museum. She had to name the most populous city in the nation. How could she be wrong? It's a needle in a haystack."

They resumed walking. McIntyre reached for his pack of cigarettes, debating whether to pull it out. He was desperate for a smoke.

"You smoke?" Iris asked, surprised.

"Occasionally." He paused. "Want one?"

She looked at the pack he held out to her and surprised him by taking the whole pack. Instead of taking one, she shoved it in her pocket.

"Oi!" he cried. "What are you doing?"

"You can have it back later. When we're done with this whole thing."

"Mrs. Flynn—"

"I'm sick of being called 'Mrs. Flynn.'"

"It wouldn't be right for me to use your Christian name. Not while we're, well, investigating the case."

"What is yours?"

"I beg your pardon?"

"What is your first name, again?"

"Rob."

"Well, then. I won't use yours, either." She stuffed her hands in her pockets. Her cheeks were crimson from the cold. "I have a question for you."

"What?"

"If you knew you didn't believe Mrs. Foley, why did you tell her you'd send someone there to make a sketch?"

"Would you really be able to sleep tonight if you didn't see it?"

"No," she admitted.

"I'll phone now." He took his mobile from his pocket and dialed a number. She waited, putting her hand over her left ear, which was beginning to sting from the cold. While he made the arrangements, she pulled the red scarf over her head to shield her ears from the wind.

"There," he said. "They're sending someone over this afternoon, and then they'll fax the image to us. By tonight, we should know if Vanessa Foley really saw a vision of Karen Peterson or not."

FIVE

"Miss Roy, would you take care of this index sheet, please?" Mrs. Harrington asked.

Madeline Roy looked up from the reference manual she was reading. Not only was the woman who had spoken to her older than she was, in the sense of having worked there for years, even decades, but also she was nearing retirement age. Her clawlike fingers had catalogued and indexed and shelved the many books in the Reading Room of the British Museum for a long time before Madeline was even born, though her stern, sharp eyes had lost nothing with age. A pair of spectacles hung about her neck and were rarely seen perched on her nose. Under her watchful eye and those of her predecessors, the Reading Room successfully met the needs of the British public, as it had since 1857. She had been one of several trusted employees who coordinated the library's move into the Great Court in 1997.

Mrs. Harrington suffered no illusion that the Reading Room ran smoothly due to the mere efficiency of its staff. Instead, she held that those who sat behind the round desk were divinely appointed for the immense responsibility. Madeline felt privileged to be among their number. She knew that she was on probation as a new employee, though her references were flawless. She took care to please her superior, even emulating her wardrobe of sensible, low-heeled shoes and skirts and jackets from Marks and Spencer. It wouldn't do to come into such a desired position and make the mistake of dressing or acting in an inappropriate fashion.

Taking the index sheet from the wrinkled, extended hand, Madeline nodded. As she walked around the desk, she noted that it was after five o'clock. Two of the other employees had begun to put away their work, but not Madeline. She worked late every day to ensure the good opinion of Mrs. Harrington. It was a task, she was certain, that could take some time.

Taking a seat near the older woman, she bent her head over her papers, checking her work on the computer and transferring information to the sheet she'd been provided. She checked her figures twice, taking a calculator from the well-organized desk drawer in front of her and then replacing it in the precise position she had found it. When she finished, she set the form on top of Mrs. Harrington's file and proceeded to pick up a handful of books. She knew, already, that one should never lift large stacks, which could potentially cause one of the books to fall. Four was the proper number of books to shelve at one time. Never five or six.

"Where did you say you come from, again?"

"Canada, ma'am. Vancouver."

"Lovely gardens there. My sister lived there for a time," Mrs. Harrington said. She looked up at the clock. "It's after five. Shouldn't you be leaving?"

"Oh, no. I don't like to leave work undone."

Her only answer was a curt nod, but it was acknowledgment enough. She hadn't expected to win them over right away. Carrying the books, Madeline pulled her cardigan closer about her, though the room was not cold. Two things buoyed her spirits, and both of them were found in the pocket of her woolen skirt: a postcard she'd purchased at the museum, and a print-out of an email she'd received only the day before. When she got home, she would prop the postcard on her small table and read the email again. Life, which had improved in the weeks since she'd taken this position, held even greater possibilities, and on these she reflected while returning Pepys' diary and a battered copy of Greek history to their respective shelves.

It was 5:40 before she left the desk. She put on her coat and strode out of the museum, heading through Russell Square to the Tube. Despite the cold, she took her time walking through the park, appreciating it in winter as much as in summer or spring, with its bare-limbed trees standing sentry over Bloomsbury like soldiers in front of Buckingham Palace. She made her way to the edge of the park and down Guilford Street. The crowd was thick with people in a rush to get home. On the Tube, she felt as though half of London was headed for Islington and her small flat in Hawes Street. She clung to a pole in an attempt to balance herself as the crowded car jerked forward. Some minutes later, she disembarked, made her way up the steps into frigid air, and stopped into the Tesco. It had been a long day, though the crowds in the Reading Room had been somewhat thinner in anticipation of Christmas. She wandered the aisles with a mild headache, thinking about what to make for supper, deciding upon fish. After making her purchase, she walked the last two streets home.

Inside her flat, she went into the minuscule kitchen and deposited the bags on the table. Laying her coat over a chair, she pulled her prizes from her pocket. The museum postcard featured a photo of the bronze figure of a seated cat from Saqqara, Egypt, Late Period. She propped it on the small table where she would later eat her meal, and she put the email next to the postcard.

Her mind full of unexpressed thoughts, Madeline began to peel potatoes, taking as little skin off as possible before dicing them and putting them in a boiling pot of water. She liked cooking, but one day, she hoped someone might prepare dinner for her. She imagined being served roast goose with baked apples and sage on antique Spode plates alongside Waterford goblets poured with water and wine. Silver forks and spoons, polished that very day, would grace the table. She sighed. It was a fantasy, but at least one could dream.

For now, Madeline took the sole filets from the bag and began to cut them with a knife. As she did, she heard a key in the lock and frowned. It would be Brooke Turner, who had been staying with her. Although Brooke had only been with her for a week, it seemed much longer. Madeline longed to ask if she'd found a flat of her own yet but held her tongue for now. The holidays weren't the best time to find a place to live. It would be ungracious to nag, and she held herself to a high standard these days.

"Come in," she called. She'd made enough food for two.

Brooke struggled through the door with a heavy-looking parcel. Although she was only in her twenties, Brooke attracted attention because she carried a cane. She'd told Madeline about an automobile accident at age fifteen that had damaged her spine. Surgery had corrected her condition enough that she was now able to walk, though with a noticeable limp. Her hair was straight and brown and she wore black horn-rimmed glasses. She came into the kitchen with her package and watched Madeline turn the filets in the pan.

"Don't peek," she ordered, setting the box aside. "It's a Christmas present."

"You shouldn't have," Madeline admonished, taking down two plates and bringing them to the table.

Inwardly, she cursed. Now she would have to get a gift for Brooke. She'd already told her that she would be out of town for two days after Christmas in order to take care of some personal business. The last thing she wanted to do was to entertain a virtual stranger for the holiday.

"Can I help?" Brooke asked, watching her progress in the kitchen.

"No, that's all right. I've got it." The space was too small to allow two cooks, particularly when one of them used a cane. "You can sit there, if you want, and talk to me."

"I was hoping to look at a flat today, but the agency was closed. They won't open again until next week. I hate to be the bearer of bad news, but there probably won't be anything in my price bracket until the New Year, perhaps even February."

"Don't worry about it," Madeline said, trying not to get angry. Her mother, who was acquainted with Brooke's, had extended the invitation before checking with her. She couldn't let them both down by trying to push Brooke out too soon. "Any luck on finding a job?"

"I'm not sure what I want to do," Brooke said.

"What have you done in the past?" Madeline asked.

"Nothing earth-shattering. I worked as a receptionist in a clinic once."

"There should be positions like that around."

"Hmm." Brooke got up from her chair and walked into the sitting room, where she began going through a stack of CDs in a bin. "Mind if I put on some music?"

Madeline didn't answer, stabbing the filets with a fork and turning them with more force than necessary. She'd been feeding the girl for a week without receiving so much as a pound for her expenses.

If she had to put up with it until February, she'd go mad. She took the boiled potatoes from the stove and mashed them. Her mother was a wonderful cook, and it had been her favorite thing as a girl to work with her in the kitchen. In fact, if she hadn't been working toward her own goals, she might have become a professional cook herself.

When the fish had been seared to perfection, she set a plate for Brooke on the table and stood in the doorway with her own.

"If you don't mind, I'll eat in the bedroom. I'm working on something at the moment."

"Go ahead," Brooke said, smiling. "I don't mind. I'll listen to music."

Madeline snatched her postcard and letter from the table and proceeded to the relative quiet of her bedroom. Through the wall, she could hear the music throbbing. She tried to ignore it, putting the plate on the desk, and then sat down, arranging the postcard in front of her. Once again, she unfolded the paper. As the potatoes cooled, she took a bite of the sole and began to read.

Dear Madeline,

Thank you so much for your email. It isn't often that I hear from someone who reminds me so much of myself. It would appear that we have a great deal in common, and your book sounds quite interesting. Have you finished it, or only just begun? I want to encourage you to continue. Don't let anyone or anything get in the way of your dreams. Your work at the Reading Room sounds interesting, too. It is one of my favorite places in London. I am pleased that you saw my advertisement about hiring an assistant and would be quite interested to meet you. I'm free on the day after

Christmas, if that is not terribly inconvenient, and we could discuss the feasibility of such an arrangement.

Best regards,
Alison Kendall

The day after tomorrow, she would be meeting Alison Kendall, whom she admired a great deal. Madeline owned three copies of her book: one to pour through daily for insights into her thought life, and two spare copies to be kept in pristine condition for the future. One day, a book of her own would be published, perhaps about the impact of modern novelists on English Literature. She hadn't begun it, but knew she would, and there was a mystery novel for which she was making notes. She was talented, of course; her letter to Alison had brought the intended result, and anyone with such talent would one day be noticed.

Pulling a file from her desk, she perused the articles she'd collected on Alison already. It was surprising how much one could learn about someone if diligent enough. Alison had been in a long-term relationship with a police detective and had left him after writing her book. Perhaps she'd come to distrust men as much as Madeline. They could be heavy-handed and cruel. No doubt a man who worked as a police detective would be even harder than most. One of the magazines had shown an inset photo of Alison's home in Lincolnshire, and she was pleased that she would get to see it for herself. She stared at Alison's photograph: at her blonde hair and pale eyebrows, the faint rose of her lips.

She knew from the articles she'd carefully researched that Alison had grown up in London and was fond of du Maurier; that she did not have children but devoted herself to her career; that her next mystery was to be set in a country house in Caithness; and that her desk was a century old and had belonged to her great-grandmother. One photograph showed her sitting in front of it in an upholstered chair of faded yellow, with a board for tacking up things overhead, where postcards of Vienna and snapshots from a recent trip to Scotland hung for inspiration. Much was made in the news of the fact that Alison had taken to writing in her late thirties, as well as the fact that she had studied at City University in London rather than a more prestigious school, and lacked the sort of training that should have been requisite for composing a novel of such high acclaim. Of course, Madeline was certain that in spite of the accolades and attention, Alison would not be spoiled by her success, and she hoped she would find in Madeline a willing and eager assistant who would do anything for her.

It was a relief, at last, to know exactly what one was meant to do in life. The Reading Room was a plum job, but one which could be abandoned if it worked out for her to work with Miss Kendall. The Mrs. Harringtons of the world had their place, but others would rise like stars in the evening sky to shine on everyone around them.

There was a knock on her bedroom door. "Shall I do the dishes?" Brooke asked.

"That's fine," Madeline answered, irritated at the intrusion.

"I can take your plate."

"I'm not finished. I'll bring it later, thank you."

"Let me know if you want to watch a video or something."

"Thank you."

The sound of Brooke's cane scraped against the wall as she left, probably leaving a mark as well. Thank goodness tomorrow was Christmas. She would board a train for Lincolnshire the day after, and if everything went as expected, she might just have a chance at a whole new life.

SIX

THAT EVENING, IRIS FLYNN sat across from DCI McIntyre in his office at the Truro Police Station in Tregolls Road. It was half past seven and there was a small holiday party going on in the lounge. The sound of noisemakers drifted down the corridor to McIntyre's office, where she sat holding the fax they had waited for all afternoon. Iris watched a young couple talking near the small, makeshift Christmas tree covered in blinking lights and tinsel that looked as if it had been purchased several decades ago. The spirit was lively, but the atmosphere, with its institutional gray walls and desks piled with paperwork, was not conducive to the mood. Christmas wasn't her favorite time of year, anyway. She preferred spring, when everything frozen and dead came back to life. If she'd been in Sydney, she would have been going with Nick's family to Christmas dinner. The Flynns went to the same restaurant every year, eating lobster and shrimp with heads bent over their plates in a ritual that never deviated. She was glad she wasn't there, but Nick would miss the family routine, she knew.

Men grieved differently than women. Of course, he would argue that brooding in front of the girls brought nothing but harm, but what else was a mother supposed to do after the death of her child? Eat lobster and chime in the New Year? Get pregnant again, as if another child could take Sophie's place? She looked at the sketch in her hands, suddenly angry. The clock on the wall ticked off the minutes, and she realized that McIntyre was waiting.

"Well, that's it, then," he said. "It's not her."

"No," she admitted. "There's some similarity, like the dark hair, but Karen's not as beautiful as this girl. She's, I don't know … ordinary. This girl could be a model or something."

McIntyre took the paper she held out and folded it twice. "I've had Dugan send it out to see if there's a match with any known criminal, but it seems unlikely."

"I'll wait."

"Nothing more will come in tonight. It's late. You should go to your brother's house. Do you want me to drive you?"

"I'll get a cab." She stood. "Are you going back to London?"

"No. I'd rather go home."

"I've ruined your Christmas."

"My brother and his wife have been taking care of her mother." He tapped the fax before leaning over to lay it on the desk. "You're not having much of a Christmas, either."

"Finding Karen is the only thing I care about." She looked up at him. "You do think she's alive, don't you?"

"It's possible. Of course, without physical evidence, we can't be certain."

"What will you do next?"

"I'm contacting the US State Department again to find out if she's gone back. What's the name of the town there where you lived when you met her?"

"Astoria. Near the Washington border."

"How long did she live there?"

"I have no idea," Iris answered. She was starting to realize that there were many things she hadn't known about Karen Peterson.

"Give me a description of what she was wearing when you last saw her."

"It's in the file. I've given it already."

"Tell me again," McIntyre insisted, narrowing his eyes. "You might remember something new this time."

"She was wearing a pleated skirt, plaid. The main color was blue. She wore tights and black boots."

"Black tights?"

"Yes. And a black jumper. Her coat was red, with those, what do you call them? Barrel toggles or something."

"Give me a physical description."

"Five foot two. Short dark hair, chopped to her chin. She has brown eyes and a full face."

"I know you're tired," he said, standing.

She felt a catch in her throat as she realized he was dismissing her.

"I've got your number," he said. "I'll ring if I get any information. I'm going to have Dugan take you home."

"Thank you."

He walked her out of the office and down the hall, raising his hand to get someone's attention. A man in his mid-twenties came over and nodded at his superior. He was tall, with short, disheveled hair and a pleasant face.

"Sergeant Dugan, this is Mrs. Flynn," McIntyre told him. "You'll be taking her to her brother's house."

"Yes, sir," Dugan answered. "I'll get my coat."

Ten minutes later, she was sitting in DS Dugan's car and they were driving across Truro. After giving him directions, Iris sat back, looking at the familiar buildings, relieved that the sergeant didn't attempt a conversation. Once again, she'd failed Sophie and was being sent away. It was humiliating. McIntyre had made her feel like a complete idiot, if not a terrible mother, with his air of artificial sympathy. She hated sympathy anyway, his or anyone else's. No one could possibly understand how she felt unless they'd lost a child themselves.

Silently, she watched street signs and finding the one she wanted, leaned forward.

"Pull over there, to the curb."

"Let me take you to the door, Mrs. Flynn. It's a cold night."

"No. This is fine."

When Dugan turned off the engine, he sprung out of the vehicle and went around to open the door. Iris got out of the car.

"Are you sure you're all right?" he asked.

"Yes, of course."

The new moon was shrouded behind the clouds, which were thick and heavy with the threat of more snow. A pool of light illuminated the street.

"Which door is it?" he asked.

"Just there." She pointed across the road. "Thanks for the lift."

Hefting her bag over her shoulder, she turned and began to walk away from the car, listening for the sound of Dugan's engine behind her. When she crossed the road, she looked back. He started the car but waited, watching her in the rear view mirror. No doubt he would have to report back to McIntyre that he'd discharged his duty as requested. She walked up to a door and knocked. When it opened, Dugan eased the car away from the curb.

The man on the other side looked at her with a raised brow. He was in his thirties, holding a martini in one hand. Another loud Christmas Eve celebration was going on inside. "Yes?" he asked, looking her over. "May I help you?"

"Sorry. Wrong house," she answered. She turned and began to walk in the other direction.

"Wait!" he called after her. "You're welcome to join us anyway, luv."

"No, thanks," she muttered under her breath. She walked faster, turning the corner and heading south. Of course, she hadn't given Dugan her brother's address. She didn't plan to see Jonathan at all. Crossing the street, she turned in the direction of a large gray building and stopped to read the sign. *Hostel, Vacancies,* it read.

Clutching her sole piece of baggage, Iris opened the door and stepped inside, rubbing the back of her neck. Exhaustion permeated every fiber of her being. There was nothing to do but try to come up with a new plan.

At least Truro was familiar territory. Cornwall was home. Her mother lived an hour away, though she had no desire to see her, either. Going to Australia had been not only the beginning of a new life, but an escape from a difficult past. Marriage had led to children and the opportunity to live in exotic places, though she hadn't had a moment to think of anything but nursing babies and following Nick around the world. She'd never had any idea of what she wanted her life to be, and all of that uncertainty had led to the death of her three-year-old child. Sometimes it felt as if her life had been hurtling toward one horrible incident, and there had never been anything she could have done to change it.

59

Inside the hostel, smells assaulted her: chlorine and steam from the showers, sweat and antiperspirant and powder and cologne. It combined to make a rank stench. Trying to ignore it, she went up to the desk where a young woman was talking on the phone. It was obviously a personal call and she turned away from Iris, as if to make her go away. Iris shifted her bag onto the other shoulder and waited.

"Can I help you?" the girl finally asked, cupping her hand over the receiver.

"I need a room for the night."

"Twenty-two pounds. Do you have any ID?"

"Yes," Iris answered, rummaging through her bag and holding it out for the woman to see.

The girl glanced at it and pulled a key from behind the desk. "Women's toilet and shower are that way. Towels on the rack."

"Thank you."

Iris went into the toilet, her duffle thrown over her shoulder. She turned the tap and looked in the mirror, letting the water run over her hands before washing her face. Stripping off her clothes, she turned on the shower. When the water was hot, she stepped in and lingered for a long time, not letting herself think about anything at all. Afterward, she toweled her hair and body and dressed in her spare clothes, a pair of jeans and another white tank. The wet ends of her hair were cold on her neck. She brushed her hair back and looked closer in the mirror. There were small red blotches along her throat. The stress was getting to her again.

When she was dressed, she went to the small room which she noted to her satisfaction was a single. She couldn't have stood the sight of anyone at the moment except, perhaps, for Nick. Plugging in her phone to recharge, she sat on the narrow bed and switched on a lamp. After a moment, she took out the handful of photos she carried with her and laid them out, looking at each one: Nick holding India, with Charlotte and Sophie hugging his knees; her three girls lined up in a row on an upturned crate, looking red-eyed and sleepy on a hot summer afternoon; and last, one of herself with Sophie a year ago, at the cottage in Truro. *It's an adventure,* she'd told the girls when they left America to come to England, but no one had believed it, least of all her. Charlotte had been old enough to go to school and had taken the move particularly hard.

Exhausted, Iris glanced at the clock on the table next to the bed. It was nearly nine o'clock, which meant almost six a.m. in Sydney. The girls would get another hour and a half of sleep before they would be woken and dressed for breakfast. In Sarah's perfect, ordered world, even Christmas Day would have a routine. Iris wasted no time being angry about it. She also knew that Sarah would have gotten presents, even at the last minute, for them to open. No doubt they would all read "From Mummy and Daddy" on the card.

Comforted, she lay back on the bed. There was nothing to do now but sleep. Tomorrow, she would figure out what to do next.

SEVEN

McIntyre's house seemed quieter than usual when he arrived home. He turned up the heater and hung his coat in the closet, tossing his bag on the floor next to the sofa. It was good to be home, with stacks of his favorite CDs in the cabinet and the shelves piled high with books. A framed photo of Alison on a table caught his attention. She hadn't phoned him again, not that he expected her to. He switched on the lamp before walking into the kitchen to put on the kettle and check the cupboards for chocolate biscuits.

He wandered into the living room and sat down in an old leather chair that had belonged to his father. Alison had hated it, and even he couldn't dispute the fact that it had seen better days, but it was both sentimental and comfortable, two reasons he stubbornly refused to get rid of it. The truth was, they hadn't argued often. Alison had suffered silently through his frustrations over various cases and whenever he was stymied by his Superintendent or a lawless murderer or both. He was an expert brooder, by any standard; the sort of police inspector that needed coffee, silence, Scotch, and more coffee to get through a difficult day.

That said, he had his good qualities. He was faithful, as he imagined anyone with Alison Kendall would be. She was beautiful, and if she had a tendency to be a little cold, he knew precisely the way to thaw her out. Since she'd been gone, he'd had to admit he missed the challenge of it. She was sensitive to slights, but forgiving when forgiveness was required, and particular about certain things that made no sense to him, although he felt that must be true of most women. Of course, he hadn't expected her to be perfect. He certainly wasn't. The house had gone to seed somewhat in her absence, and he'd resisted Dugan's prodding to have someone in to clean for him. If Alison decided to come back, he would, but in the meantime, he presumed he would eventually get around to it. Until then, the post was dropped on any spare surface he could find and there was a sink full of unwashed cups, and nothing had been sorted in ages.

After the long day spent with Iris Flynn, he wasn't in any mood to do it now, either. He turned on the television, looking for something interesting, although *Britain's Got Talent* or Graham Norton interested him not in the least. While waiting for the water to boil, he settled on a program about the fate of dormice after a twenty-year experiment to reintroduce the creature to the countryside. It didn't hold his attention. He turned off the television and went back into the kitchen, where he picked up the new copy of Alison's book that he'd purchased on the way home.

The kettle shrieked and he reached for a mug. He realized he didn't mind being home alone late on Christmas Eve instead of in London. He'd felt overloaded the last few weeks, and the prospect of a day or two with no expectations was appealing. He found the box of biscuits and poured a handful into a bowl, thinking in spite of himself of Iris Flynn. She was the grain of sand in the oyster, trying to force change through constant irritation. In spite of it, he felt sorry for her. She'd lost something that she could never get back. The realization stoked his feelings of guilt. He should have taken her to her brother's house himself, instead of making Dugan drive her.

A few other things bothered him, too. Why hadn't Nick Flynn come with his wife to England? The man had no business letting Iris badger the Truro Police or look for Karen Peterson alone. No wife of his would undertake something like that alone as long as he was alive to help. It was hard to understand the sort of relationship that allowed two people to spend so much time apart. He didn't know them, but from everything he'd seen, all the responsibilities of parenthood had been thrust on Iris. No wonder she'd responded to a friendship in a strange place, even allowing the woman to come to England with her. One couldn't live completely without support. Perhaps he'd been too hard on her. The question was, did Nick Flynn blame Iris as well?

The shrill ring of the telephone broke the silence. He picked up the receiver. "Yes?"

"It's me," Dugan said.

"What is it?" he asked. Something told him he wouldn't be getting his biscuits.

"Mrs. Flynn told me to go to Kenwyn Street."

"Kenwyn Street? I thought her brother lives out past Station Road."

"She went to a hostelry, boss. She gave me the wrong address, so I parked the car and followed her."

"Did she see you?"

"No, sir."

"The one on Castle Street?"

"That's the one."

"Thanks for calling. Are you headed home now?"

"Yes, unless you need me for something else."

"No, thanks," McIntyre answered. "Go home and have a good Christmas. At least one of us should."

He hung up the phone and turned toward the kitchen where the kettle was shrieking. Turning off the flame, he leaned against the counter, trying to decide what to do. What had happened between Jonathan Martin and Iris Flynn that kept her from seeking his help when she had nowhere else to go? No one deserved to spend Christmas alone in a hostel, especially not someone who'd gone through as much as Iris had.

Grumbling, McIntyre grabbed his coat and went out to start his car. He knocked snow off the bonnet while the car warmed up to a tolerable level. Of course, it was meddling to reappear in the woman's life once he'd sent her away, but even though he knew it, he couldn't stop himself.

"You've lost it," he muttered to himself as he pulled out onto the road and drove across the city. Few people were out that evening, mostly those who were braving Mass on the cold night. He knew the locations of each hostel in Truro, though he'd never been inside this particular one. After a couple of minutes, he found a place to park and went inside, kicking the snow from his boots.

"I need to see Iris Flynn," he told the girl behind the counter. She was young and wore too much makeup. She looked up from the small television she'd been watching and frowned.

"Guests aren't to be disturbed."

He drew his identification from his pocket and held it out to her. "DCI McIntyre. Where can I find her?"

"There's no trouble here," she told him.

"I didn't say there was."

After a moment, she puckered her lips and raised a shoulder. "She's in Room 113. Upstairs."

He looked in the direction of the staircase and nodded. It's not too late to back out, he thought, but instead of retreating to his car, he walked upstairs and knocked on the door of Room 113.

Iris opened it right away.

"What are you doing here?" she asked in surprise. The thin white shirt she wore left nothing to the imagination.

He fidgeted, embarrassed, and looked away. "I could ask you the same thing. Why didn't you go to your brother's?"

"What business is it of yours?" She had a stubborn streak, he'd noticed. She never answered any question she didn't wish to.

"Get your things. You're coming with me," he said.

"To London? Hampshire? The police station? Are you going to arrest me for renting a room?"

"We're going to my house. You can't stay here."

"I most certainly can. I paid for it."

"You know what I mean," he said. "You can't go to a hostel on Christmas Eve."

"I don't want to owe you anything. Everything you've done has already been off the clock."

"Forget the bloody clock."

"I had an idea," she said, "though you've probably already thought of it. CCTV. Have you looked at any footage yet?"

McIntyre crossed his arms. "That's not in police jurisdiction. The recordings kept by various civilian agencies. And in case you don't recall, we don't have a photo of the suspect."

"Can we look at them now?"

"In a major case, we can request them, but we don't generally. No one has time to go through all of those hours of footage."

Iris gave him a look. "I do."

He frowned, rubbing the top of his nose with two fingers. "I suppose you do," he said at last. "In fact, I can't think of anyone better. I'll set it up after Christmas, even get someone in to help you. Maybe Dugan and Ena Warren, one of our clerks."

His phone rang and he tugged it from the breast pocket of his shirt. "McIntyre."

"Inspector McIntyre, this is Alan Hogarth of the Identity and Passport Service. I'm contacting you about your request for information about a woman named Karen Peterson who entered the country in November of last year. I'm sorry to inform you that we have no record of any such person coming into Britain from the United States at that time, or at any time last year."

He looked at Iris Flynn, who was watching him intently. "Are you certain?"

"Quite sure, Inspector. No one by the name of Karen Peterson at all."

"Thank you for letting me know."

McIntyre ended the call and rubbed the space between his eyes. "What is it?" Iris asked. "Tell me."

"Did you ever look at Karen's passport or driver's license?"

Iris frowned. "I don't think so. Why?"

"According to Immigration, there's no such person as Karen Peterson," he said, shaking his head. "She's a ghost. Whoever came with you to England has completely disappeared."

EIGHT

IRIS AWOKE THE FOLLOWING morning disoriented. After waking several days in a row in different locations, she sat up in the bed, trying to remember where she was. The room was ordinary: a bed, table, wooden chair, a few pictures on the walls though nothing personal, a dresser and a lamp. Outside, a light rain pattered against the window, washing away the last of the snow.

Suddenly, she remembered. It had been good to be spared thought, to float without purpose even for a few seconds. She got out of bed and walked to the window, rubbing her arms as she stared up at the cloudy sky. McIntyre's house was old, having been built before the war. There were low ceilings and narrow passageways, the kind of house that had been conceived as a summer cottage with children running in and out, traipsing sand and mud from the garden. In previous winters, it had been boarded up when the family went back to London, forgotten along with the paint brushes and the wooden trug littered with decaying leaves.

The smell of toast made its way into the room, which she found she could not resist. As she perched on the edge of the bed to dress, she knew going downstairs meant facing Rob McIntyre.

He was something of a mystery. He didn't want to work on a case with no leads, and he didn't want to be drawn in by sympathy toward her, but he was drawn in just the same. It had been his decision to bring her here, and so she'd let him. Every twenty-two pounds she saved meant another day she could look for Sophie's killer. Her only other plan was to go to London and stand in the streets of St. Pancras until Karen, or the woman who called herself by that name, was found. However, she didn't expect McIntyre's good will to last for long, and then she would have to think of other options. She looked into the mirror, smoothed her hair with her hands, and went downstairs to the kitchen.

"Good morning," he said when she stepped into the room. He stood there, spoon poised in mid-air. "Are you hungry?"

"Yes," she answered. "Thanks."

She sat at the table, where two places had been laid and a teapot steamed. "May I pour?"

"Please."

She watched as he placed eggs and toast on a plate and came to sit beside her. There was barely room for two people. Ignoring his proximity, she filled his cup and then her own.

"What's the story with your brother?" McIntyre asked. "I know it's none of my business, but why couldn't you go there?"

Her eyes narrowed as she lifted the jug of milk. "I don't have to stay here, you know. If you have a problem, I'll go."

"I just wondered."

"We were closer when we were young. People change. Sometimes there are fundamental differences in their characters. You have a brother, don't you?"

"Yes. We usually get on, although sometimes things are a bit competitive between us. Do you have any other siblings?"

"Just my sister in Australia."

"And she's watching your children, instead of your husband." McIntyre made a wry face and shrugged. "I'm sorry. I'm used to interrogating people. My mum would thump me for that one."

"It's all right. Nick's decided to work for his father's company for a while," Iris said. "He'll be fishing for the next few months."

"Has he fished before?"

"When he was much younger."

"What did he do in the States?"

"What is this? Twenty questions?"

"More like conversation. Usually, when two people share a table, they discuss various subjects in an effort to stem the boredom."

"Are you often bored?" Iris asked.

"I suppose. Aren't you?"

"Never."

"What shall we do today?" McIntyre changed the subject.

Iris put down her fork. "What would you do if I wasn't here?"

"Probably read a book."

"Then, by all means, read it."

"What about you?"

"There's not much else we can do today." She avoided using the word *Christmas*. "Perhaps I'll read, too."

She stood and began to collect the dishes. It was therapeutic to set the kitchen in order. He had a dishwasher, but she didn't use it, preferring to take her time and wash each dish and cup by hand. Afterwards, she went into the front room and looked at the bookshelves.

McIntyre sat in a chair by the window, reading. Iris was relieved to see that he was so engrossed that he seemed to have forgotten she was there. It was difficult, always being the focus of attention. If things worked out, she would track down Karen and then go home to her family and live the quietest life possible, a life where none of them were ever written about in the newspaper again; a life where she had no reason to push and prod and argue to get something done.

The morning passed in silence. After a while, Iris went upstairs and looked at the books under the eaves in the guest room, selecting one, *Exotic Plants of India*, and thumbing through the pages. The book, all brown pages with a water-stained cover, was nearly as old as the house. It had a musty smell, but the drawings roused her interest: jacaranda, lepidagathis, matricaria, with their lush, intense colors and odd leaves and twisting vines. She lay on the unmade bed, pulling the quilt around her as she read.

McIntyre didn't disturb her with polite enquiries as to whether she would like a cup of tea or slice of cake or anything else. She refused to think of her children, for one day at least, or of her husband and the state of their marriage. This day, if nothing else, represented a Sabbath from pain and suffering. She concentrated on the book, letting the dullness and minutiae wash over her like a warm bath, and eventually fell asleep. Later, she heard McIntyre once again in the kitchen and disentangled herself from her perch to see if she could help.

"Fried eggs again, I'm afraid," he said when she went into the room. "The shops aren't open today."

"It's fine."

Without asking his opinion on the matter, she took an apron from a hook and tied it around her waist, wondering to whom it had belonged. It was patterned with muted violet flowers. Then she recalled a photograph of a blonde woman in the other room and wondered who it was. A girlfriend, perhaps, or an ex-wife. It certainly wasn't his sister. Men didn't keep photos of women unless they were in love with them.

McIntyre left the room for a couple of minutes and returned with one of his large, bulky cardigans. She raised a brow.

"Here," he said. "It's cold."

Iris accepted it without comment, putting it on over the apron. It hung well below her hips, but she didn't care. She turned the eggs, aware that he was watching her.

"What are you going to do when all of this is over?" he asked.

She shrugged. "I can't think past looking at the CCTV footage."

"Dugan's going to have it ready for you to look at in the morning."

"I'm glad we don't have to wait long."

After the meal, he made coffee, and then they sat in front of the fire, reading. The telephone rang once when his brother phoned, and she listened without interest to the muted conversation. The clock on the mantel ticked off minutes, and a light dusting of snow fell for an hour before it finally stopped. She must have fallen asleep, for some time later, she woke in an empty room. She turned off the lamp and crept up the stairs, trying not to wake him.

At seven the next morning, by unspoken agreement, Iris and McIntyre were dressed and ready to go. They ate unbuttered toast, standing in the kitchen. Afterward, she followed him to his car and got in, her duffel bag tossed on the floor in front of her.

He looked at the bag at her feet. "You packed?"

"I don't know what will happen today," she answered.

"No one does," he said, starting the car.

"Tell me what you know about CCTV," she said, changing the subject. "Was it a government plot to supervise the comings and goings of ordinary citizens?"

"That's a bit far-fetched, isn't it?" McIntyre asked, backing out into the street and putting the car in gear. "The truth is, it was actually developed in response to IRA bombings. Then it was used for surveillance in public areas, like banks. Now it's inexpensive enough to be used for home security."

"Does it really prevent crime?"

"Sometimes, but not as much as we'd like. The Home Office finds it more effective for deterring theft in car parks than crimes against people."

"There must be thousands of cameras in Britain."

"More than four million. In the bigger cities, like London, the average person is caught on tape more than three hundred times a day."

"Three hundred! Then we'll surely find Karen."

"It's doubtful. No one could possibly watch all of that footage. I've got special permission to view the Truro railway station for twenty-four hours after the she took Sophie. That's all we can do, for now."

"Why just one day?" she protested.

"The footage is monitored for illegal access by the Data Protection Act. For all they know, you could be seeking out Miss Peterson to commit a crime against her."

"That's ridiculous."

"You'd be surprised," he said. "Some people will do anything for revenge. We have to take what we can get."

He parked outside the station and led her inside to a large room. No one else was there. They walked over to a table and McIntyre turned on the computer. Iris unbuttoned her coat and sat down.

DS Dugan walked in. "Did you find it, sir?"

"Yeah, thanks," McIntyre answered. "What time did you come in?"

"About four a.m."

"Knock off at noon, then," McIntyre said. "And could you find Miss Warren for us?"

"How does this work?" Iris asked when Dugan had gone.

"There are four cameras at the Truro Station. These two computers are set up for you to view the twenty-four hours following her disappearance."

Iris looked at the screen, which read 6:15 p.m. in the corner. "I guess we'll start here."

"You're on your own. I have to get back to my office. Dugan will bring Ena around later. Give her a description of Miss Peterson, and then you'll at least have another set of eyes."

Iris looked up at him. "Thank you for arranging this. Even if it is just one place, for twenty-four hours."

"I'll send in coffee," he said.

"Pots of it, I hope," she murmured. "It looks like I won't be going anywhere for quite a while."

NINE

WITHIN THE FIRST THIRTY minutes of watching the CCTV footage, Iris got a cramp in her neck. She folded her coat to use as a cushion on the hard metal seat, but could never get comfortable. She moved the chair four times. Her right knee ached from the way her leg had been tucked under her in the cold room, and she was getting eye-strain from squinting so close to the screen. McIntyre had told her she could fast-forward, but she refused, fearing that she might miss the briefest glimpse of Karen. The police station coffee was too strong, but she drank it anyway, aware that it was her only hope of concentrating.

Around eight thirty, a pretty young woman with blonde hair, wearing a fleece jacket and jeans, opened the door of the screening room. Iris shut off the machine to look up at her.

"I'm Ena," she said, taking off her jacket and hanging it over a chair. "Inspector McIntyre sent me."

"I'm Iris. Thanks for coming. I appreciate having some help."

Ena pulled a chair up to the computer next to Iris's. "Let me get some coffee and then you can tell me what we're looking for."

"It's strong," Iris cautioned.

"It's practically lethal. That's what keeps us going around here."

"It's good of you to help."

"That's all right." Ena smiled. "I enjoy it. Gets me off the phones for a few hours."

"You might not be so glad after you've done this for a while."

"Rather like reality TV, isn't it?"

"Only more mind-numbing," said Iris. "I think I'll have to take back something I said to McIntyre. I've found I can become bored after all."

"Well, I won't be bored, especially if Alex Dugan comes in later."

"I've met him," Iris said.

"He's quite nice, he is." Ena put her cup on the table between them. "Do you want more coffee?"

"I'll get it later, thanks."

"So, what are we looking for?"

"A woman, twenty-something, with short, dark brown hair. She was wearing a blue plaid skirt with black tights and shoes, and a red coat with toggle buttons."

"Red coat. Great. That should stand out pretty easily."

"Well, you can't just look for the coat. I mean, she could have changed clothes. Look for the young woman, her dark eyes and round face."

"Striking or ordinary?"

"Ordinary. Makes it much harder."

Ena sat back in her chair and took a sip of coffee. "I need a few more details. Was her hair wavy or straight?"

"Straight," Iris said. "Here, start with this one."

They hit play on their computers, and Iris squinted in concentration.

"Ho," Ena murmured. "It was busy that day at the station, wasn't it?"

"That's what makes it hard."

Neither of them spoke for nearly half an hour. Even so, Iris appreciated the company. She paused the footage often, scrutinizing every person who walked through the railway station, aware that Ena did the same. As she concentrated, she wondered how she would feel if she actually saw Karen. No matter what McIntyre said, she knew Karen had killed her daughter, and she'd deliberately left Charlotte and India alone by the Truro River. But how had she taken Sophie miles away, to the Tresillian, without a car? And what did one do after taking a life? she wondered. Eat a meal in a café? Call someone they knew? But Karen didn't know anyone in Britain, and certainly not in Cornwall. She'd gone out on her own from time to time after they arrived, but no one had ever come to the house. There'd been no sign she'd been seeing anyone. Then again, perhaps Karen had met someone and simply not told her about it.

"What did you do for Christmas with your family so far away?" Ena asked, interrupting her thoughts.

"It was a quiet day. There wasn't much we could do about finding her on Christmas."

"You were with Inspector McIntyre?" Ena asked, glancing at her.

"Yes. He let me stay for the night."

"That's surprising."

"Why?"

"Well, he's not known for his soft heart, shall we say?"

Iris looked at her and raised a brow. "What is he known for?"

Ena settled back into her chair, her eyes never leaving the screen. "Oh, nothing bad, of course. He's good at his job. But terribly impersonal, if you ask me. Not the sort to get involved."

"Then he may not want that bit of information shared around," Iris said. "I shouldn't have said anything."

"Of course. I won't tell anyone." Ena leaned closer. "So, what's it like at his house? Is it a shrine to his ex?"

"What do you mean?"

"His ex-girlfriend. She left him last Christmas and—"

The door opened and McIntyre stuck his head into the room. "Ah, Miss Warren. Glad to see you made it. No sightings yet?"

"Not yet," Iris said, "but we've hardly started."

McIntyre drummed his fingers on the door frame for a moment. "Well, looks like you're set. I'll check in again later."

Ena stopped the playback and took a pair of black, rectangular-framed glasses from her bag before resuming it. After a few minutes, she sighed, lifting her mug. "This coffee is especially bad today."

"But it's hot."

"Scalding." Ena suddenly sat up in her chair. "Take a look at this. I think I saw something."

Iris paused her footage and turned to look at Ena's screen. "Back it up a minute."

Ena reversed the video and stopped it a few seconds later. "Look, here, on the corner of the screen. Check out that woman."

"She has a gray coat and a knit hat," Iris said. "I can't really see her hair."

"She has a round face, though, and looks young. Wait here. Let me find out if someone can enhance it for us." Ena got up and left the room, leaving Iris alone with her thoughts. If this was Karen, how had she managed to change clothes? She'd only had her small handbag with her when she left the house. There were so many unanswered questions.

Ena returned a few minutes later with a tall man in tow. "Iris, this is Dhanesh. He's one of our IT techs."

"Show me which image you're talking about," he said.

"This one," Ena answered, pointing out the figure on the screen. "The girl in the gray coat."

He sat down and worked on it for a few minutes before standing. "Okay, got it. I'll enlarge it and see if we can get a usable image for ID purposes. Maybe you'll get lucky."

Iris watched him leave the room and turned back to her screen. "I'm going to keep going. That might not be her."

"Good idea. I will, too."

"How long will this take?"

"He said maybe thirty minutes."

Iris rubbed her eyes for a second and took a last sip of her coffee. "Want a refill?"

"I'll get it," Ena answered.

"No, that's all right. I need to get up and move around for a couple of minutes." Iris took the cups and walked over to the coffeemaker. "It's getting low. I'll make a new pot."

A few minutes later, Iris brought two fresh cups to the table and sat down. She was going to get chest pains if she drank much more. Turning on the screen, she backed up the footage five seconds to get her bearings. "What were you saying earlier about a shrine?" she asked.

"Oh, I wondered if Inspector McIntyre wasn't harboring a certain amount of angst. Let's just say that after the breakup, he wasn't the same."

"What did she look like?" Iris asked.

"She was pretty, of course. Blonde, a natural beauty."

"I've seen a photo of her," Iris said. "At least, I assume it was of her."

"Aristocratic bearing?"

"Definitely."

"That's her." Ena gave a wry smile. "I mean, how many aristocratic blondes could he possibly know?"

Iris leaned toward the screen and watched the people as they came into view. Over the past hour, she'd seen innumerable travelers pulling tickets from their pockets and checking railway times, plugging coins into machines for stale coffee, and talking on mobiles. A few people in wheelchairs had made their way through the crowd; children wandered away from tired parents and threw tantrums. She watched as young couples clung to one another, and unruly youths with spiked hair and mismatched clothing walked around the station as if to intimidate everyone else by their attitude and appearance. And everywhere, there was luggage. It all began to run together.

"God, I wish we'd get a break," Ena muttered.

"I don't know if he brokers deals, as such."

"Are you religious?" she asked.

"I don't know. Are you?"

"Dunno, really," Ena said. "Sometimes. At Christmas or Easter. Whenever there's a major life problem. Not so much otherwise."

Iris's mind went back to the day when Sophie was born. Her middle child had to be coaxed into the business of living. She'd certainly prayed then. Iris hadn't felt maternal before the birth, merely irritable, unwieldy, and uncomfortable. For most of the last ten years, she had identified more with being a wife than a mother. Yet she had those moments of astonishment that something so small and perfectly formed could have come from her. One look at tiny, newborn fingers made the world seem a symphony, heard only by those who knew its secrets. There was then, she supposed, a God, but his ways were not her ways, his thoughts not her thoughts, and Iris Flynn wasn't fool enough to ever believe they could be.

"You may not know about the book," Ena said, interrupting her thoughts. She stood up to stretch.

"The book?"

"McIntyre's ex wrote a book."

"Really?" Iris asked, not particularly interested.

"I've read it myself. I would swear one of the characters is him."

"What sort of book is it?"

"It's a murder, obviously." Ena clapped her hand over her mouth as soon as she realized what she'd said. "I'm sorry. That was really insensitive."

Iris caught her breath and looked at Ena. "It's an ugly word to me now. I hardly thought about it at all until it became personal."

Before Ena could speak, the door opened and Dhanesh stepped inside, holding up a print-out of an image.

"I've enlarged the frame," he said, walking over to Iris. "It's grainy, but you can get a pretty good likeness."

She leapt from her chair and went over to inspect it, a knot growing in her throat. She blinked at the photo, frowning. "It's not her," she said, not certain whether to feel relieved or upset.

"Are you sure?" Ena asked.

"Yes." She handed back the image. "Thanks."

"I'll hold on to it, in case you want to see it again," he said.

"Oh, I forgot to stop the footage," Iris said, rushing back to her computer. She ran the video back a few seconds. "No wonder the police don't use these for every case. How could they ever get through all of these hours of nothing happening?"

"Would music help? Or Prozac?"

Iris gave a slight smile. "Maybe a combination. You know, I can't drink any more coffee. Is there something cold around here? Juice or anything?"

"There's a café next door. Shall I get something for you?"

"I think I'll do it. Do you want anything?"

"No thanks. I haven't drunk enough bad coffee yet."

Iris put on her coat and left the building. Walking to the café helped clear her head, trying not to be angry. Ena hadn't meant to mention murder. Most people couldn't comprehend what it meant to have a member of your own family snatched away and killed. It was too great a tragedy to imagine. She wouldn't have, either, if her own child hadn't been a victim. She thought of Sophie reaching up to take Karen's hand. What were her final words? Her final thoughts? Had she been crying, in pain or fear? Perhaps McIntyre was right. Perhaps her own motives weren't as altruistic as she'd thought, not that she would admit that to him. Her mission in life was to see Karen caught and punished.

When she returned, she went to the windows to see if they could be opened. Only one would budge, and in spite of the cold, she opened it a crack.

"Find anything?" she asked Ena, trying to smile.

"Not so far, I'm afraid," Ena replied.

She sat down in front of her monitor, sipping the juice, watching faces go by on the screen.

Two more hours passed slowly, and Iris realized that she hadn't expected it to be so difficult. She felt deflated and angry. If they could get a glimpse of Karen, it would vindicate her decision to come to England and force McIntyre to reopen the case. After four long hours of staring at the relentlessly boring footage, all she felt was guilt for wasting everyone's time.

McIntyre came into the room and looked up at the clock. "You need to knock off for a while," he said.

"I should stay."

"Your eyes are probably shot. You have to rest, if only for an hour." He turned to Ena. "You too, Miss Warren. Take your lunch break."

"Thank you, sir." She looked at Iris. "I'll be back in a bit."

Iris nodded. She pulled on her coat and walked over to stand by McIntyre at the door.

"You should get away from the station altogether," he said.

"I'm starting to think it's pointless," Iris answered. "Between the two of us, we've covered nearly eight hours of recordings, and there are so many more to go."

"Karen might not have gone through the Truro station at all. She might have gotten a ride up to St. Austell."

"That's the scary part. Or what if Ena saw her but didn't recognize her? Or even me? It's hard to tell what people look like when they're rushing about with their heads down."

"I know there's no derailing you about this, but I have to warn you. If you do spot the Peterson woman, the only chance we have is if she's heading toward a train going away from London. If she went to the city, it would be easier to find a needle in a haystack than to ever lay eyes on her again."

"If I didn't know better, I'd think you were trying to discourage me."

"Even I know that's not possible."

Iris nodded and left. She decided to take McIntyre's advice and get out of the building altogether. The air was still cold, but the wind had died down and she was glad to get away from the stale, airless room. She stopped in a restaurant and ordered a bowl of soup, though she was not really hungry.

Sitting in the nearly empty room, she thought about Karen. She'd been a quiet, solitary sort of person. If she'd met someone that night, who might it have been? Iris dismissed the idea of a man right away. Karen had been escaping a difficult relationship with her previous boyfriend. She'd seemed to want nothing to do with men at all. Her relationship with Iris was distant as well. There were local concerts and art shows, and Iris had often seen Karen sketching, so it made sense that the girl might have attended one of those on her nights off. At the time, Iris hadn't cared enough to ask. Now she regretted that more than anything.

She watched as people passed by outside, wondering if any of them had anything to hide. Trying to find a murderer made everyone seem suspicious. Losing Sophie had made the entire world a frightening place.

When she was finished, she put on her coat and went back to the station. It was as busy as usual. She didn't try to look for McIntyre, heading instead back to the computers. Ena was already sitting in her chair.

"How do you feel?" the clerk asked.

"Better, thanks," she answered. "How about you?"

"Ready to get back to it."

Less than four minutes after she'd returned to the hard metal chair and resumed the footage, she saw the figure of a woman in a red coat come into view. The coat was unbuttoned, and a blue plaid skirt was visible beneath it.

"Oh, God!" Iris shouted, her heart suddenly pounding.

Ena jumped from her chair. "Is it her?"

"It's her! Red coat, dark hair, dark tights and shoes."

"We'll get Dhanesh to enhance it, just to be sure."

"Get McIntyre!" Iris said. She ran the video back and replayed the few seconds where Karen shuffled through the station, holding a black scarf in her hands with a black handbag over one shoulder. Apart from the red coat and the distinctive blue skirt, nothing about her stood out.

Within minutes, McIntyre came running into the room, Ena at his heels.

"It's her!" Iris cried, pointing at the monitor. "Karen Peterson!"

He stared at the screen for a few moments and then cursed. "Bloody hell. She's taking the train to London."

Iris sank into her chair, struggling to stay composed. He'd said if Karen had headed into London, they had little to no chance of finding her. Now she would have to stand in the streets of St. Pancras for days or weeks on end watching for her.

"It's not hopeless," McIntyre said at last.

"What do you mean?"

"At least now we have an image of her. That's something. We'll circulate it around London. In a city with eight million people, someone has to have seen her."

TEN

THE STUMP, OR MORE correctly, the medieval parish church dedicated to St. Botolph, with its high and distinctive tower, could be seen from nearly any location in the port town of Boston in Lincolnshire. Alison Kendall found herself looking for it as a reference point whenever she came back home. Although she'd lived there for a year, she hadn't entirely settled in and familiarized herself with the city or adjusted to living on her own. Navigating her compact Lexus through the narrow roads, she drove along Norfolk Street amidst the late afternoon traffic.

Boston was historically interesting to her as the home of John Cotton, once vicar of St. Botolph's and a pilgrim father who organized the Massachusetts Bay Company and helped found the city of Boston, Massachusetts. It had also been the home of John Foxe, author of *Foxe's Book of Martyrs*. Her grandmother, who had been the only religious person in the family, had read it with much enthusiasm. Alison, as a young girl, had found the apocalyptic material both frightening and fascinating. After her grandmother's death, she'd inherited the book and sometimes leafed through the pages, looking with dread and lurid thrall upon accounts of martyrdom that had taken place during the reign of Mary Tudor. Although she was not religious herself, she looked upon her grandmother's legacy as one that could aid her writing career. All ghosts and memories of the past could be laid bare as fodder for stories and books to come. After completing her second book, she planned to write the story of an older, mystical woman and the influence she had upon her young granddaughter. That had been part of the reason she'd moved to Boston when she'd left Rob.

She was keen to get home. Her car sloshed along the wet streets in a long line of slow-moving vehicles. The heater in her car emitted sporadic bursts of hot air, which left the windshield foggy on the inside of the glass. She wiped at it with a gloved hand, trying to get a better view of the car in front of her. Rob would have chided her about that. He'd always insisted she do things the correct way. He was intractable, even in the small things. Cars were heated before driven, windscreens clear. She was far too impatient to care about details.

The winter, though hardly begun, had already palled. She longed for summer and the smell of newly mown hay, and for sandals and ice cold martinis. Summer brought the clamor of birds and frogs and crickets and people bustling about in the outdoors. Summer, too, meant the absence of dull hothouse strawberries in favor of piquant ones pulled fresh from the vine. She felt very spoiled with the earth's riches in summer, something that felt very remote in the dark days of December.

At last, she arrived home. She wrested her luggage from the passenger seat of the car and hurried to unlock the door. Even before she removed her coat, she went to the sideboard in the front room and poured herself a sherry. Prior to removing the woolen beret from her hair, she unbuttoned her coat and looked at herself in the mirror. Her cheeks were flushed with cold, her fingers pale and bloodless when she removed the gloves. Alison took another drink and decided to lay a fire.

Shivering, she struck a match and held it to the logs on the hearth. She hated laying a fire. One always ended up with sooty, ashen fingers. Rob had done it when they were together. Of course, it was natural that she should think of him sometimes; after all, they had been together for ten years. Nearly every thought she had was filtered through the lens of his opinions and beliefs. It was why she'd had to leave him, though she still had conflicting emotions on the subject. He was an ordinary man, which was a strike against him. Settled in his ways, another strike. He seemed to have idealized a version of their life together that was quite separate from the reality. She could see the day-to-day ugliness of life, of which there had been much. There had been frequent disagreements about whether to stay in or go out; she, being more social, preferred a large company with whom to spend the evening, while he would have spent every night at the pub with the same three mates if she'd let him. There was constant friction about their personal habits, as well. He was an early riser; she, late. Their dissimilar tastes in food and music and art and politics rendered them, in her view, incompatible. Rob, however, was never irked by their differences. He was never riled, and she sometimes wished he was. Yet she thought of him often, and missed him.

There were messages on the answering machine, and she kicked off her heels and went over to play them.

"Alison, it's Sheila. Roger and I are planning our usual Christmas fete and we'd love to have you join us."

Alison frowned at the machine. Sheila was an old friend from university days that she hadn't seen in at least five years. Her husband,

Roger, was a rather pedantic sort who'd enjoyed taking shots at Rob for the failures of the police in modern society. After one particularly miserable evening, she and Rob had decided not to see the couple anymore. Alison had never liked it when people looked down on Rob because of his work. She, of all people, knew how seriously he took his job. Of course, she wasn't surprised to hear from Sheila now. Since her book had received such acclaim, old friends and relatives had come out of the woodwork, wanting to see her and to renew their friendship. They also wanted to talk endlessly about the book. It was one thing to write books, but another thing completely to have to talk about them to people who hadn't bothered with her in years.

Another two calls were from acquaintances she'd made here in Boston. One was more promising; he taught at the college and wanted to get together for drinks. She would probably meet him, and if he was witty or interesting or accomplished in some way, he might be added to her group of intellectuals. She collected them the way other women collected handbags. The newest was always the most exciting.

"Alison, it's Madeline Roy." The final message caught her attention. "I got your email, and I'll be arriving tomorrow around noon. See you then."

Alison put down the glass and replayed the last message. Madeline had a low, pleasant voice. She wondered if the girl was pretty, too. The letter she'd sent was quite flattering, like most of the applications for the position, but Madeline's had a tone that was quite intriguing.

At the least, meeting her would make a nice diversion for a couple of days. At best, she might have found a personal assistant. Alison locked the door and went upstairs, looking at her favorite pieces as she walked by: a gilt mirror, a striking Louis XVI console, and an early work of one of the minor Impressionists. The house itself was not grand, but she expected large sums of money in the next year or two and the opportunity to find something better, perhaps a Grade II in the Lake District, something with presence, which would be a good showcase for the antiques she was collecting. One had to look the part, naturally; serious authors couldn't reside in seaside cottages in Cornwall with moth-eaten cardigans and a pack of dogs, even for a man like Rob McIntyre. Alison wanted to entertain in style, and for that life, she had to indulge in finer things. But for now, she contented herself with good sheets and good wine and a long, hot bath.

The next morning, she rose early, eager to meet Madeline and discover if her hope for a more than adequate assistant would be realized.

The house was spotless. Luisa, her maid, had come a couple of days earlier and seen to the scrubbing and dusting. Nonetheless, Alison ran her finger along the mantle just to be certain. Upstairs, fresh linens had been put on the beds, the bath had been readied with fresh towels, and cakes of gardenia-scented soap were placed in porcelain dishes. There were only three bedrooms, and she didn't often have guests, but if Madeline passed the interview process, she would consider letting her live in.

Alison had only advertised in the London papers, of course. Girls from Boston, even those who had gone to university, were not likely to be as sophisticated as London girls. Madeline, although Canadian, had not only gone to Oxford but was presently employed at the British Museum, a position most difficult to obtain. She wondered if Madeline would be willing to leave the British Museum and live in Boston. She hoped that Madeline would not be the tiresome sort, but didn't worry about that a great deal. The girl's letter had represented her quite well.

It was a fine day. The sun was out, mirroring her good mood, as she arrived at the station. And when passengers disembarked the train, Alison's concerns were allayed immediately by the sight of Miss Roy. She wasn't certain what she'd expected: most likely an average young woman who was attractive, alert, and reasonably well-dressed. As Madeline Roy stepped from the train, Alison realized she was all of those things and more, catching the eye of every man in the vicinity. She wore a black skirt with long, narrow boots and a bright crimson scarf over her woolen coat. Her dark hair was long and wavy, her eyes large brown, bottomless pools. Something stirred inside Allison, but shaking it off, she walked up to her and extended her hand.

"Miss Roy," she said, smiling.

"Miss Kendall, it's so good to meet you." Madeline took her hand with her own manicured one. "Thank you for having me."

"My pleasure," Alison said. An odd sensation crept up her arm, and she studied the young woman. Next to her tall, slender frame, Madeline was small, round, and feminine. She couldn't help noticing how Madeline's lips were touched with a shimmer of restrained lavender gloss. "How was your trip?" she asked.

"Very nice, thank you."

"Would you prefer to lunch at home or at one of the restaurants in town?"

"At home would be nice," Madeline said, surprising her. She'd expected the girl to answer "whatever you like," the bland, common response. Judging from her eyes, this girl was neither bland nor common.

"Home it is, then," Alison answered. "This way."

The conversation on the drive home was exciting, an actual discussion of books. Too often people passed themselves off as intellectuals or book lovers when they knew little of either world events or literature. She herself was a voracious reader and critic of literary works. Though she didn't reveal her motive, the conversation was no less than a litmus test of Madeline's suitability.

"What are your favorite types of books?" Alison asked.

"I primarily read the classics," Madeline said. "I'm particularly a fan of Henry James, although I have favorites among his works. I prefer *The Portrait of a Lady* to *Washington Square* or the others."

"Why is that?" Alison asked.

"It has such a darkness about it. Isabel Archer is torn between good and evil. The characters brood in the shadows, and I like brooding characters. James uses the same structure throughout his writing, and yet all of his stories have a vastly different feel."

Alison noticed that Miss Roy never said "I think." This girl knew what she thought and declared it with a spark, an almost physical quality to her self-confidence. While she drove, she noticed that Madeline's hands lay still in her lap while she spoke, showing her to have a more formal demeanor than many women she knew.

"And what sort of book are you writing yourself?" she asked, fidgeting with her scarf with her free hand.

"I'm making notes on a mystery," Madeline said. "Of course, it would be nothing like yours. Like 'Portrait,' you have a central character who longs to be free and yet is held to the standards a man has set for her. She's rejected every good man available and finds herself chained to the one man she could never really love. You were quite unique, using that framework with a character who becomes a murderer."

For a moment, Alison couldn't speak. No one else had made that connection.

"That sounds familiar," she said, as evenly as she could.

Madeline turned and smiled. "Oh, of course I'm familiar with your novel. Mine will take a different approach. But naturally I'm intrigued to learn more about the woman who accomplished such an interesting feat."

Alison hardly knew what to say. It had been an adjustment being thrust into the spotlight, one that she had long desired. Yet there was an odd rankling whenever she felt someone knew her too well. She wasn't quite sure what to think of the clever Miss Roy.

"Not to worry, Miss Kendall," Madeline continued. "No one can write like you."

"We're here," Alison announced, her cheeks growing pink. In an effort to disguise her emotions, she parked and got out of the car.

She regained her composure as she opened the front door, lit a fire, and led Madeline to the kitchen. The meal, a thick beef soup made by Luisa, was soon simmering on the Aga while she cut the bread. Alison worried that it wouldn't impress her guest, and then was piqued at herself for wishing to impress a mere hireling. If she were to employ Madeline Roy, the girl would type letters and sort files and reheat Luisa's soups. They would work in close quarters and eat ordinary meals. There was no reason to feel uncomfortable. This would only be the first of many such meals if she were to employ her.

They talked of art over soup, of London and favorite paintings. Alison noticed the details that Madeline added to each thought. Particulars interested them both, and it became obvious that someone of Madeline's interests and qualifications would make an excellent assistant. She was well-endowed with organizational skills and knowledge that would be most beneficial to someone in Alison's position.

"I have to tell you that it's possible I'll leave Lincolnshire within the year and look for a home elsewhere," Alison said. "Of course, there would likely be quarters for you in the house, if that would be acceptable to you."

"Where do you think you will move?" Madeline asked.

"I'm looking in the Lake District," Alison replied. "I'd prefer a fairly substantial property where I can write in peace."

"Won't that be wonderful? You'll be visited by the ghosts of Wordsworth and Coleridge."

Alison was once again pleased, both with the girl's knowledge of the Lake Poets and with her approval. Together, they sorted the kitchen after the meal and spent the afternoon looking through her study, which would have to be organized before a move could be made. That evening, Alison knew she would offer the position to Madeline, but an impulse kept her from offering it on the first day. Let us get through another day together first, she thought. It gave her the upper hand.

It was getting late. She would soon have to drive her guest to the hotel where she was staying.

"I'm having a drink," she said suddenly. "Would you like one?"

"Love one," Madeline replied.

Alison felt, rather than saw, Madeline behind her as she walked to the sideboard and busied herself pouring drinks. "Gin or Scotch?" she asked.

"Scotch."

Alison poured the drinks and then looked up into dark, unreadable eyes. Their hands brushed as she passed Madeline the glass, and she felt her heart begin to race. Was it her imagination or had her life just taken a completely unexpected turn? And what would Rob think? She couldn't help but wonder.

ELEVEN

"THE SUPER WANTS TO see you, sir," Dugan said the next morning as he came around the corner.

McIntyre could tell it took some effort for Dugan not to raise an eyebrow. He nodded, and then walked with some annoyance down the corridor and into the office of his superintendent, Patrick Quinn. Quinn was the third superintendent he'd worked for in his tenure for the police and by far the most demanding. He wanted cases solved yesterday. He expected the paperwork completed and on his desk before the tankards were emptied in the pubs. The man had little response when something was done well, and never in his four years in Truro had he given unequivocal praise to anyone. No one liked being called into his office, for it meant ten times out of ten that some fault was being brought to one's attention when one's time was best spent pursuing every possible lead. Morale flagged at times, particularly among the junior staff, and it was the responsibility of men like McIntyre and Miller and the other DCIs on the team to encourage their sergeants and DIs while taking every hit the superintendent could lash out.

He knew, too, that his mind wasn't on the rest of his caseload at the moment. Iris Flynn had seen to that, but he was distracted for other reasons, too. Alison, of course, was one. After meeting a woman like Iris, he found it ironic that he'd been so eager to change Alison, a woman whose main fault was that she was focused on herself and her writing when he wanted children and marriage. There, he thought, I've admitted it; I want a family just like my brother's, and Alison doesn't. Now Iris had taken over his life like a typhoon, unsettling everything in her path. In spite of the fact that they had little to go on, nothing would stop her from trying to find Karen Peterson, if she had to knock on every door in Britain.

Quinn sat at his desk among tall stacks of files, four cups of old coffee, and an assortment of gadgets ranging from compasses to small retractable telescopes. It was impossible to tell the importance of his position from his desk. While McIntyre's office was not entirely tidy, it was worthy of a prize compared to Quinn's. The superintendent's office needed to be gutted and reassembled by someone with a keen sense of organization. It wasn't likely to happen any time soon, however. Quinn was in his mid-fifties, with a graying beard and thinning hair. His rumpled suits indicated that he spent too much time in his office each day trying to run a police station and stop crime in this small corner of Cornwall, a task that even McIntyre had to appreciate.

"I've had a call from the Home Office," Quinn said the moment he was at the door.

McIntyre entered and stood behind the chair, waiting to be waved into it by his supervisor. He didn't have to wait long. "You wanted to see me, sir?"

"I understand you've opened the Flynn case again. Has some new information come in that I wasn't aware of?"

McIntyre cleared his throat. "I've been investigating a new tip. After reviewing CCTV footage from the railway station last year, we've identified the prime suspect."

"Who authorized the request of the footage?"

"I did."

"On what new information did you base that request? In case you didn't know, there's a staff shortage at the moment. We don't have the ability to waste valuable hours in front of screens on the small chance you'll see a suspect."

"I utilized volunteers for the effort, and we got lucky," McIntyre answered, refusing to mention Iris by name.

"Trained volunteers, I trust." Quinn poured coffee from one of the old cups into another in an effort, McIntyre hoped, to dispose of them all. "Not just ordinary people off the street."

"Of course." He wondered if his boss would ever come to the point.

"Immigration says that you've been looking for a woman named Karen Peterson, and that according to their records, no such person was found to have come into the country during the past year."

"That's correct."

"What do you know about the suspect?"

"Not much more than we knew before. She lived with the victim's family and was asked by them to take the children for a walk. Two of them, a toddler and a five-year-old, were found by their mother on the bank of the Truro River. The three-year-old's body was found washed up a few miles away on the banks of the Tresillian. Until we got positive identification of the suspect, we didn't know whether she herself had been a victim that night. In my book, she's gone from a person of interest to prime suspect."

"Who made the identification?"

"The child's mother. She's recently back in the country after staying with family in Australia, and she's the only person who can identify the woman we're looking for."

"Well, if you have a positive ID, that's something, but make sure you don't waste time chasing your tail if nothing turns up. There's plenty of other cases that need your attention."

"Yes, sir," he said, standing.

"And I want a report as soon as you have any concrete information."

"Of course." McIntyre turned and walked through the open door. Bloody bureaucrats, he thought. Always wasting time when there was work to be done. They wanted nothing more than to impede an investigation by their unwanted interference. One thing he knew for certain, he wouldn't advance much farther in the ranks, if at all. He had no desire himself to run the operations of a police station, or to stick his nose into the business of every detective on the force.

He headed to his office. Iris had her faults, he mused, but he knew she loved her children, having seen the photographs she put on the bedside table in his guest room. He wondered how her two surviving daughters were managing without her. She never mentioned them, as if it would break down her last ounce of reserve. On the other hand, perhaps being separated from them for now was the only way she could get through the day.

As he rounded the corner, he saw Iris waiting outside his door. "How did you get here?" he asked.

"There's nothing to do at the house, so I took a cab," she replied. "We have to do something. Karen was on that video. She killed Sophie and then got on a train like nothing even happened."

"And went to London, of all places." He began to walk toward the stairs.

Iris followed after him. "We have to find her. I don't care where she went."

"We'll find her," he said, though privately he doubted it. Too much time had passed since Sophie's death.

"But London is a gateway to Europe or Africa. She could have gone anywhere."

"We have the photo now," he said. "That's something." His mobile rang and he took it out of his pocket. "Hold on," he said, catching her eye. "Would you wait a second?"

He stepped a few yards away to answer it.

"Rob, it's Alison," came the voice on the other end of the line. His heart began to thump just hearing her voice.

"Alison? How are you?"

"I'm fine. I wanted to talk to you, that's all."

"I'm up to my neck in work at the moment," he said. "But if you give me a few minutes, I can ring you back."

"All right."

He shoved the mobile in his pocket and looked at Iris. "Dugan will have to drive you back to the house. The superintendent is on my case and I don't have time to come up with things for you to do."

"Could I take your car?" Iris asked suddenly. "There's someone I need to talk to, myself."

"Well—"

"Please. I'll pick you up later."

His first instinct was to tell her no, but one look at Iris and he could see she'd been told no all of her life. Her child was gone, but it wasn't her fault, and it wasn't his place to punish her further.

He sighed. "Be back here at six," he said, holding out his keys.

"Thank you," she answered.

He stood and watched her walk away, hoping she was going to make up with her brother. Not only could she move out of his house, but she would have someone to look after her while they chased the slim lead of finding the Peterson woman in London. Her speculation that Peterson had moved on to Europe or even a more distant location was more than a possibility. Whether the woman had killed the child herself or merely been an accomplice, Karen had plenty of reason to leave the country altogether. If Iris went to stay with her brother, he could be the one to hold her together when it all came apart. And he had no doubt that it would, indeed, all come apart.

McIntyre turned and went back into his office and closed the door. He sat down in his chair and pulled out his mobile, wondering what Alison was going to tell him. He remembered the day he met her in New Bond Street more than a decade ago. He'd seen her entering Georgiana's Tea Room, and he spent some minutes trying to get up the nerve to go inside to speak to her. She was beautiful, but back then, before she'd become so self-assured and independent, there had been a vulnerability about her that attracted him. He'd watched her through the bow window, checking her watch as if waiting for someone who hadn't arrived. No one ever showed up, and eventually he went inside and made an excuse to talk to her. It had been one of the best days of his life.

Now he took a deep breath before dialing her number. If he were to ever be with her again, he would have to face the fact that he'd made mistakes and be willing to change. Of course, that was part of the process of living—learning to change, correcting one's mistakes, growing stronger in the face of adversity.

He reached into his desk and took Alison's photo from the top drawer. In it, she wore brown woolen trousers and a silk blouse with very small buttons. He remembered those buttons, and the way she'd laughed and slapped his hand away whenever he tried to undo them. Over it, she wore a thick cardigan with sleeves that tapered all the way to her fingertips. Suddenly, he realized how much he'd longed for this moment. They could forgive each other, he decided, and they could start again.

He dialed her number and waited. She answered on the first ring, which pleased him.

"Alison," he said. "How are you doing? Are you still in London?"

"I'm back in Boston, actually," she answered.

"Were you in St. Pancras?" he asked, getting an odd feeling in the pit of his stomach. He dismissed it at once. He was in the business of discovering facts. He didn't believe in coincidence.

"Yes, as a matter of fact. Why?"

"Nothing. It's just part of a case, that's all."

"Anything I've heard about?"

"Undoubtedly."

"But you won't discuss it, of course," she said.

"Well, we're putting a photo out to the news outlets from a murder case from last year, if you must know," he answered.

"Not the child murder?" she asked.

He wasn't surprised she remembered. Sophie's body had been found a couple of weeks before she'd left him, and the entire city was focused on the murder.

"Yes, as a matter of fact, it is." He wanted to change the subject. "What's happening with you? Are you writing your second book?"

"Yes. I'm hoping to finish it by the spring. I'm doing the research for the background of an upcoming one now."

McIntyre suddenly wished for a cup of coffee. Or perhaps something stronger. "I've seen the first one in all the shops."

Alison clicked her tongue on the top of her mouth. "Yes, it's doing well. I've been lucky."

He could imagine a torrent of admirers raining down on her. She probably had loads of letters from fans, both British and American, from what he'd read in *The Times*, with the requisite number of photographs and mobile numbers attached.

"Why did you ring?" he asked. He tried to sound casual, but it came out clumsy all the same.

"I've been wondering how you are. What have you been doing with yourself?"

"Not a great deal. I've had an awful lot of free time on my hands the last year or so, in case you've forgotten."

Her slight pause told him she was wounded by his jab. "You have all the crime in Truro to keep you busy."

"That I do. Too busy, unfortunately."

"There was something I wanted to tell you." He could hear her take a deep breath on the other end of the line. "Right after I came to Lincolnshire, I had a miscarriage."

It took a moment for it to sink in. "You were pregnant?" he asked, incredulous.

"I didn't know until I was losing it."

"Why didn't you call me?"

"There was really nothing you could do. It was an overnight in hospital, and then I went home."

"I had the right to know."

"You did, and I'm sorry I didn't tell you. It happened so soon after I left that I thought you'd still be angry, and I couldn't handle the thought of disappointing you about a child, too."

On the other side of his door, people were talking loudly. Some sort of argument had broken out. McIntyre felt like punching something himself.

"Are you all right?" he asked after a moment.

"I'm fine. I was only six weeks along, and there weren't any complications. It's been on my mind, though, and I wanted to tell you."

"I'm really sorry. I wish—"

"Did you ever fix the back door?" she asked, interrupting him.

He shook his head and grunted. He hadn't even opened the back door since she'd been gone. Alison used to throw it open in good weather while she was cooking something atrocious with balsamic vinegar and wine sauce, but without her, he was wont to eat takeaway, sitting in a dark room. She'd taken all the life with her when she'd gone. Of course, he hadn't known how true that statement was until now.

"I didn't think you would," she replied, interrupting his thoughts. "I miss the house, you know. It's so quirky. The halls are too narrow, and the doors! God, the squeaks. And you never had time to fix them. Still, I miss it a little."

"You never said anything about squeaks."

"Yes, I did. You never listen."

"It doesn't matter now."

"I'm sorry. I only meant to say there are good memories, aren't there? Even the little things."

"Yes. There are good memories." He cleared his throat. "You never really told me why you left. It was so sudden."

"To research the next book, I suppose. I wanted time to figure out what to do with my life. I found the house in Lincs and hit the ground running. I could focus on my work and write five or six hours a day."

"I've read some of your book. You changed some chapters, bringing in one of my cases."

"That's how it works, Rob. You hear an idea and then take it from there. Every writer does."

"You might have told me if you weren't happy," he said, changing the subject. "We could have tried again. It's not exactly fair to walk out on someone without a word."

"Look, I don't want to argue with you," she said. "Perhaps I shouldn't have called. I thought it was time to clear the air."

"I'm sorry." He sighed. He hadn't wanted to start an argument. "What are you doing right this minute?"

"Sitting in my car, staring out the window."

He knew her. She liked to watch the world go by. No doubt she stole ideas from everyone who passed down the street. McIntyre suddenly recalled that she often jotted notes in a journal she kept in her bag, and he felt tempted to ask if she still carried it. It was a kind of theft, he thought.

"Tell me about where you live."

"The house is nice," she replied. "Bigger than yours, with a grander fireplace. Not as cozy as the cottage, of course."

"Is there a garden?" he asked.

"There is, not that I can do much with it. I'm too busy to think of things like that right now. In fact, I've hired an assistant to come and organize my notes. That's the thing I really hate, keeping track of the endless bits of paper. I need someone to take care of everything. I put an advert in *The Times* and found someone I like with the right references. She has excellent qualifications."

"Someone from London?" he asked, barely paying attention. Her work was not the subject in which he was most interested. "Is she moving to Lincolnshire?"

"She's moving in with me for the time being."

"You're too trusting," he argued, getting up from his chair. "I don't care what her qualifications are, she doesn't need to move in with you. You don't meet someone for the first time and ask them to stay in your house. Not in this day and age. Don't you read the papers?"

"Stop worrying. I'm a big girl."

He suddenly realized he'd done the same thing, taking in Iris Flynn when he hardly knew her. He was hardly the one to scold Alison now.

There was silence for a moment on her end. Then, "Are you seeing anyone? Not that you have to tell me."

"Of course not," he snapped. He regretted it the moment it came out of his lips.

"Well, maybe you should."

"You walked out on me, Alison. I don't think I need to take relationship advice from you."

"I thought your anger might have abated a little over the past twelve months, but I see I was wrong. How are David and Susan and the kids?"

"They're fine," he grumbled. "Susan's mother was ill, so they went to be with her at the holidays."

"I'm sorry. I didn't realize you would be alone."

"I wasn't alone."

"Really?"

He ignored her surprise. "All right, we've caught up now. Is there anything else?"

"I don't like to talk when you're angry."

McIntyre lifted a file from his desk. "Fine. I have work to do. If you want to talk to me, you know how to find me."

He tossed the mobile onto his desk and sighed. What had he expected, anyway? For Alison to admit she'd made a mistake and was coming back home? That he would drive to Lincolnshire, stow her bags in the boot of the car, and bring her back to the house they had made together? That she would go into their bedroom and take the heather shawl from the bottom drawer and wear it when she slid into bed next to him on a cold winter morning? He missed the smell of her and the feel of her. He missed the way the sun caught her hair and reflected its golden hues. And now he'd learned that he'd almost been a father. If only she'd found out she was pregnant before she left, it might have changed everything.

He'd expected too much. He hadn't been ready for yet another rejection. Women, he decided, were more trouble than they were worth. He would throw himself into this impossible case, solve the Flynn murder, and then do everything in his power to eliminate women from his life altogether.

TWELVE

BEFORE SHE'D ASKED McINTYRE for his car keys, Iris hadn't even realized she was going to do it. Karen's grainy image was being sent to the newspapers, yet she felt deflated despite having accomplished the very thing she'd hoped to do. Techs and lab assistants were working to produce the best quality image possible, and McIntyre and his team would get it in the right hands … which left her, for the moment, with nothing left to do. She drove away from the station, having no desire to rattle around in McIntyre's empty house. If she'd done everything she could at the moment for Sophie, it was time to take care of something she should have done days ago. It was time to see her mother.

Turning McIntyre's car onto the A39, she headed straight into the abyss that she had escaped at seventeen. She hadn't come all the way from Australia in order to mend fences with her mother and her brother, but to deal with the unresolved issues in her life, and her mother was nothing if not an unresolved issue. She hadn't thought she had the strength to deal with it, but some indefinable emotion, long buried, somehow drew her back in.

Until now, life had always carried Iris along without much thought. She'd married and given birth and never dreamed of having any kind of career. In retrospect, she'd enjoyed the years between school and marriage, when she'd lived with Jonathan and worked for him in his antiques business, learning odd bits of information on Regency and Queen Anne furniture and the differences between various pottery manufacturers in Staffordshire. It had been interesting, though not nearly so much as the company she'd kept in those days: a group of friends who danced in clubs to Justin Timberlake and the Cheeky Girls and who clustered under the stars smoking cigarettes late into the night. They went to the cinema en masse, often laughing and making remarks that drew attention from the crowd, and when they were asked to leave, went to cafés where they pooled their shillings for cups of tea and pints and the occasional sandwich. They had lofty conversations, disparaging the likes of Tony Blair though they knew little of his politics, although Evie, one of the girls, threw around grand terms like "the Belfast Agreement" or "the House of Lords Reform" until they shamed her to silence with their laughter. They'd crowd around the telly, watching the *EastEnders* at Derek's house, which was the largest by far of anyone's in the group.

None of them worked regular jobs. Iris's hours at the antique shop were irregular, to say the least. One of the nicest things about Jonathan was that he never reprimanded her for sloughing off a shift to spend time with friends. Both of them knew it was her first and only time for youthful indiscretion and complete irresponsibility. Yet none of these things had tied her to Truro, or even Cornwall, and boredom had eventually set in. So she'd gone to stay with Sarah in Sydney, where she'd met Nick.

Nick Flynn was like no one Iris had ever met before. He was aggressive and physical, the kind of man who made his presence known. When he laughed, everyone in the room turned their head to see what was amusing. When he shouted, everyone froze. The young men of her experience were placid, dull-witted, and easy to control. None of them had been interesting or accomplished, particularly when it came to sex. The boys she'd been with were all tongue, insinuating their wet muscles into the fleshy parts of her mouth, fishing around for God knows what; exploring, in reality, not her but womankind and the orifices provided by that office. None of them moved her in the slightest. Nick, however, was different. He knew what he wanted and took it before she realized what had happened. Her mother had hated him, but she would have hated anyone who'd kept Iris away from Cadgwith, and there was nowhere further one could go from Cornwall than the wild shores of Australia.

Her father wouldn't have liked Nick either, Iris knew. She wasn't certain he liked anyone. Gerald Martin had been handsome but aloof, preferring his own company to anyone else's, spending hour upon hour hoeing weeds in the plot of land at the back of the house and devising on paper the perfect English garden. It was years before Iris realized there were many different sorts of gardens, all beautiful in diverse ways, none which could definitively be considered perfect. Her father had disagreed. He calculated the number of seeds and saplings he needed each year, weighed the difficulties of having too much pink in one area or an overabundance of aroma in another. Her mother said later that he'd spent seven years trying to choose a bench for the rock path. His thin, dark hair was always tousled, falling into his eyes as he labored over clay pots and leaky watering cans. Iris had grown up believing that he was a good listener, but now, after having children of her own, she realized that he listened because he'd had no other choice, and that if one listened without interruption, the speaker would soon tire of their monologue and leave one in silence. His nails were always stained from potting soil, and the shoes he wore when gardening were the same ones he wore her entire life. The holes that developed in the toes bothered him not in the slightest, and even in winter, when he walked his dormant trails, plotting whether to add hyacinth, he didn't wear boots or even good shoes but his worn garden pair.

He was no different with Sarah or Jonathan. They just didn't try as hard as she did to receive his acknowledgment and attention. Her siblings were happy to be left to their own devices, ignoring both of their parents to the best of their ability, but Iris had loved her father best. She felt as though she'd somehow let him down by not being more intelligent or more interesting, or more helpful in the garden. She was burdened, even now, by knowing that she hadn't made a difference in his life, and his death when she was thirteen left her not only bereft but aware that she'd failed him. For two or three years after he'd died, she'd tried to take over the garden in his place. It was an utter failure. She hadn't the strength to hoe a large plot of weeds or to prune trees. Most of all, she hadn't the knowledge of what to do about the ever-growing shrubbery and flowers, which, over time, grew over the paths and trails and became so tangled and haggard that she could no longer bear to try.

In the wake of her father's death, she'd noticed her mother as if for the first time. She had no recollection of when she first realized her mother was a drunk. The house had always been dim and tomb-like, cluttered beyond redemption. Stacks of unread magazines were piled in short towers around which she learned to walk. Coffee mugs, stained from years of caffeine and too few washings, along with hard glass ashtrays, dominated the surface of every table. Stale smoke clung to curtains and furniture, and the rugs reeked of urine from a cat that escaped long ago. Everything about her childhood seemed dreary, especially the woman who sat day after day watching the telly or sometimes staring at the walls like a patient in a sanitarium. Iris brought her glasses of water and cardigans and packets of cigarettes, and then escaped to the privacy of her room. Her father must have done most of the cooking, she realized later, until she herself was old enough to do it.

She was forced into the role of caretaker, though through sheer willfulness, she refused to take on everything. She cooked the meals—one had to eat, after all—but she had no interest in becoming the household drudge. Sarah took her beauty and talents off to Australia, marrying well; so well, in fact, that she could forget she'd ever come from this remote corner of Cornwall, raised by two doddering parents. Jonathan quickly began his own life. He'd inherited a small bequest from a distant uncle and began his antique business in Truro. Iris yearned to leave, too. Jonathan wanted to teach her the business, and Sarah wanted her to come to Australia and choose a husband from the eligible men of their acquaintance and buy decent clothes and settle down. By marrying Nick, she'd let them both down. To Iris, a rich husband and fine house in Sydney were almost a prison. She was eager to see the world and to escape the life she'd always known. She didn't know then that she would miss Cornwall so much, or realize that wherever she went, she would always feel alone.

Cadgwith was beautiful, she decided as she rounded the curves of the road into the village where she'd been born, a tired fishing village on the eastern side of Lizard Peninsula, all gray stone houses and boats in various stages of disrepair pulled up along the sea's edge. In the distance, the chimneys of thatched-roof houses churned out small clouds of smoke in the waning light. The hillocks were dotted with melting snow and dead, withered vines. She drove McIntyre's car down to the sea, where she got out of the car and sat on the bonnet, looking westward over the water. America was over there, some three thousand miles away, Africa to the south. She'd lived in both places. When she was a girl, she'd dreamt of going away, anywhere, as far as the winds could propel her. Still, she couldn't help but wonder: what good had it done her to leave, after all?

The sharp sea smell rose around her, and she wished that Nick had been willing to fish here instead of Australia. Cornwall was good for little else. Half of the people she'd grown up with had gone into fishing. Of course, she knew the answer. Nick was no fisherman. He would abandon that scheme like all the others.

"Stop, Iris," she said to herself. She had no right to criticize him. She'd known the type of man he was when she'd married him. Hadn't she been willing to follow him around the world, dragging their children from continent to continent? Then she shook herself. It didn't do any good to think like that. She couldn't change anything from half a world away.

After a while, she got back into the car and drove to her mother's house. The door was unlocked, as it had been most of her life. Iris walked inside, looking at the familiar, dingy rooms, wondering at first if the house was empty. Cleanliness had never much concerned her, but as she looked about, she shuddered at the odor of filth. It wouldn't have been surprising to find mice trails in the dust. She walked into the kitchen, a jumble of used glasses and empty plates. A quick perusal of the cupboards yielded a few tins of potted meat and a half empty box of Weetabix.

From the other room, she heard someone stirring, and a moment later, her mother appeared in the doorway, a loose housecoat draped over her thin shoulders. Her hair was wild and gray. One hand hung over a hip and the other held a packet of cigarettes. She looked at Iris without surprise.

"It's you."

"How are you, Mum?"

Helen Martin snorted, revealing nicotine-stained teeth. "Stupid question. What are you doing here?"

"Nothing." Iris held up a tin. "What are you doing for food these days? This isn't fit for a cat."

"Ten year or more you've been gone, and now you wonder what I'm doing for food? Why aren't you with your Aussie and those children of yours?"

Iris shrugged. "I had business here."

Her mother turned and walked into the sitting room and Iris followed, sitting opposite her on a worn, faded chair. Her father had often sat there in the evenings, engrossed in seed catalogues. She stretched out her fingers and gripped the arms, longing for him so much it almost took her breath away. Why hadn't she been able to get through to him?

Why was her mother so difficult?

"I should ask how you are," Helen said, extracting a cigarette and playing with it. "I imagine it's not very well."

"No," Iris answered, surprising herself. She hated talking about her feelings to anyone, least of all her mother, but it tumbled out, anyway. "I'm not doing well at all."

Helen looked at the window, and Iris followed her gaze. The curtains were parted but the panes were too grimy to see through. The place was a shambles. It needed to be cleaned, and Iris wondered if she had the energy to even try, not that it was her responsibility.

"What was her name again?" her mother asked.

"Sophie. You might have remembered."

"You weren't around enough for me to know them."

"What do you expect?" Iris asked. "My children didn't need to be around you when you were drunk."

"Aren't you touchy? Nobody asked you to come."

Iris sighed. She hadn't meant to start a row. That was the trouble with seeing her mother. She always thought she could handle it, but she never could.

Helen lit her cigarette. "Have you seen Jonathan yet?"

"No."

"Looks like the two of you had quite the falling out." She looked at Iris, raising a brow. "You always used to be so close."

"Do you see him much?" Iris asked, hoping to change the subject. She would deal with Jonathan later.

"He's the dutiful one, I suppose," Helen said, plucking at her sleeve. "He comes now and then with a sack of food. He never stays long."

Iris wondered for a minute what it would be like to have your children despise you as much as Helen's did. But then, after what they'd gone through, what would Charlotte and India think of her when they were grown? The thought left her cold.

Her mother looked at her and frowned. "What did you say about food?"

"What?"

"I believe you said you didn't want me eating this food. Perhaps you should go to the market and get something decent for supper. That is, unless you have something else to do that's more important."

Iris looked at her mobile, knowing neither McIntyre nor Nick would ring. Whether she liked it or not, there was nothing she could do at that moment about Karen Peterson or her children or anything else. It was up to Immigration to find Karen's true identity, and to the news stations in London to publicize her photo. She had hours before she had to pick up McIntyre, so she might as well do the shopping and make her mother something decent to eat. She looked up at her mother, who was watching her expectantly.

"No, Mum," she said at last. "There's nothing else I have to do."

THIRTEEN

MADELINE WAS BACK IN her small bedroom in Islington, packing for her move. Alison Kendall had offered her the position of a lifetime and she'd turned in her notice at the Reading Room, something she would never have done for a lesser reason. For once, everything was perfect. For once, the planets aligned and the bitter disappointments of daily life were obliterated from her horizon.

Apart from one. She listened now with irritation to the sound of Brooke banging pots in her small kitchen, no doubt preparing another garlicky meal. Bloody fool, she thought, with her bland personality and horrendous taste in food. The woman had taken over her flat as if she owned it, and the cloying odor of spices might never be eradicated from her kitchen. Sitting alone with a single lamp burning, Madeline realized she was hungry. In spite of it, she wouldn't eat the revolting meal of whatever Brooke was making. There was something more important to think about. In the morning, she was going back to Lincolnshire.

Pulling herself to her feet, she decided she would go to her favorite restaurant for a meal. She took her time getting ready, brushing her hair, applying mascara and eyeliner, and then choosing a special dress, a black sleeveless sheath with a matching jacket. It made her look quite trim and attractive. Around her neck, she wore an old set of pearls that had belonged to her grandmother and which came out only on special occasions. Her beaded and somewhat frayed black clutch was a particular favorite, having been found in a jumble sale. It looked to be forty or so years old. She loved classic pieces—they made her feel as if she'd been an heiress to a grand fortune who owned an estate in Hampshire and went riding on the weekends, instead of a working class girl who had put herself through university.

She left the flat, ignoring Brooke's shrill, nasal voice calling out to her and nearly tripping over the girl's cane as she made her way out the door. Outside, she wrapped a scarf around her head, then buttoned her coat and slipped her clutch into its wide, deep pockets. There wasn't an empty cab to be had at that hour, and she was forced to walk into the brisk wind, which bit her cheeks. Madeline was not deterred. Two roads down, there was an Italian café where she went on special occasions, and she headed in that direction.

With relief, she found the café and opened the door, her eyes having some difficulty adjusting to the dim, candlelit room. Jorge, the waiter who had worked there for more than thirty years and never forgot a patron of any regularity, recognized her by sight if not by name and saw her to a table far from the door. There was no crowd. She waited for him to supply one of the ancient menus, which she studied for some time before choosing the linguine along with an inexpensive wine.

After ordering, she set the menu to the side and sat, ramrod straight, observing the other patrons like a spinster who lives for years in a hotel in Bayswater without ever learning the other residents' names. But she would be living with Alison Kendall, and as more than just a mere assistant.

While she waited for her meal, Jorge brought her a serviette and a glass of wine. As usual, Madeline took her time, setting down the glass between sips, glancing at the décor, or lack thereof, and wondering about the silent couples around her. At school, most of the other girls had dreamed of marrying, with visions of elaborate ceremonies and long, meringue-like dresses and lace trains. They wanted children, not out of maternal desire but as a solid claim to a dashing solicitor or banker with a holiday home in the Seychelles or the Bahamas. The dream included the services of an important interior designer, an unlimited wardrobe, and a small but potent stream of lovers who kept them company while the requisite husband paid for the lifestyle they required.

Madeline wanted none of those things: no meringue, no interior designers, and no men, married or otherwise. It had taken her twenty-nine years to discover her purpose in life, but now it was obvious to her. The spark she and Alison had felt on that first day had been unexpected but welcome, and had led to a couple of intimate days together. The conversation alone was electric; the lovemaking tentative at first, and then exciting. She'd rambled around Alison's house, exploring her books and paintings with great interest. In spite of what Alison had said about buying a house in the Lake District, Madeline thought her home in Lincolnshire was already perfect. Books filled the shelves but weren't designer chosen, straight and rigid and lifeless; they were read and consulted and shoved in at odd angles, a sign they were truly enjoyed. There wasn't anything new or special about anything in the house, but, in its entirety, the splendid, undesigned originality made a beautiful whole, an exquisite, authentic form of Alison herself. That was the world Madeline belonged to—the intellectual world, the world that appreciated art and literature above all else.

Jorge brought the food and placed it in front of her. She spread the serviette over her lap and sat there thinking. She believed in Fate. It was true, she'd been infatuated with the Alison whose book she adored, who had been so lovely in the interviews she'd read, but nothing compared to getting to know the woman herself and to the closeness they now shared. Madeline had never experienced a connection like that before, even when Alison had been reticent the first morning after. Madeline had cooked breakfast for them, enjoying the country-house kitchen instead of the minuscule one in her small flat. Alison had come downstairs before Madeline finished turning the eggs, her glasses perched on her nose. She'd been hesitant and nervous; it was clear she'd never been with a woman before. In fact, she'd said very little at first, ignoring the eggs and toast in favor of hot, strong coffee, and Madeline, realizing the delicacy of the situation, had said nothing about the food.

"It's a beautiful morning, isn't it?" she'd asked.

"Hmm," Alison answered. Even that was too much effusion for her.

"More coffee?" Madeline ventured after a long pause.

"No, thank you." Alison looked at her over her spectacles. "You know, you're a guest. You shouldn't have to do the cooking."

"I was happy to do it. Will we get to work today, or just discuss moving arrangements?"

"Arrangements?"

"To have my things moved from London. I'm anxious to get started."

"Well, after last night … " Alison blushed, fumbling for words. "It's possible there might be some awkwardness if we attempted a working relationship now."

Madeline scrutinized her face and then attempted a light tone. "I certainly don't think so. I'm qualified for the position, aren't I?"

"I don't believe that is at issue."

"There. You see? There's no problem. I'm a very good assistant, and we have the benefit of finding, shall we say, a mutual satisfaction in one another personally?"

"I'm afraid I didn't really think it through."

"Of course you didn't. It was purely an emotional reaction. How often does that happen between two people, anyway? Weren't we lucky to feel it?" Madeline reached across the table and touched Alison on the hand. "It was magical."

"It was reckless. I'm not usually like that."

"Neither am I. But I felt something the moment we met."

"I'm sorry," Alison said, extracting her hand. She stood. "I should never have behaved so unprofessionally. I'm sorry I mislead you, but I don't believe we would be comfortable working together."

There'd been a moment of silence. Madeline looked at her eggs, which were now runny and ruined. She tried to think of a way to salvage the situation. She rose from her seat and walked around the table and then reached up and touched Alison's face. She leaned into her slowly. Despite everything Alison had said, she gasped and then accepted Madeline's kiss. It was slow at first, then became more insistent.

"This is madness," Alison whispered after a moment.

"Give into it. It's lovely."

They stood that way for some minutes. Madeline could feel Alison's indecision with her lips. It was a matter of winning her over. At last, Alison pulled away and turned to face the window. She touched her lips as if to erase what had happened.

"I'm not a lesbian."

"I'm not, either," Madeline answered. "I'm just a woman who is interested in another woman."

"I don't know what to do." Alison turned and looked at her, searching her eyes for the answer.

"You don't have to do anything," Madeline said. "Why not enjoy the moment? I'll work with you on the book, keep you company, that sort of thing. There is one thing."

"What?"

"You really ought to keep the maid. I'm a terrible housekeeper."

In spite of herself, Alison smiled. It was soon decided. They would attempt a trial relationship, one that wasn't strictly defined. Alison couldn't admit it to herself yet, but it was certainly a beginning.

After her solitary dinner, Madeline found a cab and went back to her flat, cursing the fact that she had to return even for a single night to a flat with an unwanted flatmate. There was no privacy to be had in such a small space. She unlocked the door, hoping that Brooke had gone to bed, but found her sprawled across her settee watching the telly, feet propped upon a small but expensive wood table that Madeline had carried several streets from a local shop, and upon which she'd never, even when exhausted, propped her own feet. She was about to complain when Brooke spoke.

"You didn't eat my supper."

Madeline took her key from the door and closed it. "I don't actually care for spicy food. Besides, I had some business."

"At this time of night?" Brooke inquired.

She shrugged. She owed Brooke Turner no explanation of her life. "What are you doing?"

"Watching some news programme. These presenters are stupid, aren't they? They predicted snow for today."

Madeline glanced at the television, where the word *murder* caught her attention. A woman's face came on the screen. It was a strong face, with dark hair that was pulled back. Madeline had never seen anyone look as desperate in her life. Next to it, there appeared a photo of a child of three or four.

"That's a shame," she remarked, putting her keys into her handbag.

"I know," Brooke answered, nodding her head. "That poor little girl."

"Sad." Madeline pulled off her coat and folded it, laying it across a chair. "So, do you plan to look for a flat of your own, or are you going back to Canada?"

Brooke shrugged. "I haven't decided."

"Well, I wouldn't stay here if I were you," Madeline said. "Winter in London can be so horrid."

"You're forgetting Canadian weather. Those famous Arctic winds."

"Still," Madeline persisted, changing the subject, "wouldn't you be happier at home if you don't plan to work?"

"You're subtle, aren't you?" Brooke said, sitting up. "Don't worry. I'll find something in the new year."

Madeline sat down across from her and sighed. All she was doing was making the situation worse. She was going to Lincolnshire anyway. She might as well be gracious to a family friend, for her mother's sake if nothing else.

"Well," she said, her tone softening, "I suppose there's no rush. I'm taking a new job out of the city for a while. If you like, you're welcome to stay a while longer."

It was the right thing to do. She had much more important things on her mind.

FOURTEEN

AT HALF PAST SEVEN the next morning, McIntyre was standing outside his office at the station, looking at the evidence board. The chat with Alison the day before, while not forgotten, soon would be, if he was lucky. It was time to turn his mind to other things, like the fresh lead in the Flynn case. They'd spent the last couple of days making calls and going through the physical evidence again, and now it was time to go out and see who remembered the Peterson woman.

Dugan arrived a few minutes later with a packet in hand. The sergeant looked bleary-eyed and tired, as he often did before noon. Most young men his age slept in until all hours whenever they could get away with it after a long night out. Dugan wasn't that sort. He was more prudent than most, but still, he was young. His trousers were never pressed, and buttons that had come loose were sewn on with the wrong color thread. He lived on takeaways and stale cakes and whatever else was left in the break room. He was a typical twenty-seven-year-old bachelor who played Xbox in his spare time, killing imaginary villains when he wasn't at work pursuing leads on real ones.

Oblivious to the fact that he was late, Dugan held up the packet and gave him a lopsided grin. "Got 'em."

McIntyre nodded. Enhanced prints of the blurry train station photo of Karen Peterson were inside, he knew, along with copies of the artist rendering of the subject Vanessa Foley had described. He thought the psychic, in spite of her normal appearance, was a nutter. People couldn't divine information psychically. It defied logic, and logic was the key to any good police work. However, because he did not want to disappoint Iris Flynn any more than she'd already been, they would show Peterson's photo and the sketch to everyone they could over the next eight or ten hours.

"Are you ready, sir?" Dugan asked.

"Yes," he answered. "I want to pop 'round as many shops as we can. It's been a year, but there's always a chance someone may remember her."

Unlike when they were searching for leads a year ago, at least this time they were armed with actual evidence. With Dugan in tow, he headed down the stairs.

McIntyre had lived in Truro all his life, apart from his university years, and he knew every inch of the city. In fact, he sometimes took it for granted. His parents had been married in the cathedral on St. Mary's Street, and he and David had been christened there, two and five years later, respectively. His first job was at the grocer's on Charles Street, and his second at the railway station, where for a brief time he thought of training to become an engine driver. Instead, his parents had talked him into going to university and he'd found himself interested in police work. There were problems in towns like this, of course. Lack of housing for the growing community

124

was frequently brought before the city council, and while crime was significantly lower than in many other areas of Britain, there had been a steady rise in violence, theft, and antisocial behavior. The murder of Sophie Flynn had shaken the entire county, with mothers everywhere now fiercely diligent in the care of their children, lest they, too, fall victim to a crime.

There weren't many places that a woman like Karen Peterson could have spent time in a town of this size. The younger crowds clustered in the cafés and bars. That was the sort of thing that would have attracted someone young, places where a woman could have met men. Even from the little he knew about Karen, which amounted to little more than her age and general description, he felt certain she would have been interested in the opposite sex, particularly in a town with as few diversions as Truro.

The air was frigid as they left the station, and McIntyre zipped his coat to his chin. They got into the car and Dugan turned onto St. Clement Street. The traffic was the usual for this time of day; people going to work or to the local café for a good, strong coffee. It would have been business as usual, he realized, if they weren't searching for a child murderer. Dugan drove to Kenwyn Street and parked the car.

"Here's your set, sir," his sergeant said, handing a folder to McIntyre.

"Thanks."

They got out of the car and McIntyre surveyed the shops. "I'll take the north side of the street and you can take the south. We'll figure out which way to go next when we get to the end of the road."

"Are we at it all day, then?"

"Why, Alex?" he asked. "Do you have somewhere else to be?"

"Not until later," his sergeant answered, shrugging.

"Big date, then?"

Dugan smiled. "Wouldn't you like to know?"

"Oh, I know, all right. When we get a break, you can phone Ena and tell her you'll make dinner or whatever plans the two of you made. We won't let police work interfere with young romance."

"A, how'd you know it was Ena? And B, you're sounding a little jaded there, boss."

McIntyre raised a brow. "Anyone who works around the two of you knows it's Ena. And no comment to your second remark."

He headed across the road to the chemists' shop with a wave of his hand.

The first hour yielded no results. They went up and down several roads, showing the photo and sketch in every shop, salon, or business they passed. It was repetitive and boring asking the same question to everyone they saw. When he came out of an estate agent's office, Dugan appeared at his shoulder.

"Should we get a coffee, sir?"

McIntyre nodded. They stopped for coffee and then parted less than a quarter hour later with the same strategy on Chapel Hill. It was nearly three o'clock in the afternoon when Dugan showed the photo to a man in an electronics shop who recognized Karen Peterson. He crossed the road to find McIntyre, and the two went back to the shop to question him.

"Do you recognize this woman?" McIntyre asked, holding up the photo again.

The shop manager was a heavyset man in his early fifties, with gray hair and ruddy cheeks. He looked like he needed an extended holiday, McIntyre thought. In the glaring fluorescent light of the shop, he was pasty and tired-looking.

"I used to see her from time to time," the man replied. "She was going around with one of the men who works here."

"What's his name?"

"Kevin Hughes. He's been here for a couple of years. She started coming around to see him when his shift ended at night. They must have broken it off, because one day I didn't see her again."

"Tell me about Hughes," McIntyre asked. He leaned against the wall, rubbing his finger against his nose. "What sort of bloke is he?"

The man shrugged. "Don't know. The usual sort we get in here. He's quiet, he works, and he gets the job done without breaking too many things. That's all I care about."

"Do you know where we can find him?"

"He's due in tonight at eleven."

"Have you got an address?"

"Mary will, up in the office."

"Thanks," McIntyre said. He looked at Dugan. "Come on. Maybe we can catch him at home now."

Ten minutes later, they were driving to Hughes's house. They pulled up in front of a small cottage, painted gray. The garden, buttressed by a short stone wall, was well-tended, with frost-covered leafy winter ferns. It certainly wasn't the sort of place Hughes would have owned on his own. McIntyre led Dugan up the steps to the front door and then knocked.

For a few moments, there was no sound apart from the wind rustling the branches of the tree overhead, and then a young man opened the door. He frowned, closing it again part of the way so that McIntyre could just barely see his face and the collar of his shirt.

"Who are you?" he asked, glancing from McIntyre to Dugan and back.

McIntyre pulled out his identification and held it up. "DCI McIntyre, Truro Police. This is Detective Sergeant Dugan. Are you Kevin Hughes?"

"Yes."

"We'd like to ask you a few questions."

"What about?" Hughes asked. He was obviously uncomfortable having policemen on his doorstep.

"It would be easier to talk inside," McIntyre said.

"I haven't done anything."

"No one says you have."

After a moment, Hughes stepped back and opened the door, allowing them to enter. It was a tidy house, with a sofa facing the telly and handmade afghans on the backs of two yellow chairs whose velvety sheen had faded years ago. There were a few magazines on the table, *Country Living* and *Garden Inspirations*. Clearly, he lived with one or both of his parents.

"You live at home?" McIntyre asked.

"Yeah," Hughes answered.

"Where are your parents?"

"At work. I do night shifts, so I'm home during the day."

"We must have woken you," McIntyre said, unapologetic.

Hughes shrugged.

Dugan took the artist's sketch from his pocket. "Do you know this woman?"

The young man gave it a brief glance and then shook his head.

"Give it another look," McIntyre said, watching Hughes's face as he gave the sketch a proper once-over. There was no discernible change in his expression.

"Never saw her before," he said. "Not that I wouldn't like to."

McIntyre remembered that Iris had called the girl in the sketch as pretty as a model. It hadn't been what he'd expected, either.

"All right, then. Take a look at this one."

He pulled out the photograph from the train station. Although it was grainy, Karen's round face and bobbed brown hair would be recognizable to anyone who'd spent any amount of time with her, he was certain. Not to mention that the distinctive coat and skirt she wore were easily identifiable. In the original investigation, when the Flynns' house had been searched, they'd discovered that Karen hadn't owned more than a suitcase full of clothes. If someone knew her, they would know that outfit by sight.

This time, as he held out the photo, he got the result he was waiting for. Hughes said nothing at first, but the flash of recognition was unmistakable.

"You know her," McIntyre said.

"I used to," Hughes replied.

"What is her name?"

"Karen. Karen Peterson."

McIntyre nodded at Dugan, whose eyes had narrowed at the admission. "When was the last time you saw her?"

Hughes put his arms up, lacing his fingers and putting them behind his head. "Ages. A year or more, I think."

"Was she your girlfriend?" Dugan asked.

"We went out a few times," Hughes said, lowering his arm. He flexed his neck muscles as though they were tense.

"How'd you meet?" McIntyre asked.

"Down at the pub," Hughes said. Despite the fact that he shrugged, he looked nervous. His face colored. "She came into the Crown one night, alone. We ended up talking."

"What did she tell you about herself?"

"She was from America, staying with a couple, working as a nanny or such."

McIntyre nodded. "Did you ever see her with anyone else? Anyone at all? Friends?"

"No," Hughes answered. "Like I said, she came into the pub that night and we met a few times after that."

"Where did you meet?"

"Mostly the pub."

"What did you talk about?"

Hughes looked uncomfortable. "Look, I don't know anything about what she's up to now. We had a casual thing, that's all."

"How long before she went missing?"

Hughes hesitated before answering. "When did she go missing?"

"Around Christmas."

"A week, then, maybe. I'm not sure."

"Why didn't you call the police when you learned what happened?"

"I didn't want no trouble. You blokes tend to get the wrong end of the stick."

"Mr. Hughes, we have reason to believe she's involved in the murder of the young child. If you have any information about it, you need to tell us. It's a crime to withhold information in a murder case."

"I don't know anything, I tell you," he insisted. "I knew the girl and got tired of her. She was tired of me, too. Neither of us was in it for a real relationship, just a few laughs. I don't know anything about the kid's murder."

McIntyre looked him square in the eye for a moment and then held out a card. "This is my number. I want you to call if you remember anything. Anything at all. We want to retrace this woman's steps as closely as we can during those last few days."

Hughes took the card without looking at it. Whatever he knew, McIntyre realized, he wouldn't tell. They were going to have to have him followed. The girl had left Cornwall, but it was possible Hughes might still be in contact with her. He would also get a warrant to search the house.

"Thank you for your cooperation," McIntyre said. "We'll be in touch."

———————

When the police had gone, Hughes went back into his room, kicking at the piles of clothes on the floor until he found a clean shirt. Pulling it on, he put on his heavy jacket and locked the door on his way out of the house. He was rattled. He hopped on his motorbike, fastened the helmet under his chin, and set out on the road. When he felt upset, he often went for a ride.

It occurred to him that he was upset quite often. He felt like a complete non-starter. It was hard living at home with his parents, listening to them complain to each other about household tasks that needed doing or whether or not to go to the pub on Friday night. They never seemed to be happy, no matter what the circumstances. He was sick of his job at the electronics shop, too. Shifting boxes wasn't the way for someone his age to make a living. Unfortunately, he had no idea of anything better. He'd been keeping his head down, hoping to scrape a few pounds together, but he never seemed to be able to save anything. It was too easy to piss it all away on drink and nights out with friends. He should have been more careful and gotten out of Truro, to London, perhaps, before the police connected him with Karen. Now they'd figured it out. Enough time had passed that he'd thought he was in the clear. He'd almost been able to put it out of his mind altogether, but suddenly it was back, in living detail: Karen's face on that fateful night, begging him to agree to her plan.

Worse, the face of that child haunted him, crying and clinging to Karen for dear life.

Out of nowhere, a horn sounded and he slammed on his brakes, narrowly avoiding being hit by a bus. Heart racing, he pulled over to the side of the road.

"Fucking wanker!" he shouted at the driver, though he knew it was his fault. Everything was always his fault.

He drove to the river, even though it wasn't the best place to think things through. There weren't many options. He parked the bike and ripped his helmet from his head, throwing it down on the rocky bank. He sank down beside it. As he tried to calm down, the river gurgled along over rocks and stones, winding its way to somewhere else. He wished he could follow it and get out of here. Of course, if he left now, it would only arouse more suspicion.

How could that child's murder have come back to haunt him after all this time? A faint memory wrestled in his consciousness for a moment before he could recall what it was. Then he knew. His mother had made a random comment a day or two before. He'd submerged it as soon as he'd heard it, hoping it had no significance. It was something about the child's mother. She'd come back to Truro and wanted the police to reopen the case. It was all over the local papers. He always tuned his mother out as much as possible anyway. Now he realized that by returning and forcing the police to take another look at the case, the Flynn woman had the potential to take him down. If he didn't do something soon, the police would have him in custody before he even knew what hit him.

FIFTEEN

McIntyre parked in front of his house that evening wanting nothing more than an empty house, a hot meal, and a warm bed. None of them were waiting for him. Even worse, Iris was sitting in his favorite chair, reading one of his books, waiting for him to start something in the kitchen. It had been six days since she'd showed up on his brother's doorstep in London. He wasn't used to houseguests, and he'd had about all of it that he could take. She looked up in surprise when he came inside, as if she hadn't realized the time.

"You're back," she said.

"Yeah," he answered. "I live here."

He went straight to the kitchen and inspected the cupboard thoroughly. There was an old packet of crisps, a half-empty bag of sugar, and a tin of biscuits he'd been given the Christmas before. He sighed. He couldn't remember the last time he'd shopped for food. He could either go out for a takeaway or to trudge down to the pub, but after talking to people all day long, all he'd wanted was peace and quiet.

He stood there, unable to make a decision. While he was thinking, Iris put the book on a table and walked over to him.

"It's probably time to eat," she said. "You look tired. Shall I get something for us?"

Ordinarily, he wouldn't have let her, but it would achieve two of his goals: to have five minutes alone and then to eat. He reached into his pocket and extracted his keys.

"If you don't mind … "

She took the keys and went to put on her coat. He stood rooted to the spot until he heard the engine turn in his car. When she'd gone, he walked upstairs to his bedroom and lay across his bed.

After interviewing Kevin Hughes, he and Dugan had gone back to town and spent the rest of the afternoon showing Peterson's photo to anyone they could find. No one else recognized her. It would be hard to go as unnoticed as she had during her weeks in Truro, but somehow she'd done it. As he pondered the odds, his mobile rang in his pocket and he put it to his ear.

"DCI McIntyre speaking."

"Detective McIntyre, this is DS Michaels. We've had a tip on the Flynn case, sir."

McIntyre sat up. "I'm listening."

"It was an anonymous tip, but we knew you'd want to hear it. The caller said that Joe Ellers is responsible for the child's murder."

"Joe Ellers," McIntyre repeated, surprised.

He knew the Ellers, as did nearly everyone at the station. Joe was a twenty-two-year-old man who lived on a farm north of town with his mother. He was mentally challenged, and from time to time was caught vandalizing a neighbor's car or stealing from the local shops. His widowed mother had refused to put him in care, yet she couldn't control him around the clock. Usually Joe had done something harmless, but that didn't mean anything, as far as McIntyre was concerned. Perhaps everyone had underestimated what the man was capable of.

"What exactly did the caller say?"

"That's the odd part, sir. He was very specific. He said that Joe Ellers had been seen with Karen Peterson and that he'd taken the child from her. The caller said the child's coat has been spotted in a chicken pen behind the Ellers property. It's green."

"Was the call made from a mobile or a call box?"

"Call box, city center."

"I'll get out there immediately," McIntyre said. "Thanks for calling."

After he hung up, he dialed Dugan's number. "Alex, I'll pick you up in five minutes. We've got a tip on the Flynn case. We're headed to the Ellers' farm."

"The Ellers?" Dugan asked. It wasn't what he'd been expecting, either. "Yes, sir."

"Bollocks. The Flynn woman has my car. Can you pick me up?"

"I'll be right there."

In less than ten minutes, they were heading north. It had gotten dark and McIntyre realized that in his haste, he'd left no note for Iris, who would be coming back to an empty house with packets of food. His stomach growled and he wondered what he was missing for supper. Pulling out his mobile, he punched in her number.

"Yes?" Her answer was rapid and breathless, and he realized at once that he couldn't get her hopes up. They had no idea what they would find once they got there.

"I had to leave," he rumbled. "There's a tip, not that we expect it to turn out to be anything, but we're checking it out anyway. I'm trying to make sure we leave no stone unturned."

"You could have waited for me," she said accusingly.

"No, I couldn't. You can't be involved in a police investigation, particularly when we're weeding through tips. Most of them lead nowhere, as we've already seen in this case."

"Where are you headed?"

"Out of town. I'll see you later." He hung up without waiting for a response. She probably would have tried to follow him if he'd given her any more information. In his own car, no less.

"Turn there," he said to Dugan.

Dugan pulled off the A30 and headed west. Within a few minutes, they were pulled up in front of the property and he cut the engine. Even though there were lights on in the small house, it was too dark to see much beyond the path in front of them.

"Do you have a torch?"

"Yeah," Dugan answered. "Two in the boot."

"We'll need them."

"Do you think they'll let us look around without a warrant?"

"If not, we'll get one."

McIntyre opened the door and stepped out into the cold night air. The muted sounds of animals and distant cars could barely be heard above the gusting wind. He pulled up his collar and walked across the gravel drive to the front door, with Dugan behind him. He knocked three times and then took a step back. They heard heavy footsteps coming to the door, and it opened to reveal Joe Ellers' mother. She was a gray-haired woman in her fifties with a tattered purple cardigan pulled over her broad shoulders. She was solidly built, someone who could handle farm work, he imagined, and she frowned when McIntyre pulled out his badge.

"Police, Mrs. Ellers. May we come in for a moment?"

"What is this about, Inspector ... ?"

"DCI McIntyre, ma'am. We need a few minutes of your time."

"Has there been trouble?"

"We have a few questions."

She stepped back and let them enter. It was a small house by any standard, and barely fit to live in. There were tools and farm equipment on every surface, clothes piled in heaps, and the detritus of several meals scattered about the small room. The smell of bacon wrapped around them like a snake.

"I'm sorry," she said, raising a shoulder. "We're not used to company."

"Is Joe here?" McIntyre asked. "We've received a complaint."

"Oh, no," she murmured, pulling the cardigan around her. She looked from McIntyre to Dugan and then back again. "What is it this time?"

"Do you remember a year ago, when a little girl went missing?"

"The one they found in the river."

"That's the one. What was Joe doing that evening?"

She looked startled. "My Joe? He wouldn't hurt a fly. He's got a mischievous streak in him, to be sure, but he wouldn't hurt anyone. As for that night, he was with me, of course. He's almost always with me."

At that moment, McIntyre suddenly noticed that a figure had crept to the edge of the room and stood without a word in the doorway. Joe Ellers was an odd-looking young man, tall and thin, with long blond hair combed in an odd, sweeping pattern around his face. His clothes, like his mother's, were worn and in disrepair, and he wore oversized wire-rimmed glasses on his expressionless face. His eyes looked vacant and his hands were in his pockets, rubbing against his thighs.

"It's all right, Joe," his mother said. "I'm talking to some nice policemen. They want to know if anyone has any information about an old case. Go have some milk. There's a fresh carton in the kitchen."

They watched as he slunk off in search of milk and McIntyre looked at Dugan for a moment before continuing.

"Do you mind if we have a look around outside for a few minutes?"

"There's nothing to see but piles of manure, but if you think you need to, I won't stop you. We've got nothing to hide."

"Thank you," he said. "We'll be back in a few minutes."

They stepped back out into the frigid air and Dugan hurried to the car to get the torches. The sky was dark, the moon half hidden behind the clouds. McIntyre glanced back at the house and saw Joe Ellers watching him through a filthy window.

"Christ," he said. Ellers was a creepy little bastard, whether his mother thought so or not.

Dugan made his way through a rubbish-strewn path and directed the light from his torch toward a large pen.

"Pigs," he said.

"Where are the chickens?"

"Over there," Dugan said, gesturing to the right. "You can smell it."

They followed the path to a penned area with a wooden structure in the center. Dugan lifted the latch on the gate and McIntyre followed him inside, mud oozing around his shoes. He tried scraping the worst of it on a fence post before following Dugan. There were feathers and dung and sharp bits of wood protruding from the ground, and the coop itself looked as though it would cave in on itself. The pen was large, at least fifteen by twenty feet, and more rubbish was piled up against the west side as though in an attempt to block the harshest winds. McIntyre kicked at an abandoned shoe and looked at the mess in front of them.

"Do we know what color the coat is?" Dugan asked, interrupting his thoughts.

"Green," McIntyre answered. He'd happened to look at the police report the day before and knew the tip was correct. "Not that you could make out a color in this darkness."

Dugan, however, was undeterred by either the darkness or the smell. He walked toward the pile of garbage and lifted an old wooden crate. Tossing it to the side, he reached back and pulled out an old rod and reel and looked at McIntyre.

"I don't understand people, sometimes," he muttered.

McIntyre shook his head and walked around the back of the hen house, kicking at the empty tins and boxes clustered along the wall. Then something caught his eye. It was some sort of fabric, though he couldn't discern the color at first. He walked over and saw a little sleeve protruding from beneath a discarded plastic bin. Shining the light on it, he saw that it was green. He slipped on a latex glove and pulled it from the spot. A green coat, small enough for a three year old. He turned to Dugan, holding up the article for him to see.

"Well," Dugan said. "It looks like we'll be making an arrest after all."

————————

Iris fidgeted after McIntyre left, pacing back and forth across the house. She wasn't afraid to be alone, but she was nervous waiting for McIntyre to return. There were moments when she didn't think she would survive this investigation, and on nights like these, she couldn't help but think about how it felt the night Sophie went missing. She remembered the bitter cold and the fear so palpable she could feel it. The police had never found a single trace of Karen Peterson after that night, and she wondered why she thought there would be now.

Someone knocked at the door and Iris opened it without hesitation. Ena Warren was standing on the other side, shivering in the cold night air. She was a welcome sight. Iris had no desire to spend another minute alone, thinking about the fleeting image of Karen at the railway station and wondering if McIntyre had found her. Ena smiled and held up a bottle of wine.

"I figure they'll be out for the evening," she said, stepping inside. "We might as well do something. Which way's the kitchen?"

"Through there," Iris answered, gesturing to her left. She closed the door and followed Ena with some curiosity. "By 'they,' you mean McIntyre and Dugan?"

"Yes. Alex and I had plans tonight, but that went out the window. I suppose that's the nature of police work."

Iris propped herself against the door frame, watching as Ena searched the cupboards for wine glasses. She didn't seem to notice that Iris wasn't helping. Finding the right one, she took two glasses down from the shelf and opened the bottle.

"I hope you like red. It's all I had," she said, pouring.

"Red's fine," Iris replied. It had been a long time since she'd had anything stronger than tea. She and Nick had always been too pinched for money to buy anything much, and when they had, he'd spoiled things by getting drunk.

Ena led the way back into the sitting room. It was dark apart from one lamp and the fire, with its orange-red flames sparking blue. Iris put her glass on the trunk in front of the sofa and put on another log so it wouldn't go out.

"I'm relieved to see you," she said to Ena.

Ena pulled off her coat, but instead of tossing it over a chair, she kept it around her shoulders. "It's cold in here," she said. "And lonely, too, I imagine."

"Sometimes," Iris answered, lowering her eyes. It didn't do to think about it too much.

"I thought you might like some company. I know I would."

"How long have you worked for Inspector McIntyre?" Iris asked, to change the subject.

"Almost two years. And I've had my eye on Alex the whole time. He only just got up the nerve to ask me out this week. Finally!"

"He seems nice," Iris ventured, not knowing what else to say. She didn't do lunch or nights at the pub with friends. Her life had been one long sludge after another. Socializing ranked near the bottom of her list of priorities.

"He is," Ena said, unaware of the mental struggle going on inside Iris. "He's nice, he's kind. He's loyal to the core. But the problem with the nice ones is that they're afraid to ask you out. And you can't push them too hard or they won't take you seriously."

"You're probably right," she said.

"How did you meet your husband?" Ena asked.

Iris sighed and took a sip of the wine, which was too sweet. "I was visiting my sister in Australia. She'd been living there for a year with her husband, and I was going to spend the summer with them. I met Nick on the beach one afternoon. He was surfing that day. He's the rugged type."

She didn't want to say he hadn't been the nice type. He was tough as old boots when she met him, and dangerous for a girl like her. Of course, she thought, look how it turned out. Sarah's children hadn't been taken from her in her posh suburb, where they went to private schools and had a mother and a Swedish au pair to look after them. Dragging her children around the world without purpose had cost Sophie her life.

"You must miss him," Ena continued, oblivious to the irritation that was rising in Iris. It was a statement, not a question. "All the more reason to have some of this."

She poured another inch into the top of their glasses. "What did you do before you were married?" she asked.

Iris took a sip of wine and mulled the question. Ten years was a long time when you lived the kind of life she did.

"It's hard to think back that far," she said, running a finger around the rim of the glass. "I worked with my brother for a while in his antique shop."

"That's promising. Did you like it?"

"I remember how much I liked seeing things I would normally never see, like inlaid wood boxes with their scrollwork designs. And African masks and shrunken heads sitting on a walnut cabinet that was a hundred years old. There was a sense of history there. Everything had been touched and loved before."

"Have you thought about working with antiques again?"

"Not really," Iris said, hoping to change the subject before she had to think any more about Jonathan and their complicated relationship. "Tell me about you."

"There's not much to tell. Before I got this job, I worked in a PR firm, just working the front desk and taking messages. I thought for a while that I might want to learn the business and work my way up, but then a friend told me about this job and it was intriguing, to say the least. I like knowing that everything we do at the station helps someone. My part might not be important, but every little bit, as they say."

Iris nodded, looking at the girl. She looked younger than her age, with her wavy blonde hair pulled back and tied with a navy ribbon that matched her blouse. She was pretty and pleasant, quite suited for someone like PC Dugan. McIntyre, on the other hand, would never have been with as uncomplicated a girl as Ena Warren, as was evidenced by the photo of his previous partner. Iris had seen Alison Kendall's book sitting on a table and wondered if it would unlock any of the mysteries of DCI Rob McIntyre. He was taciturn on occasion, not that she cared. She was frosty enough herself, she knew. Sometimes life didn't lend itself to happiness, and one had to cobble together sanity any way one could.

They talked for the next two hours, Iris managing to keep the focus of the conversation off her own life. They finished the bottle and then made coffee in McIntyre's kitchen, an unspoken agreement, perhaps, to wait for McIntyre to arrive home. Iris had to admit that it was good having someone to talk to, someone whose life hadn't been tainted with death and suffering. She couldn't remember the last time she had.

McIntyre returned before midnight. Iris, sobered by the coffee, stood when she heard him open the door. Ena came up behind her and she could see his surprise at finding the clerk in his house.

"I'm glad you're up," he said, looking back at Iris.

"What's happened?" she asked.

The door was still open behind him and she rubbed her arms. It was cold outside. Bone cold. Sometimes she felt she would never be warm again.

"Are you up for a trip to the station?" he asked. "We've got a suspect in custody, and I have an article of clothing for you to identify."

Iris grabbed her coat and slipped it over her shoulders. "Let's go."

"I'll be going, then," Ena said. She picked up her coat and nodded at Iris before she left.

They didn't speak in the car, the companionable evening now spoiled. Her mind was on what they would find once they arrived. She hoped it wasn't one of Sophie's tiny red shoes. She wouldn't be able to stand it.

McIntyre parked the vehicle and they hurried inside. She followed as he walked through the corridors with a purposeful stride.

"Who's in custody?" she asked.

"It's a local, a young man who has been in minor scrapes with the law from time to time. Nothing serious, but we found something and need you to take a look at it."

He led her into a cold, clinical room with blinding fluorescent lights and walked up to the counter. The arms of the small coat were spread open as if it were ready to go back on its tiny owner. It was smudged with dirt, though it hadn't been particularly clean when her daughter had worn it for the last time. It took no effort to picture Sophie buttoned up in its warmth, her arms reaching for her. Iris reached out a hand to touch it, but McIntyre held her back.

"Is it hers?" he asked.

Iris began to cry, a low moan that rose from a dark place deep inside. She hadn't known there were still tears left to shed. Nick should have been there to see it with his own eyes. Then he just might have felt a fraction of the pain that she was going through.

After a minute, McIntyre led her to a chair.

"What's happening with the suspect?" she asked after she got control of herself.

"We're holding him for now. He denies any knowledge of the coat or of having anything to do with your daughter's murder." McIntyre sat down on the desk opposite her. "There are problems with this lead, to be honest," he continued. "The suspect can't drive. Someone else would have had to be involved to get them to the scene of the crime and back, and we know Karen didn't have a car. There's no information tying him to Karen or him even being in Truro on the day of the murder, not to mention how he could have gotten a few miles away on the other side of the Tresillian in an area of woods and ponds. And he's mentally challenged. He lives with his mother on a farm outside the city."

"I may not have known her well, but that doesn't sound like someone she would have been involved with."

"We have officers at the house and grounds now looking for more physical evidence. At the moment, it's the best we can do."

A tall, uniformed sergeant walked into the room. "I've got something for you, Inspector."

McIntyre looked at Iris. "This is DS Willis. He's been running tests on the coat."

"We've got the fingerprints back," Willis said, holding up a file. "There were none on the fabric, as we thought, but we got several good prints off the buttons and the brass buckle on the back. None belong to the suspect you took into custody tonight. We're running them through the database for possible matches. Also, upon inspection, there's no way that this coat was left in the elements for the last week, much less the last year. It's been alternating rain and snow, and this coat hardly has anything on it. It's pretty clear it was planted at the Ellers farm for you to find."

"Planted?" Iris demanded. "Who would do something like that?"

"You'd be surprised," McIntyre answered, drumming his fingers on the table. "If it's not the man we questioned tonight, then someone else is trying to throw us off track. And I think I know exactly who that might be."

SIXTEEN

McIntyre was standing in the kitchen when Iris came down at six thirty. She must have been awakened by the smell of coffee, if she had slept at all. She wasn't a coffee drinker per se, but now he watched as she grabbed the pot and poured a cup in haste.

"I'm coming with you," she said.

"You can't," he argued. "There's nothing you can do anyway. I can't let you watch me question a suspect."

Hughes had been arrested overnight and McIntyre was going in to give him the once-over. Sophie Flynn's coat had been planted on the Ellers property, and there was a high probability that Hughes was involved. In any case, he would get to the bottom of it. Without a doubt, the man was hiding something, but if nothing else, he was their only true lead to Karen Peterson.

"I don't care if you make me wait in the car. I can't sit here any longer."

"You can wait in my office. I'll let you know if anything important happens. But the truth is, it's a long, drawn-out process. It usually takes hours, sometimes days, to get to the bottom of a situation."

"There's something else."

"What?" he asked, rinsing his cup in the sink. He dried it with a cloth and set it on the shelf next to the mug that Alison had always used.

"I want her coat," she said. "Sophie's coat."

"Sorry," McIntyre said, shaking his head. "It's evidence. If we find Karen Peterson, it may well be the only physical link to your daughter's death."

"When you find her," Iris corrected.

She pulled on her coat and took the red scarf from the peg as he grabbed his own from the back of a chair. He could see his own breath as they walked out to the car. He clicked the button to unlock the doors and they got in. Iris was frowning, concentrating on some memory, perhaps. He couldn't even imagine how it must have felt to see her child's coat, rescued from a dump of a chicken pen in the back of nowhere. If that didn't upset her, he had no idea what would.

There was no morning traffic. The lanes were quiet, as though a hush had fallen on the entire city. He took a right onto St. Clements Hill Road and a few minutes later, pulled up behind the familiar gray building and found his space in the car park. They walked into the station and took the stairs to his office. None of the other detectives were in yet, and neither, fortunately, was his superintendent, who was sure to have opinions about Iris Flynn hanging about the station.

McIntyre's office was one of the largest on the floor, which wasn't saying much, with a wall of bookshelves stuffed with reference materials and stacks of files waiting to be returned to their proper place. Next door, in Miller's office, his fellow inspector had potted plants and pictures of St. Andrews hung on the walls, and an antique walking stick stand held a couple of nice putters in the corner. It was a regular paradise. Miller's wife had turned it from a squalid box into a professional-looking office. His was still a squalid box. Alison had never even been in his office, much less offered to decorate it.

He turned on his computer and waved Iris to the chair by the window. It wasn't comfortable, but of course he could have Dugan take her back to the house when she got tired of waiting.

"Want some coffee?" he asked.

"Not until I get desperate," she said. "I've tasted it."

He turned away from her and smiled to himself. It was the first light-hearted remark she'd made in his presence. He hadn't thought her capable of it. Picking up the phone, he punched in a number.

A familiar voice picked up the line. "DI Parsons."

"Jake, it's McIntyre. I want to interview Kevin Hughes a little later. Can you take care of that for me?"

"What time do you want me to bring him to the interview room?"

"Go ahead and bring him now. We'll let him cool his heels for a while. He has some things he needs to think over. And I'd like to talk to Joe Ellers now."

He set the phone back in its cradle. "I've got to go. Coffee's in the lounge down the hall if you need anything."

"Isn't he the one you arrested last night?" Iris asked. She hadn't removed her coat or scarf. She just sat there staring at him.

"Yes. I need to get his full statement." McIntyre coughed. "I also plan to show him the coat and get his reaction to it."

She blanched at the mention of the coat. "Then maybe I—"

"No," he interrupted. "I can't let you have it."

She started to protest.

"And no, you can't speak to him, either. Trust me, it wouldn't do any good." He checked his emails and then logged off the computer, so she wouldn't be tempted to look through his emails while he was out. "If you want to go back to the house, let me know. Stick your head out and somebody will find me."

"Thanks," she murmured.

She walked over to stand in front of the board where he and Dugan had pinned up photos and clues for the case. She reached up and touched the photo of her daughter. There was a card underneath it that read *SOPHIE Flynn, 3 Years OLD* in Dugan's messy scrawl, to remind them she'd been but a child when her life was so unfairly stolen from her. There were copies of the artist's sketch of the woman who'd turned out not to be Karen, and an enlarged copy of Karen at the railway station in her red coat with the toggle buttons. McIntyre hadn't thought about how difficult it would be for her to sit in this room for hours staring at them.

"Are you sure you'll be all right?" he asked.

She nodded without turning around. "Yes."

He shrugged and left the office, pulling out his mobile and dialing a number. "Dugan?"

"Right behind you, sir."

He turned to see his sergeant walking toward him. Dugan unzipped his coat and took off his knit cap.

"So, who are we talking to first?" Dugan asked. He was always ready to get down to business. There was nothing like working with people who took their job seriously.

"Ellers," McIntyre answered. "Make sure his Appropriate Adult is present. We're going to let Hughes sweat it out for a while."

"Will do." Dugan raised an eyebrow as he hung up his coat and tossed his cap onto his desk. "So, what do you think? Did Hughes throw the coat in the pen intentionally to implicate Joe Ellers?"

"It didn't get back there by itself, and I doubt Ellers is someone Karen Peterson would have turned to for a crime like this. There's no record that they ever met, and he isn't the type to talk to strange women at any rate."

"And neither of them had a car," Dugan added. He suddenly stopped, cocking his head. "Look, boss."

Joe Ellers' mother was standing in the corridor, arguing with another officer about her right to see her son. McIntyre had no desire to speak to her and ducked down another hall. They went to the interrogation room where Joe was waiting. Even in the light of day, in a room well-lit by fluorescent bulbs and an entire police force coming to life around them, Ellers was oddly menacing. His glasses, too large for his face, drooped down his nose. His nose needed blowing and his clothes were too loose for his frame. He watched them come into the room, his mouth open and his eyes squinting, concentrating on them as if trying to remember where he'd seen them before.

A middle-aged woman with graying hair sat next to him, and McIntyre nodded at her. "I'm DCI Robert McIntyre. And you are … ?"

"Brenda Chapman," she answered. "I'm Mr. Ellers' Appropriate Adult. I was called about an hour ago and asked to be available in case you wanted to start the interview early."

"That's fine, thank you," McIntyre replied. He waited until everyone was settled in their chairs before he turned on the recorder and began to speak. "This is an interview of Joe Ellers. Who is present: myself; DCI McIntyre; DS Alex Dugan; Brenda Chapman, acting as Appropriate Adult; and Joe Ellers. The date is 29th December, 2015. The time is 8:32. Joe, I need to remind you that you're still under caution. You don't have to say anything unless you wish to do so, but anything you do say may be used in evidence. Do you understand?"

"Yes," Ellers answered. "You want to talk to me."

"I'm DCI McIntyre. I spoke to you last night. Do you remember?"

Ellers looked at him again and nodded.

"I need you to speak your answers, please."

The young man frowned.

"Do you remember me coming to your house last night?" McIntyre repeated.

"Yeah." Ellers was sitting completely still, watching him.

"All right, Joe. Do you remember why you're here?"

"Probably 'cos I looked at the girl funny."

"What girl?"

"The one at the café yesterday. She didn't like me."

He glanced at Dugan for a minute. "No, you're not here because of a girl at a café. I want to talk to you about Karen Peterson."

"Who?"

Dugan pulled out a copy of the CCTV image and put it on the table in front of Ellers.

"Do you see that woman in the red coat? Have you ever seen her before?"

"Short."

"What?"

"She looks shorter than the other people."

McIntyre looked at the photo, frowning. She didn't seem shorter at all. "Look at her face, Joe. Have you ever seen this woman before?"

"Is she from the café? Will she be mean to me, too?"

"No, she's not from the café. She was taking care of a little girl."

"I don't like kids. They point and stare."

"Did this woman point at you?"

Ellers looked at him and then at the picture again. Finally, he shook his head. "Don't know her," he said.

"Joe, I want to talk to you about the coat that was found in your chicken pen. A child's coat. We want you to have a look at it."

McIntyre nodded at Dugan, who disappeared into the hall and returned a half minute later with the small green coat. It was zipped into a plastic bag to protect it from any additional fingerprints.

"Have you seen this before?"

"It's a coat."

"Yes, it's a coat. Do you know where it came from?"

"It's not mine. It's too small."

"Did you ever see anyone else wearing it?"

Joe shook his head. "I don't like kids."

"Yes, Joe, we know. Do you know a fellow named Kevin Hughes?"

"Who?" he repeated.

McIntyre looked over at Dugan. "Looks like that's a no."

"Can I have an ice cream now?" Ellers asked. "Mum said if I'm good, I can have an ice cream."

"When you go home," McIntyre said. He stood and spoke into the recorder. "I'm terminating the interview."

He and Dugan walked into the hall and closed the door behind them.

"What are you going to do, boss?" Dugan asked.

"The only thing that ties him to the case is that coat, and all evidence points to its having been planted there."

"Are you ready to talk to Hughes?"

"I'll head over there now. He knew Karen Peterson, and was probably even sleeping with her, for Christ's sake. In case you didn't notice, he was more than a little dodgy during our chat yesterday." He started walking. "Why don't you check on Iris Flynn? Just don't tell her anything."

Dugan nodded and turned down the hall. McIntyre went back in the direction he'd come and opened the door to the interview room of Kevin Hughes. The young man looked the worse for wear after a night in jail. His hair was in his eyes and he needed a shave. He gave McIntyre a scathing look as he came in.

"No sleep?" McIntyre asked. He gave the caution and turned on the recorder but didn't sit at the table right away. He didn't want Hughes getting comfortable. There was something intimidating about looking up at a person who was grilling you that made it impossible to get your balance.

Hughes shook his head instead of replying, and McIntyre knew it meant he was afraid of saying the wrong thing and being locked up for a very long time. He bent down and got in Hughes' face. "Let's get this out in the open right now. Did you kill Sophie Flynn on December 17th of last year?"

"No!" Hughes insisted, almost coming out of his chair.

McIntyre narrowed his eyes at him. "Then you have nothing to worry about. We just need you to answer a few questions so we can piece together what happened. I want you to tell me about the last time you saw Karen."

Hughes rubbed his face and sighed. "Fucking 'ell. This is such a mess. She came to the house."

"The night she took the child?"

"Yes."

"Had she ever been to the house before?"

"No, we always met at the pub."

"How often did you meet?"

"A couple of times a week, from the time she came to Truro. We'd struck up a conversation the first time we met, and we liked each other a lot."

"Was she alone the night she came to the house?"

Hughes hesitated. "No, she wasn't."

"So the child was with her?" McIntyre's heart suddenly beat a little faster.

"Yes."

"She brought the child. This child," he said, pulling a photo of Sophie Flynn from his pocket and slapping it on the table. "Was she alive?"

"'Course she was. Why wouldn't she be?"

"Why did she come to see you that particular night? Was the child hurt? Was Karen hurt?"

"No. No one was hurt."

"Then what did she want, Kevin? Did she plan to harm the child?"

"No, she wanted to keep it, I think. But of course I knew she couldn't. It was one of them brats she was taking care of for the Flynns."

"Tell me everything you can remember about that conversation."

Hughes sighed in resignation and leaned forward in his seat. "I let her in the house. My parents were at the pub for the evening. I was playing video games and was going to go to see some friends later, around ten. When I opened the door, she was standing there, all agitated. She pulled the little girl inside and sat her down in a chair and then we went in the kitchen and started a fight."

"What happened, exactly?"

"She got really angry. She thought we were like a real couple or something. That's probably my fault. Sometimes you say things when you're with a girl, you know. She had some money and wanted us to take the kid and leave together. I'd talked about being bored at my job and wanting to go to London. She expected me to take her, and started crying when I refused. I mean, I couldn't go, even if she hadn't brought the stupid kid to the house. She got so angry she hit me in the face. Busted my lip, actually."

"What about the little girl?"

"When we came out of the kitchen, the front door of the house was open and she was gone. Her coat was there on the floor, but she'd disappeared."

McIntyre tried to remain calm.

"What did you do?"

"Karen started screaming and then left the house to find her."

"You didn't go after her?"

"Are you kidding? She was fucking scary, when it came down to it. I didn't want anything to do with her. And I was bleeding all over my shirt."

"What did you do with the coat?"

"I didn't know what to do with it, so I tossed it under the bed in my room before my parents came back."

"And why did you take it to the Ellers' farm?"

Hughes squirmed in his seat. "After I heard the kid was found dead, I was afraid someone would connect me to Karen. I didn't have anything to do with it, I swear. I even forgot about the whole sodding thing until my mum mentioned she saw it on the news. Then you showed up at the door and I got scared."

"You didn't know Joe Ellers personally, did you?"

"One of the blokes at work is his cousin. He talked sometimes about the scrapes Joe gets into."

"And you figured you might as well implicate someone who is mentally challenged and always getting in trouble for one thing or another."

Hughes shrugged and looked down at his hands.

"Are you the one who called the tip in to the police?"

There was no reply. McIntyre stood and walked to the door.

"Where are you going?" Hughes asked. "And what's going to happen to me?"

"You've obstructed a police investigation. We're not going to take that lightly," McIntyre growled. "In the meantime, I have to get someone some fucking ice cream."

SEVENTEEN

ALISON'S DESK WAS PERCHED under the best upstairs window, where she could look out onto the small wooded area behind the house and write without distraction. It was more of a library table than a desk, deep and wide, with a subtle carved pattern on the narrow apron. She loved everything about it: the glass lamp she'd brought home from her recent trip to London, a floral china cup filled with pens, a wooden bin holding writing pads, and a small white Coalport china castle that had belonged to her mother. She ran her hands over the smooth wood surface before opening her laptop and preparing to write. There were no drawers to hide papers. She was useless when it came to papers, anyway. With her, it was always out of sight, out of mind. Instead, she had a shelf in the room with open baskets holding various files, including ones marked *Research, Ideas,* and one quite intriguing folder labeled *Murder.*

The *Murder* file, a cheerful if incongruous polka-dot manila folder, bulged at the seams, full of clippings and notes she'd compiled over the last couple of years. It was society's fault, she thought;

if there weren't so much injustice in the world, there wouldn't be so many books to write. Poverty, overcrowded schools, divorce: children barely stood a chance in the postmodern world. They were raised on violent video games and hair-raising movies. No wonder so many of them grew up misfits. At the moment, she was interested in a case she'd been following in the newspapers and online about a woman who had killed the assassin her husband had hired to take her life. There was a poetic justice about it. Murders were interesting things, always prompting questions: What had that person done to provoke murderous thoughts in someone else? Was it an act of passion or planned to the last jot and tittle? Could murder be justified in the right circumstances? As she contemplated it for the hundredth time, she heard the door open behind her and a cup and saucer was placed at her elbow.

"Tea," Madeline said.

"Thank you," she replied, giving her a slight smile. She preferred to keep things professional while she was writing. If she got off task for even a few minutes, she would lose her train of thought and have to stop altogether.

"Any plans to go out later?"

"I hadn't given it any thought. Is there something you want to do?"

Madeline shrugged. "Not really. Just checking on you."

When she left, Alison looked out over the trees in the distance. Now and then, a deer or rabbit could be seen foraging for food, but at the moment, everything was still, just as she liked it. She turned back to her computer, thinking. Her current book involved spousal abuse, and she hadn't yet decided who would kill whom.

The husband, Keith, was hard, selfish, and had a temper, but Laura, the wife, while meek, was impulsive and reckless. The friction between them had begun, as many of these things do, at a dinner party.

Keith was celebrating a promotion, and the company for which he worked had gone to great lengths to make it an evening to remember. Laura had been introduced to all of his colleagues and then, as was her custom, went to hide at the buffet table. There were plump little shrimp and planked figs with pancetta, not limp carrot sticks and cubed cheese, the kind of uninspiring things she served when she hosted a party. There was crostini, smeared with extra virgin olive oil and covered in cheese and mushrooms. It was almost enough to soften the blow of having to stand at his side and smile when she wanted nothing more than to leave him. He'd been a bully, always wanting his way and expecting her to shut her mouth and do his bidding. She'd harbored thoughts of divorce, but he wasn't the kind of man one could easily leave. He'd threatened her, even slapped her the last time she'd mentioned it. There wasn't a home to go back to, either. Her parents had been killed in a crash not long after they were married, and she'd recklessly put the money she had inherited in Keith's hands. He held all the cards—money, power, influence—and he had both the ability and will to strip her of everything if she tried to leave. At the buffet table, she lifted a shrimp, contemplating the thought of him choking to death on one as she stood by and watched.

As she took a plate, one of Keith's colleagues came up to speak to her and she knew without looking that her husband's eyes were boring a hole through her back. She knew better than to stoke his jealousy by prolonging a conversation with another man in his presence. It made her appear standoffish, but she didn't care. It was a matter of survival. The man at her elbow was persistent, and in an effort not to be rude, she gave short answers, hoping she wasn't encouraging him. Minutes later, Keith ended whatever conversation he'd started and walked over to her. He reached for her plate and set it down on the table, then took her arm at the elbow in a tight pinch that would leave marks and walked her to the corner for a dressing-down. Two hours later, one of them would be dead. Alison only had to decide which of them it would be.

It was a delicious choice. She decided to write it both ways in order to see which she preferred. She was leaning toward killing Keith, wondering exactly how Laura would do it. A woman can only take so much before she snaps, and Laura was rife for snapping. Alison understood her, because she had sometimes been rife for snapping, herself.

Writing about murder brought Rob to mind. In fact, she knew she wouldn't have written her first mystery if she hadn't been living with a detective chief inspector. His work, tedious as it was to live with in the everyday slog, was intriguing at times. At the few dinner parties he allowed himself to be dragged to, the conversation somehow always managed to be brought around to the life of a detective and the rich mine of lurid tales he accumulated over time. Of course, he didn't ever share anything specific about his cases. Perhaps that was part of the allure. He refused to play the game. He himself was a man of mystery, caught between a life of duty and the secret life he hid, even from her. It was on the rare occasion when he talked to her, sharing thoughts and feelings like a normal person, that she learned something about his work. But mostly he kept things to himself, bottling them up, including his emotions. It was maddening.

She frowned, thinking of how close she'd come to telling him what was going on with Madeline, who had now moved in with her. She'd stopped herself as she realized he would never understand. He wasn't capable of it. He had a rigid, narrow view of life that served him well as a police officer but not at all as a human being. When Carl Linnaeus wrote his taxonomy and organized his three kingdoms with classes and orders, he must have gotten something wrong. Men and women were too different to be the same species. Of course, she thought, there were similarities. Mammals have a four-chambered heart, and lungs that breath oxygen. They have five senses and a covering of hair and a lower jaw made of bone, but men and women are vastly different creatures. When it came to their brains, the differences were even more evident. Men tended to reflect on things and then quickly move onto another task. Women, however, with a more natural blood flow through the brain, ruminated on and revisited emotional issues, which rendered them a different type of species altogether.

She'd often accused Rob of not caring about things that were important to her, but she now realized that he simply wasn't hardwired to do so. She couldn't expect him to care about her writing or her dreams or even a great deal about her physical well-being. Certainly not her emotional state. He was a hunter-gatherer of the highest order, who punched the clock and at the end of the day expected nothing more than to be fed. It wasn't how she wanted to live. She felt suffocated going through the motions of being a good helpmeet and partner when she really wanted to stretch herself creatively and emotionally. He hadn't understood, but she'd begun to see that it wasn't only Rob, it was men in general. There might be some exceptions, some rare men who could empathize and understand what a woman was feeling; the ones who changed nappies and went with their wives to romantic movies. But in the end, she supposed, perhaps they'd simply gotten a higher dose of estrogen in the womb.

The sun came out from behind the clouds, where it had been obscured for most of the last few weeks, and she stood, stretching. She'd gotten up too early once again. It had been ingrained in her since childhood, when she'd been raised by grandparents after losing her mother in an automobile accident when she was nine. Her father had disappeared before she was born. He was seldom mentioned and never missed. Settled and happy with her grandparents, she lived the routine of sixty-year-olds as she grew up: rising early, eating three proper meals a day with napkins and forks—never fingers—and going to bed long before any of her friends. She awoke to the trill of sparrows outside the window in spring and to the sound of her grandmother making breakfast in the small, neat kitchen, always eggs with a soft center and toast. Her grandfather, too, was industrious by dawn, having drunk his tea and finished at least a chapter of whatever book he was reading before he went to work in the factory down the road. Before work each day, he would take her on his lap and read a page of *The Dubliners* or something by Huxley, feeding her sips of tea while they waited for their bacon and toast. She never remembered the plot of anything, but it was a good feeling being wrapped in his strong arms, listening to his deep and sonorous voice; perhaps her most vivid childhood memory.

Life with grandparents, however, was a serious affair. Socks were always to be pulled up, hems that had come loose immediately stitched, and beds made before one walked out the door. Friends were investigated before a playdate could be allowed, and not only the friends but their parents, as well. It was a solitary business, growing up, but Alison could not imagine any other life. She found her friends' homes overwhelming with the bustle of children and chatter, and was always relieved to go home. Even dating had its limitations. She was not allowed to date until age seventeen, and then it was prearranged outings with boys her grandparents had connections to, whose families were already known to them. Alison was no rebel. She knew if it weren't for her grandparents, she could have grown up in an orphanage. Yet because of her insular childhood, she never developed bonds of friendship or love with anyone in her growing-up years. She had yearnings, but for whom or what she did not know. Others around her defined themselves by virtue of their talents or leanings, but she'd never had any strong enough to give her a sense of self.

She went downstairs and poured a cup of coffee, spilling some on the counter. Luisa turned to clean it up, but she shook her head. "I'll get it, thanks," she said.

"I don't mind, Miss Kendall."

She smiled and took a cloth to wipe it. "What's for supper tonight?"

"I had planned to do your usual salmon … "

"Ah." Madeline must have interfered with the menu again. Alison was used to a schedule. She liked knowing Wednesday was salmon, Thursday pork. "What are we having instead?"

"Pasta primavera."

"That's fine, thanks," she answered. "And tomorrow?"

"You mentioned a roast."

She nodded, wondering if she would have to speak to Madeline about it. Pouring herself a fresh cup of coffee, she made a mental list of Madeline's good and bad qualities. There were many good qualities, she knew. Until Madeline came along, she'd thought herself reasonably organized, yet Madeline brought a higher definition to the word. The files Alison had entrusted to her were sorted into "written," "edits," and "rewrites," with a list attached to each one. She typed and filed and made sense of Alison's hastily scribbled notes. There was no doubt that there was much more time for writing, now that she could focus less on the running of the house and the organization of her paperwork and was free to dream and think and tap at her keyboard at any hour she chose. And there was always a cup of tea at hand even before she knew she wanted it. It was a physical encouragement, a cheerful prod to keep at it. Alison had spent too many years alone at a desk in front of a blank wall pounding out well-polished sentences, desperate for a little kindness, the sort Rob would never have given. In spite of Madeline telling her she wasn't much of a housekeeper, the house was now gleaming and tidy—far tidier than usual. In fact, she almost missed the stack of books on the floor and piles of unopened letters on the table. Madeline almost made Luisa superfluous.

The girl, however, had bad qualities as well. She was territorial, for someone who had only recently come to live with her, and a bit dismissive with Luisa, expecting the maid to do more than Alison required. Worse still, Madeline herself was a distraction whenever she came into the room. Unlike Alison's penchant for casual, warm clothing in winter, Madeline's preference for snug jumpers drew attention to her body, and Alison couldn't help but notice the overwhelming feelings it engendered in her.

She had begun to wonder: was that how she saw herself, as a lesbian? There was no doubting the instant and powerful attraction between the two of them, but had she actually made a huge life reversal, or was it a brief spark of intimacy lighting up a long, loveless winter? Unfortunately, she hadn't the energy or desire to find the answer, not when Madeline was such a ready temptation. Soon, she thought, she would grapple with that question. Soon, perhaps, but not quite yet.

EIGHTEEN

In the mist of the late afternoon, the river swelled against its banks, engorged after a week of steady, unrelenting rain. The clouds had broken. Wan sunlight played on the dappled rocks bleached gray and white over many decades of summer. Shadows fell from golden oaks over the water, until it reached a clearing where occasionally someone would discard shoes and socks and wade in the eddying pool. Water beetles scurried through marsh grasses. Across the damp ground, voles and dormice darted from nest to nest, pausing to guzzle fallen treasures of berries and nuts. If one listened closely, one could hear the swallows playing among the trees. It was as still a place as England could offer. Not a single human had ventured this way in some weeks, and the serenity was meant to be broken one way or another. Odd-shaped mushrooms sprung from the shaded ground under the trees, unsightly, poisonous fungi destined to be trampled under human feet; perhaps a hiker, taking a brief respite from the guidebook and trail to appreciate the beauty of a sheltered riverbank. Or young lovers, separating themselves from the crowds of the nearby village, would find it suitable for an impromptu picnic, sipping champagne from a bottle and making love on a blanket tossed upon the ground. In summers past, a young earl rode his chestnut gelding across this meadow at least once each year, hardly noticing his surroundings as he focused on giving the horse its head and experiencing a welcome departure from his social life and familial responsibilities.

The eventual intruder was someone quite different. A young girl stepped among the reeds, making her way to the pool which lapped against the pebbled shore, water clear enough at its edge to see minnows and the odd trout. Her hands were no larger than the petals of the flowers she picked as she passed. A breeze ruffled her hair and she shivered, pulling her jumper around her shoulders, though she was undeterred from the joy of freedom and the exploration of such an interesting place. Overhead, a wren called for its mate as the girl perched on a long, flat rock, pulling off her shoes before venturing closer to the water. It was colder now. She was quite young, without the wisdom that would dissuade her from wandering in such a place alone, yet some odd, unfamiliar instinct gave her a moment of alarm. Looking at the clouds overhead, which seemed to take the shapes of rabbits and ponies, she forgot everything else and roused herself, once again moving toward the water. Twigs, broken off a nearby tree during the week of inclement weather, lay scattered about its trunk, a plethora from which to choose. She fondled them happily, feeling the rough, thicker sticks and holding them against the brittle twigs until she found one of sufficient

166

weight and heft to poke into the water at the fish that scattered at her approach. Digging the stick into the submerged part of the bank, she jumped back as the waves touched her small, round feet.

Something caught her eye, something dark and bulky bobbing in the water a few yards away. As is the case among normal, happy children, curiosity was stronger than fear. She came near the water's edge, holding the broken branch not as a weapon but as an object with which to prod things. Small twigs jutted out from the object and she moved closer, extending the branch in front of her, making tiny swirls in the water with its tip. She was knee-deep in the pool now, goose pimples breaking out on her small, thin body. With the branch, she poked the strange dark thing, watching as it bobbed about the murkier part of the pool. She tapped it again and then stepped back in horror as it turned on its side. It was the head of another young child, hideously disconnected from its body like a bloody sword ripped from its sheath.

Iris dropped the book onto her lap. What kind of monster was Alison Kendall, anyway? What had McIntyre seen in a woman who was capable of creating such a gruesome image? The curiosity she'd felt about the woman with whom he was obsessed was doused, as if by cold water. She threw the book to the floor, drawing her limbs into a ball. She'd dreamt of Sophie again last night, of her tiny, elf-like body wriggling into bed next to her. Someone like Alison Kendall had probably never loved or lost anyone in her life. She knew nothing of how wretched it felt to be miserable and alone, to be forced to imagine day after day her child's last moments, wondering what her final words had been. Surely, she had cried for her mother, as Iris, in her agony, had cried for her.

Yet it was pointless, all of this speculation and distress. It helped no one. She'd been here nearly two weeks and nothing had changed. Coming to England had been nothing more than an expensive mistake, one that put her in debt to her sister, jeopardized her relationship with Nick, and separated her from her two living, breathing children who woke every day wondering if this was the day Mummy would return to them and everything would begin to be normal. Children were fortunate that way, she decided, capable of believing life could have a happy ending and not be the devastating ordeal that Iris and others who grieved and coped with loss knew it to be. She felt empty, bereft, spent. Karen remained untraceable. There were no answers here in Cornwall. Things could no longer be put right. She had no choice but to borrow money from Jonathan, putting herself in even greater debt, and return to Sydney to try to figure out what to do.

Iris rose from the sofa, kicking the book aside as she made her way to the stairs. She tore off her shirt and pants and tossed them on the hall floor. Turning on the shower, she felt sure there wasn't enough hot water in the world to rid her mind of the image planted there by Alison Kendall. She stepped into the spray and held her face under it, eyes closed, arms clenched around her stomach. No one could help. Not Nick, who was as powerless as she; not her mother, who lived in an alcoholic haze. She stood there for a long time. She'd done everything she could. It was time to go home.

———

At first glance, the house appeared empty. McIntyre was relieved. He'd had no peace since Iris appeared on his brother's doorstep. It

168

was the sort of thing he hated, being expected to provide a resolution to a problem when there was none to be had. Karen Peterson, or whatever her name was, had either fallen into the dark crevices of London or had left the country altogether by now. Neither Joe Ellers nor Kevin Hughes had any direct involvement with the child's murder. He would call his superintendent and ask for a leave while he sorted things out. He was sick of police work. Things had been going downhill for some time.

Tossing his keys onto a nearby table, McIntyre looked through the post, sifting through it to see if there was anything of note. There was not. Another sign his life was at a complete standstill.

He walked upstairs to change his clothes. His bedroom was quiet. The bed was made, just as he'd left it; the newspapers and magazines in a jumble on the table, as usual. He turned, surprised, as a door opened in the hallway and looked up to see Iris standing there, rubbing her hair with a towel, completely naked.

"God! You scared me!" she said. The towel she held was too small to cover anything, despite her best efforts, so she didn't try. Instead, she frowned. "Well, you don't have to stand there staring."

"What *should* I do?" he asked, ready to battle.

Neither of them moved. In the stillness, he could hear the sound of her breathing. She watched him with an indecipherable expression on her face. A strand of wet hair hung across her cheek, and before he knew what he was doing, he reached out and touched it, moving it away from her face. His fingers were now damp, and with them he drew an imaginary line down her jaw, caressing it.

This was a face that had never been caressed. She stood rooted to the spot, the lines around her mouth betraying neither expectation nor surprise. Life had been difficult for her, long before she married Nick Flynn and was carted around the world and lost a child in the

169

worst possible way. She'd never worn beautiful clothes or had a reliable roof over her head. She'd taken everything that was given without question or complaint. Touching her arm, he felt an incredible sadness. Her life was even more screwed up than his, and neither of them deserved it. He wondered if she might have been beautiful if life hadn't dealt her so many blows. He leaned forward and kissed her, watching as her eyelids fluttered closed, receiving this silent pact of atonement, as if he'd asked forgiveness for all that anyone had ever done to her.

It was only a few steps to the bed. He guided her to it, tugging at the buttons of his shirt. She smelled of lavender; the soap that Alison preferred and which he'd kept on hand in case she ever came back. He didn't want to think of Alison. Neither did he especially want to think of Iris. He wanted to feel warm lips and soft hands and round thighs pressed against his own. She was alive, after all, and responding to his touch. They were two people trapped in a world of hopelessness and dying. For a moment, it felt good to be one of the survivors. He touched her teeth with his tongue and she grasped his arms, keeping him close. A pang of guilt hit him, but he dismissed it. This was biological. This was what kept the human race from dying out. People did it every day. Not him—not Detective Chief Inspector Rob McIntyre, cuckold of a woman who stole from other people's grim realities to write her fiction—but other men. And of course, not Iris Flynn, broken, forsaken Iris Flynn, who was caught in a spinning wheel of distorted facts and clues that would never solve her child's crime because it was easier than accepting what had happened and living with the reality.

Suddenly, he realized that neither of them had moved for a minute. One of them had hit the disconnect button; perhaps both. He looked into Iris's emotionless eyes, unable to read her thoughts.

"What is it?" he asked. "What are you thinking?"

She sighed. "I was wondering if Nick has ever been unfaithful."

"Maybe he has," he said. "Maybe he fucked Karen Peterson, and that's what prompted her to kill your daughter."

The slap resounded through the room. He rolled off her at once, throwing his legs over the side of the bed, shocked at his own outburst. Since when had he been so cruel? Hadn't he felt sorry for her a moment before? Or perhaps he was jealous of her. She loved that dead child more than he'd ever cared about anything in his life.

Angry and frustrated, he stood up and bolted down the stairs. A few moments later, Iris followed him, though for what reason he couldn't imagine, wearing his robe. He had no interest in talking now. He selected a bottle at random from a cupboard and began to pour.

"What are you doing?" she demanded.

He shrugged, lifting his glass. "*Aqua vitae*. Or brandy, if you prefer. I should have asked if you'd like one, but of course you abstain, don't you?"

"From alcohol or sex?"

"From life."

She recoiled, her face as dark as the thunderclouds swelling outside, pulling the robe tighter around her body. "You have no right."

"No right to what?"

"You don't know me, McIntyre. You were supposed to help us. You're a means to an end."

"This is my house. I'm entitled to say what I like. You don't have to be here."

"You dragged me here. You wouldn't leave me alone. And frankly, I don't care where I am as long as I find Karen Peterson."

"It's over! Can't you see?"

"No, it's not. I—"

"It is. She's gone. We'll never find her. It would be sheer chance if she ever popped up again, and she won't, because she's not that stupid."

"Stop!" Iris cried, putting her hands over her ears. "It's not true."

He slammed the glass on the table, sloshing brandy everywhere, and grabbed her wrists, forcing her hands away from her face. "You've got to face it. You're lying to yourself. And what if we did get that one-in-a-million break and actually found her? What then? Your daughter is still gone, Iris. She's dead, and finding Karen Peterson won't bring her back."

She went limp in his hands and he released her, again shocked at himself. He was furious—at Iris, at Alison, at the world. Iris went over and sat on the sofa, staring through the darkened window. He spied Alison's book on the floor but didn't bend to retrieve it. At that moment, he wanted to toss it into the bin. Instead, he went into the kitchen to make tea. There was no taking back what he'd said. He hadn't even realized he'd been thinking it, but now, it seemed unmistakable. Nick Flynn probably did have an affair with Karen Peterson. He'd spurned her, and she'd killed the child in revenge. Sophie had been Nick's child, too. It happened all the time. The facts seemed to support his theory, but breaking it to Iris like that was the greatest insensitivity he'd ever shown. There was no way to ameliorate the situation, and so tea was the only answer.

A few minutes later, he brought a tray into the sitting room where Iris sat, unmoving, and poured it without speaking. He put the cup into her hands and poured a cup for himself.

"I'm an arse. I'm sorry."

Her voice was subdued. "You're probably right. I didn't see it. Perhaps I didn't want to."

"It is a possibility, but that doesn't make it true."

"You're the detective."

"Well, that's a mistake. I can't do this job anymore. I'm not cut out for it. There are too many people like you at the end of the day, people who get no satisfaction or justice. It's too hard."

"We're not alike here. Breaking up with a partner is different than losing a child. You haven't anything to be so morbid about."

"And you don't have anything to be optimistic about." He put down the glass. "I'm sorry. I didn't mean that."

"You're lashing out. What did she do to you?"

"What didn't she do?" he asked, shaking his head. "I can't believe I wasted time thinking she and I could make another go of it."

"There's no going back," Iris said.

"That's it. That's the point. There's no going back for any of us."

Iris put down the cup and dropped her face into her hands. "I'm stuck. Drowning. I've let this destroy my entire life."

"What choice do you have?"

"I don't have a choice," she answered. "But there is something you can do for me."

McIntyre set down the cup. "What is it?" he asked. At that moment, he would have done anything.

"I need you to take me to the place where Sophie was found."

NINETEEN

Thirty minutes later, they were in his car heading to Penhale Wood. A year ago, McIntyre had thought it an odd place for Sophie's body to be discovered, so far from the city. There were closer places to dump a body if the killer had been so inclined, and if she'd been killed in Truro. Of course, they had no idea where the crime had actually occurred. The police hadn't even established which side of the river the child had been on when she died.

The Tresillian River separated Truro and its environs from the sparsely populated area to the east, and the many small woods which were found up and down the river on both sides were generally abandoned to woodland creatures and the occasional birder. A lone jogger who had wandered farther down the path than usual had spotted Sophie's body and called the police. If it hadn't been for him, she might not have been found until after the winter gave way to spring, or even summer. There had been little physical evidence collected at the scene, and nothing establishing either a motive or killer.

Because the body had washed up on the far side of the shore, he took the A390 north and then east to cross the river before turning left on the long, narrow lane that hugged the river. It was morbid, Iris's request, but he didn't have it in him to deny her. She'd lost nearly everything that had ever mattered to her, and if it brought her some sort of resolution, he would help her do it.

He parked the car and got out, shoving his hands in his pockets. The clouds were thick and dark, threatening snow. The leaves were shiny from frost and the last snow had melted from the rocks and twigs underfoot, leaving everything damp and muddy. Iris hesitated before she got out of the vehicle. Perhaps she was having second thoughts. He wouldn't blame her. It took an extraordinary amount of courage to face the hardest thing a parent would ever have to. He gave her a couple of minutes to compose herself, stamping his feet against the cold.

Iris turned to look at him. "Did you see her?"

He nodded. He could still picture it, even without the aid of the photos they'd taken as they processed the crime. When the call had come in, he'd rushed to the scene to be there as the Forensics department took charge, trying to preserve the evidence.

They walked in the small space between Merther Pond and the river. The woods were silent, apart from the light wind. McIntyre saw an old raven's nest on the ground and kicked it. He cleared his throat, trying to figure out what to say.

The river, even at this time of year, was beautiful. He watched it wind its way past them, a living thing. He cocked his head and walked toward the spot where Sophie had been found, her remains so gut-wrenching that each one of the officers on the scene had to avert their eyes at first. In particular, he remembered her small hands, their miniscule nails capturing his attention. They had been painted a bright shade of pink, the polish chipping off; an odd thing for so young a child. He knew when he'd seen them that she would never have pretty nails again.

He stopped a few feet away and pointed, hoping Iris wouldn't go any closer, shaking his head when she stepped forward and walked to the very spot. She crouched, her back to him, and he was relieved that she didn't ask him to describe what they'd seen. He wouldn't have been able to do it.

After a few minutes, she stood, still facing the river. "I wish Nick were here." When he didn't reply, she continued. "Although he wouldn't want to see it, of course."

"Probably not," McIntyre conceded.

She looked at him, her arms crossed and a frown on her face. "I want to ask you something."

"Of course."

"It's about men and women, the way they grieve. I'm sure you've seen plenty of grief in your work. Why do we handle it so differently? It's been a year since Sophie died, and I spend all day, every day, remembering her smile, imagining her breath against my cheek, my breasts aching to hold her where she once nursed. Nick feels nothing like it. It's as if men don't even care."

"They care," he argued, though he'd sometimes wondered himself. "They just show it in a different way."

"I'm not sure I call it caring if they can get over the death of a child in less than a year. They focus on something else, something that gives them pleasure. A good fuck, maybe. I don't know. All I know is that they don't want to think about what they've lost. They cut off the grief like a rotten limb and move on without it."

"And women can't," he said.

"Of course they can't," she answered. "They've nursed that child, worried over her, prayed over her, some even giving their lives for their child. Nothing and no one will ever be a higher priority to a mother than the ones we give birth to."

"I wish all mothers felt the way you do," he replied. "That's one thing I've seen in my years with the police department—not everyone loves or feels the way they should toward the children in their care. Mothers leave their children to get drugs, or to meet men. They don't feed them sometimes. They let them live in filthy conditions. You weren't like that, Iris, no matter how bad this makes you feel. You didn't fail her. It just happened. It's not your fault."

She rubbed her arms and looked back at the spot where Sophie's body had been caught among the fallen twigs and branches on the bank. Without a word, she reached into her pocket and took out a piece of string. She bent over and found two small twigs and roped the string around them until she'd fastened a small cross. McIntyre watched as she went back and pushed it, with some difficulty, into the cold, hard ground.

"You're shivering," he said. Her cheeks were pink from the cold.

"Let's walk a little," she said. "That will warm us up."

They fell into step walking along the path. The city, on the other side, seemed a thousand miles away. He was frustrated that even though he'd interviewed Kevin Hughes and Joe Ellers, the little truth he'd gotten out of them hadn't helped at all.

"You're right," he said, after a couple of minutes. "Mothers always do take things harder. I hadn't really thought about it before, but it's true."

"You've never had children, have you?" she asked.

"No."

"Do you picture yourself as a father?"

He glanced over at her. "I suppose in the back of my mind, I did think that one day I'd have two or three kids and a wife, and be worrying about things like getting a bigger house. I can imagine cricket bats left lying about and getting ruddy sick and tired of an endless menu of fish fingers."

"Why didn't you have some, then?"

He was taken aback by the question, though after all they'd been through, it certainly wasn't too personal for her to ask. "I suppose Alison wasn't really the maternal type."

"What's she like?" Iris asked. She gave him a curious glance. "I've seen her photo. I know she's beautiful."

"She is," he admitted. "It's hard to describe her. She wasn't very confident, I guess you might say, when we first met. She changed a great deal over the time we were together. I think she had a vision of what her life should be like, and she pursued it with a vengeance."

"How did you meet?"

"I met her in a coffee shop," he said, but the truth was, he was sick of thinking about Alison.

"I read a couple of pages of her book. It was disturbing. Then again, maybe it's just me. I wasn't up to reading anything that similar to my own life."

"Most people haven't lost a child," he said, bending a branch out of their way. "It's impossible for anyone to know what you're feeling right now."

"She was the funny one, Sophie," Iris said. "She loved to laugh and sing. India hasn't really grown into her personality yet, but Charlotte was never like that. She's always been serious, like me. They've had a hard life. Much harder than they deserve."

She turned suddenly and began to walk back to the car. He pulled his hands out of his pockets and blew on them, quickening his step to keep up with her.

"Iris."

She slowed down but didn't turn around.

"She was lucky to have you for a mum," he said.

Iris stopped and looked at him. "That's the thing I don't believe, you see. If I'd been a good mother, she wouldn't have died out here in the godforsaken wilderness. Do you believe in hell?"

He glanced away for a second. "To be honest, I'm not sure."

"Well, I am," she said. "And I know one thing. I may never know for certain who killed her, but whoever it was who took my child's dying breath is going to spend every second of eternity burning in hell for what they've done."

Before he could answer, she got a text and pulled her mobile out of her pocket.

"Nick!" she exclaimed, until she looked at the screen and sighed. "No, it's just Sarah."

She opened the text, her face softening as she read it. Then she held the screen up for him to see. It was a photo of Charlotte and India, smiling for the camera. They were wearing matching dresses, and India was clutching a ragged stuffed animal in her arms.

"What's the toy?" he asked, knowing if he told her how beautiful they were that she would lose her self-control altogether.

"It's her quoll," she said, opening the door of the car.

"A quoll?"

"It's an Australian marsupial."

McIntyre got into the driver's side and started the car. He turned the heater on full blast, trying to drive the chill from the small, enclosed space. Iris had her mobile in her hand, staring at the photo.

He was relieved. She needed to focus on the two children she had who were alive and waiting for her, not the bastard who had taken Sophie's life.

That was his job.

A snippet of a Frost poem came to him, probably from the days of Alison's poetry group when she was always reading bits of it to him. *The woods are lovely, dark and deep.*

But the woods, he knew, were deadly. And no matter how he felt about it, he couldn't guarantee he could keep any promise he'd made to Iris Flynn.

TWENTY

THE NEXT MORNING, IRIS sat up in bed and punched Nick's number into her mobile. There was no answer again, and she was starting to feel alarmed. She was like that sometimes, completely independent of him until suddenly she wasn't. He was fishing, she was sure, and more than likely already hating it. He wasn't cut out for ordinary work. Everywhere they'd ever lived, he'd worked for a while but then would quit, forcing them to rely on the mercy of strangers. Iris was used to it; Nick was the kind of person one had to love in spite of his flaws. She'd never faulted him for it. He would fish, or paint houses, or do carpentry work until his intrinsic need for freedom resurfaced. He would leave them for a time, but he always came back. She could count on it the same as she could count on the sun rising.

Until McIntyre had linked him to Karen, she'd never believed him unfaithful. In the past ten years, he'd never shown signs of attachment to anyone else, or given any sign that his feelings for her had waned. He was married, he loved his wife, and he went on walkabouts, or whatever he wanted to call it, when his desire for freedom overtook him. It was impossible to explain to anyone, and Iris had never tried.

After a while, she roused herself and went downstairs. McIntyre had gone to work and the room was cold. She longed for the sun, remembering that it was mid-summer in Sydney. Charlotte and India were probably playing with their cousins in the garden, relishing the December heat. She wondered if they thought of her often, and if they asked Sarah when she would come back. She pulled her jumper closer, wondering what she would do when this was over. For the first time, she allowed herself to consider the decisions that lay ahead. She didn't know if she had the strength to go back to Nick and the girls and start over with the Flynns ever watching in their stern, disapproving way. She'd walked out on her children without a word and gone halfway across the world, and God only knew when Nick would return.

After a cup of tea, she made one decision. One was enough on a day like this. She would see her brother. Nick and Jonathan had argued before they'd gone back to Australia, and she suspected terrible things had been said. Perhaps it was time to do something about it. Jonathan would be home. It was Monday. The antique shop was always closed on Monday.

One of the bitterest fights she'd ever had with Nick had been because of Jonathan's interference.

"He said I'm responsible for what happened," Nick told her, just days after Sophie died.

"He can't hold you responsible," Iris argued.

"We're both responsible," Nick had said. "We left her with that fucking woman."

The conversation made her go cold every time she remembered it, but it was time to face Jonathan and clear the air. Whatever his faults, and there were plenty of them, Nick wasn't capable of hurting any of their children. She had no doubt about it. He was no more capable of it than she.

Iris grabbed her coat from the hook, pocketing the house key McIntyre had given her. It was a good three miles to her brother's house, but she decided to walk, hoping to generate some warmth with the exercise. She could have called a cab, but she didn't want to spend any of her dwindling funds, and pride kept her from asking Rob McIntyre for another favor.

She'd walked at least a mile when a small black Ford pulled up beside her. She heard the window being rolled down and looked over at the car.

"Want a lift?"

Iris peered into the vehicle at the man who'd made the offer. He was about her age, with dark hair and even darker eyes. He was a nice-looking man, someone who might have been a teacher or librarian. She was tempted, but it wasn't a smart thing to do in this day and age.

She shook her head. "You're probably not headed in my direction."

"Where to?"

"A couple of miles west."

"Hop in. You'll catch your death, as me Mum would say."

After a moment, she relented. She wasn't much for walking, anyway, and when the thermometer dipped under freezing, she was even less likely. Besides, she'd have to walk back. She opened the door and sat down in the car. He checked to make certain she was inside and then pulled away from the curb. His hands were large and strong, and he steered with his left, placing his right hand on the arm rest between them. Self-consciously, she moved closer to the door.

"I'm Simon. What's your name?" he asked, as they turned the corner.

"Iris," she answered.

"You look familiar to me, for some reason. Have we met?"

"No," she answered, suddenly uncomfortable. She was aware that her photo had appeared on the front page in the newspaper, and he'd probably seen it there. It was a sensationalist story, featuring photos of herself, Nick, and Sophie, when the last thing she wanted to do was to attract unwanted attention.

"Why don't you drop me at the next corner?" she asked.

"Sorry," he replied, keeping his eyes on the road. "I guess you don't want to talk. It's pretty early in the morning, isn't it?"

They both went quiet. She didn't say a word until they were within a few streets of Jonathan's house.

"This is fine," Iris said, hoping her voice didn't sound shaky. She pointed to a house on the corner. "I can walk from here."

He pulled the car over. "Want to get a drink later? I know a great place nearby."

"Sorry," she said. "Not interested."

"I'm sorry to hear that," he said, smiling. "But it was a pleasure to meet you, Iris."

She jumped from the car, watching until it disappeared around the corner before turning in the opposite direction toward Jonathan's street. She trudged up the snowy path toward his house, suddenly nervous about talking to him. She hesitated as she reached his door, debating whether or not to knock. Perhaps she should just find a coffee shop and warm herself before the long walk back home.

Before she could decide, Jonathan opened the door as if he expected her. She had a sudden rush of affection, looking at him. If she hadn't been so angry with him, she would have hugged him. He looked his usual self, though his hair was starting to gray. It was shorter than it had been a year ago, and his boyish face was freshly shaven.

"Well, if it isn't my long-lost sister," he said, stepping back so she could enter.

The house had changed little since she'd been away. The white stucco exterior, with its blue door and tall privet hedge, looked like many other cottages in the area, but the interior was shaped by Jonathan's love of the sea. He'd collected prints of all manner of seagoing vessels, which always reminded Iris of a lighthouse they had visited as children, bringing back the smell of the sea and the shells underfoot. He still had glass jars filled with stones they'd picked up on the beach when they were young, and seeing them gave her a catch in her throat.

Iris stood in the center of the room, taking off her coat. Jonathan hung it on a hook and they sat down, eyeing one another carefully.

"Why didn't you tell me you were here?" he asked, leaning forward. "I found out from Mum when I saw her at the weekend."

Iris looked up at him. "Do you see her much?"

"I pop 'round from time to time."

"Not often, by the looks of it. The house is a disaster. Worse than ever. And the food she had in the kitchen I wouldn't give to a cat."

"This said by a woman who has seen her a handful of times in her adult life."

"Yes, it's so easy to get here from America and Australia," Iris said, crossing her arms. "I should have been here every weekend. Maybe I could have stopped her from hitting the bottle so hard. It's entirely my fault."

"Somewhat bitter, are we?"

Iris looked down at her hands. "I'm sorry. You're right. I shouldn't talk rubbish."

"We haven't spoken since Sophie died," Jonathan said. "Were you going to ignore me forever?"

"In case you haven't noticed, I've had things on my mind."

"It wasn't your fault, you know."

"But it was Nick's, evidently."

He sat back and looked at her. "We've had our differences. I'll admit I don't trust him."

"Why not?"

"I don't like the way you've been forced to live, for one thing. He's left you and the girls alone too much."

"What did you say to make him so angry last year?"

He hesitated, looking up at her as if to gauge her mood. "It's not important now."

"Did you accuse him of sleeping with Karen Peterson?"

Jonathan looked stunned. "Did he tell you that?"

"No. He only said that he detests you. Someone else mentioned it as a possibility."

"Look, I wasn't trying to make trouble for you."

"You didn't," she replied. "Nick would never hurt me. But why did you think that? Did you have a reason to suspect something was going on?"

"Not really. It was a gut feeling. I shouldn't have said anything. I was in shock and overreacted."

Iris took a deep breath. "I wish this was all over. I want to find Karen and get a confession out of her."

"What are you going to do about Charlotte and India?"

"What do you mean?" she asked.

"I just wondered if you're going to let Sarah raise your children."

"I haven't abandoned them, if that's what you're thinking. I'm pushing the police to finish the investigation."

"I just can't imagine that Sarah's lifestyle was one you wanted imposed on your children. They might lose their bohemian ways."

"I don't need your sarcasm at the moment."

"Sorry," Jonathan said, shaking his head. "I just don't understand you leaving them behind at a time like this."

"Let me tell you about a time like this," she said, standing. "I'm crushed. Paralyzed. Hardly able to think. I've got to find Karen and find out what really happened. Until then, I don't think I'm much good for them right now."

"And what if you don't find her?" he asked. "What then?"

She went over to the window and looked out into the garden. "I don't know, Jonathan. Honestly, I just don't know."

She could hear the sound of the clock ticking on the mantle, measuring away the minutes and hours of her life that were being subsumed into this reeking mess. Her brother tapped his fingers on the arm of his chair.

"I've been thinking about Dad since I went to see Mum," she said, turning back to look at him. "Why he was the way he was, what happened between them. Why didn't they divorce?"

"I suppose they stayed together for the children. Isn't that the usual line? Besides, what would have happened to her if he'd left? Could she have ever had any kind of normal life?"

"You blame her."

"Well, she *is* a drunk. Always has been. And as much as you want to blame me, there wasn't much she would let me do for her."

"Something drove her to it," Iris said. "Perhaps an adulterous husband."

"That's the usual woman's perspective."

"Don't be condescending."

"Besides, did he seem the type?"

"He must have been interested in someone, once."

"I don't see it. He never cared about anyone. Besides, it's a little pointless to take sides now." Jonathan stood and walked into the kitchen.

"Where are you going?" she asked.

"I'm putting the kettle on. I have something to tell you, anyway." Iris looked up at him. "What?"

He stopped in the doorway and looked at her. "Mum's got cancer. Did she tell you?"

"No," she said, shocked. "She didn't say anything."

"She doesn't want to go through radiation or anything. She's given up."

"But why? Why wouldn't she treat it?"

"Nothing to live for, I suppose. And anyway, I believe it's fairly advanced."

"I can't believe she didn't tell me."

"Don't take it personally. I found out by accident, myself. I happened to find a bill from her doctor lying on a table."

In spite of herself, Iris could feel tears sting the back of her eyes. Life wasn't supposed to be so hard. She looked at her brother, who was watching her carefully. "Have you told Sarah?"

"I told her yesterday, when I called her after I found out you were here."

He filled the kettle and put it on the stove. Iris looked out the window at the sloping roofline of the house next door. Along the eaves, snow had accumulated more heavily than on the rest of the roof, and it clung to thin icicles at the ends. The sky was a dead, gray color. For a moment she wished Jonathan hadn't told her about their mother, as though not knowing about it would make it less true. Hadn't she had more than her share of death and dying?

"What are we supposed to do?" she asked, rubbing her arms.

"There's nothing we can do. She doesn't want a fuss."

"We can't leave it at that."

"It's her choice. We can't force her to do anything. Believe me, I've tried." Jonathan ran his hands through the hair falling over his brow. "She didn't even want you to know."

"So why bother telling me now?"

He shrugged. "So you don't kill me later."

"This is too much," Iris said, throwing her hands up. "All of it. How much is one person supposed to take?"

Jonathan shook his head and opened the tin of tea.

"Are you seeing anyone?" she asked, suddenly.

He went still for a moment, then scooped out the tea, considering his answer before he spoke.

"Yes, actually. He's a doctor." He looked up at her to gauge her reaction. "He's been extricating himself from an unfortunate marriage."

"To a woman?" she asked.

"Yes, to a woman," he answered. "Some people hate disappointing their parents so much they do what they think they should and hope to God they'll change."

"You didn't."

"For better or worse, I've always known who I am."

"I'm sorry," Iris said. "I didn't realize. I think that's incredibly brave."

"I had no choice, Iris. You're either born gay or you're not."

"Nick doesn't think so." Her husband had made plenty of negative remarks on the whole subject and had little to do with Jonathan.

"For your information, Nick is wrong."

Iris didn't bother arguing with him. Nick had been wrong about plenty of other things before. "So, tell me about this doctor."

Jonathan smiled. "He's everything I ever hoped to find in a partner. He's kind, intelligent. He loves to read, enjoys a good glass of wine. You'd like him. We're talking about a trip to Sydney in a few months to see Sarah and Bill. I've never met her children."

"Does she know?"

"Of course she knows. We talk about everything."

Iris didn't waste time feeling hurt that Jonathan had been closer to Sarah than to her. If she were honest with herself, they'd both given her plenty of chances.

"Move in with me," he said suddenly, taking two mugs from the cupboard. "I have a spare room. You can't stay with that policeman forever."

She shook her head. She'd no idea what to do, but she wouldn't impose on him. She'd unsettled too many lives as it was. It was time now to leave Truro and go home to the girls. She couldn't force her mother to have radiation treatment any more than she could find Karen. All doors were closed to her. Even Nick was an unknown variable now. Her children were all she had left.

"Thanks for asking," she answered, touching his arm. "But I can't."

"You know you could work in the shop again," he said. "You have a knack for it."

"How's that going these days?" she asked.

Jonathan shrugged. "Bloody Americans have ravaged the country. The continent, more like. They've got all the good stuff. Every year or so, I get to bid on the contents of a country house. It keeps me going till the next one."

"Who buys the contents?" she asked.

"More bloody Americans."

The water boiled and Iris sorted the tea. Tea civilized things: losing her daughter, discovering that her mother was dying, defining her relationship with Jonathan, and facing her anger toward the world. She felt a knot in her throat. If she'd been a different kind of mother, would Sophie still have died? When she was young, she'd had at least a semblance of faith. She'd worn a cross around her neck until her father died, but now she was faithless, angry, full of hate. She wondered if they would ever find Karen Peterson. And if they did, what on earth would she do next?

TWENTY-ONE

McINTYRE PACED IN THE sitting room, too restless to sit still. Iris had returned from her brother's house and closed herself up in his spare room, likely not to come out again that night. He wondered what had happened between the two of them. He hadn't been able to judge her mood when she returned, and she didn't want to talk about it. Things had gone back to the professional relationship they'd had before, but he couldn't pretend he didn't think about it, or about the anger he'd felt. He'd never imagined becoming so frustrated that he could act out toward someone like that. It was a new low in a year of lows. The sooner the Flynn case was solved, the sooner Iris would leave and that would be an end to it.

He picked up his mobile and scrolled through his contacts until he found David. He hadn't talked to his brother in a couple of weeks. It would be good to hear his voice.

"Rob!" his brother said when he answered the call, sounding his usual self. "Sorry I haven't rung lately. We've been so busy with Susan's mother and running back and forth to look after her that I've dropped the ball. How are you?"

"Fine," he answered. "How are the kids?"

"Great, but they miss you. Peter's suddenly interested in football, so we got him one for Christmas. We spent the last few weeks shouting at Manchester United on the telly. He needs his Uncle Rob to come and show him how it's done."

"I can't wait. And the girls?"

"Susan's got them in dance lessons. She said we started late, but they're only five, you know. They can't be that far behind. Anyway, they keep us busy. Sometimes I think the kids have a better social life than we do."

Rob laughed. "Tell them I miss them, too. You're a lucky man, David."

"I know," David answered. "But still, organizing three children is like running a circus from the house."

There was silence for a moment. Rob decided to break it before his brother apologized for having a normal life.

"I want to get there, one of these days, when I meet the right woman."

"Any luck in that department?"

"Well, I'm living with a woman now, in case I forgot to mention it."

"What?" David said, shocked.

"It's not what you think," Rob replied. "It's an odd story."

"I think you'd better tell me. Do I need a drink?"

"I think we both do."

McIntyre shuffled into the kitchen, pulled a Nut Brown ale from the refrigerator, and went back to settle into his chair. He looked out the window at the winter sky, thankful for the fire burning in the grate to take the chill from the room. Alison's book was on the table, and he turned it face down. He was done with it, and with her, too.

"All right," David said after a minute. "That's sorted. Susan's bringing me a Guinness. I want to settle back to hear this one."

"Well . . . when I came up to see you at Christmas, a woman came to see me. Her three-year-old daughter was killed a year ago, and the case had gone cold. As far as I knew, she and her deadbeat husband had gone back to Australia, where he's from. She flew back on her own and landed on your doorstep, wanting me to reopen the case."

"My doorstep? My literal doorstep?"

"Yes. She told someone at the station that she was my sister. At any rate, I brought her back here with me to Truro, because her brother's here. I thought I'd leave her with him and look into it, but no. She's barmy. She insists on being in the dead center of everything, and she wouldn't even speak to her brother, much less stay with him. We found her at a hostel the day before Christmas, and believe me, I may have a heart of stone, but even I wouldn't leave a grieving mother in a stinking hostel on the day of Christ's birth."

"I didn't imagine you would. So, she's staying with you?"

"I thought it would be for a couple of days, but things keep dragging on. She's got nowhere to go. The sodding thing is, I think I'm actually getting used to her."

David chuckled. "There are worse things."

"She's no Susan, let's leave it at that."

"Speaking of Susan," David said. "She's here with my Guinness."

"Hello, Robby!" Susan sang into the phone.

"Give her a kiss for me," McIntyre said. "You've got her trained, I see."

"And vice versa. I'll be cleaning the kitchen tonight when the tots are down. We're the modern family, through and through. But don't change the subject. Get back to this woman."

McIntyre sighed. "Her name is Iris. Her three-year-old daughter was abducted by the nanny she'd brought with her from America, and was found dead the next day. There were no leads a year ago, and no photos or positive identification of the suspect at that point. Iris has come back to see the thing through to its inevitable conclusion."

"Which is?"

"Honestly, at this point, I don't know. Every lead we get comes up short. Our suspect is possibly in London. Possibly, mind you, if she's in the UK at all. And that tip came from a psychic. It's enough to drive one mad."

"Having the victim's mother living in your house may be clouding your judgment, Rob," David said after a moment. "You know as well as I do that however well-organized a crime unit is, they can't always solve every murder. You're feeling a personal responsibility toward her, which I admire, because you're my brother and that's the kind of person you are, but the truth is, you need to remember you can only do so much."

"And here I was, ready to quit the force as a complete and utter failure."

"You're talented, you're hardworking, and you've solved dozens of cases. You do the best you can, and sometimes it comes right in the end."

"You're right, I do feel responsible for her. She's at the tipping point, and I don't blame her. As far as she knows, the police are a load of cock-ups who can't get the job done. Not that I've done much to change her mind."

"She's got to know you're doing your best." David paused. "You know, I've been meaning to ask you if you'd ever consider moving to London. It would change your life. You could work for the Met and come to dinner on Sunday nights. And as an added incentive, there's an endless supply of young, unattached women who would be more than interested in a hotshot detective chief inspector."

"I'm a Truro copper, through and through," McIntyre answered. "This is my force. My jurisdiction. I can't imagine working anyplace else. Not that Susan's Sunday dinner is anything to scoff at. By the way, I haven't told you that Alison called me last week."

"What did she want?"

"To make a confession of sorts." He paused. "She told me she had a miscarriage a few weeks after she left me."

He could hear his brother pause on the other end of the line.

"Shit, Rob," David said. "Are you serious?"

"Dead serious. But the truth is, when it comes right down to it, I've realized that I bet on the wrong horse."

"It sounds like you were with someone you weren't in love with."

"How did that happen?" he wondered aloud. "I found a girl, set up house, and in the end, it wasn't good enough. You're one of the lucky few who gets to live the dream."

"The dream is big enough for all of us," David said. "The perfect woman is out there. It's just your job to get off your duff and find her."

Rob took a gulp of his ale and decided to change the subject. "By the way, I've been thinking about Granddad's land. We've been letting it sit there without deciding what to do about it. Have you given it any thought?"

The property was forty miles west of Truro, and he didn't get out to see it often. He was supposed to keep an eye on it, but with one thing and another, it generally slipped his mind.

"As a matter of fact, I have," David said.

"You want to sell it, I suppose, to pay for all those dance lessons."

"Actually, I think it would be hard to give up, unless you need the money."

"I don't. What do you want to do with it?"

"What about fixing it up as a weekend place? Susan would love that. We like being in the thick of things here in London, but there are times when getting away would be just what we need. We could continue to co-own the property, if you want, and share it. Unless you were thinking of living there full time, and reviving it, land and all."

"Chickens and sheep?" Rob asked, shaking his head at the thought. "There are days I feel like it, and days I don't, and I don't think a half-hearted commitment is healthy if you want to run a farm. It's an all-or-nothing proposition. But I do like the idea of a getaway cottage."

"One of these days, you'll have a wife and three kids and they'll appreciate the chance to spend some time running wild there like we did."

"It would probably just take some paint and a little upgrading to the kitchen … "

"And we could hire someone to clean up the garden."

"I feel better already, just having something else to think about besides an empty house and a stalled case."

"That's it, Robby Boy. Time away gives you some perspective."

"What are you doing this weekend? We could go down there and check on things."

"Let me talk to Susan, but I think she'd love it. Of course, without another woman involved, we'll have to let her handle all the aesthetics. You can't argue with her about curtains or anything else, if you know what's good for you."

"I cede all decisions to the master."

"Dad would be proud that we've kept it, you know."

"He would, wouldn't he?" McIntyre nodded. "It's one of the reasons I can't bring myself to sell."

"I'm right there with you, old man," David said. "Now get back to work and kick ass on this case of yours. You'll solve it. Whoever that murderer is, she'll make a mistake. They always do. And you're just the one to catch her when she does."

TWENTY-TWO

SHE WAS STANDING IN an ice-cold stream, submerged to her ankles. The rocks were slippery under her feet, and overhead, in the vast ocean of trees above, the deep green leaves rustled on the hardy spring branches. She looked down at the minnows scurrying through the water; tiny, brainless creatures, unaware of their inconsequential size, driven by instinct, occupied with predator avoidance, communicating with shoalmates by a chemical smell noticeable only to other minnows. It is, truly, the smell of fear. Iris wiggled her toes in the water, causing the tiny fish to dart away, ignorant of the havoc she'd caused. As she closed her eyes to feel the warm breeze on her face, the creatures beneath the surface scattered to find algae on which to feast to last them through another day. Goose bumps came up on her arms and she shivered, unaware of the world within a world at her feet. She thought only of summer, and the bliss of wading in a cold stream, and of nothing else.

Iris awoke suddenly, startled. For a second, the dream was fresh in her mind. She remembered that stream from her uncle's farm, and longed for summer; not merely a season, but that state of life that is warm and lazy and free of burdens. It was a time she wondered if she would ever know again.

She'd always wanted a simple life, and simplicity was something she'd had in abundance. Their rudimentary, day-to-day existence had been nothing if not simple. She lived with Nick, when he was there, and she lived alone when he wasn't. She made love and got pregnant in a cycle no different than that of the seasons. Someone was always being conceived, carried in a dark and quiet womb, birthed, nursed, and weaned. Her breasts ached from the unflinching constancy of it all. They owned little but the clothes on their backs and what food they put into their mouths each day. Getting away from her life had given her some perspective, though. Living without commitments and obligations hadn't simplified it all, just created a life that was raw and painful. There was no stability or security in the life she'd lived for the last decade.

Once back to England, she'd stayed as far away from her mother and Jonathan as she could, unwilling to complicate her life further. But now, after talking to her brother, she realized that staying away from them had made things worse. She was ready to face things, perhaps for the first time. That was the simple choice. She wanted, suddenly, to see her mother again. Not to confront her; the time for that had long gone.

Her mother, that fragile, wrecked creature, who was now dying, had nothing more to answer for. Everything Iris had done in her life was due entirely to her own free will and the choices she and she alone had made. She couldn't even blame her husband.

She got up and threw on her clothes to go downstairs, her feet padding on the wood floor. McIntyre was standing in the kitchen, making coffee.

"I need a favor," she said, watching the sky grow lighter in the window, a band of red infused with gold.

"Good morning to you, too," he answered. "How about a cup of coffee first?"

She nodded, pulling a cup down from the shelf. It was strong, the way he always made his coffee.

"So, what kind of favor?"

"I'm going to stay with my mum for a while. She's not well. Can you drive me?"

"To Cadgwith? Of course. It's not that far. How long do you plan to stay?"

"I don't know. I just need to be there." She watched him pour the coffee into the mug she always used. It would be odd leaving his house. She'd grown accustomed to McIntyre, even attached, not that it mattered now. "You'll call and keep me up to date, won't you? I want to know everything that's happening."

"We're back at square one, you know," he said, walking over to sit at the small table.

Iris went over and sat down next to him. There was a great intimacy in sharing coffee, sitting at a table for two. She'd rarely even sat like this with Nick. She was more used to the long farmhouse table populated by a half dozen Flynns, all shouting over one another for attention.

"Square one," she repeated.

"If Kevin Hughes is telling the truth, Sophie removed her own coat and left it behind. Don't forget, he ditched it in a chicken pen at a farm north of here, trying to frame a handicapped man for her murder."

"Are you telling me the case is going to be closed?"

"No," he said. "I won't let that happen yet. But short of going to London to look for a needle in a haystack, I'm not sure what to do next."

"Karen is out there, Rob," she insisted. "I can feel it. She didn't go back to America. She's in London."

"We have the image, which we've circulated to police and the news outlets. We have to hope that someone will see it and recognize her."

That was all they could do. After coffee, she packed her bag and made the bed. She looked about the room, thinking. She hadn't minded being in McIntyre's house. It was quiet, and quiet was a luxury she'd long done without. Of course, because of their confrontation, the more rancorous bits now forgotten, she was able to step back and look at her marriage in a critical way, assessing the validity of it. But even that now was unimportant. There were things she had to take care of first. She went downstairs, where McIntyre was waiting.

"Are you ready?" he asked.

She nodded. They went to the car, the gravel beneath their boots crunching in the snow.

"Why the sudden urge to be with family?" he asked as they pulled out onto the road. "I thought you'd decided to avoid them altogether."

"You know I saw my brother yesterday," Iris said. "Well, my mum has cancer. I knew she didn't look well when I saw her last week. She can't take care of herself."

"You haven't talked about your childhood."

"It's not something I like to remember."

"Then why go? Why not let your brother take care of things? I assume he's been doing just that for the last year."

"Well, I'm here now, aren't I? Taking up space in your house, not contributing to anything. I want my girls, but I can't go back to Australia until we find Karen. Everything is a mess."

"If you hadn't come back, we wouldn't have the photo of Karen at the railway station. Someone will find her, and that will be due to your persistence going after her." He looked at her for a moment, and then back at the road. "How will you get around once I leave you?"

"Mum has a car. I'll use that."

They fell silent, lost in their own thoughts. Iris tended to second-guess herself, but this time, she realized he was right. They had at least identified Karen and proven that she'd headed into London, and that was a step in the right direction. The timing was right, too. If she hadn't come back to England, she wouldn't have known about her mother, and she certainly wouldn't have been able to do anything for her. She felt guilty for resenting her so much. After all, it was impossible to get inside someone's mind and understand their demons. Whether something had driven her mother to drink or whether she suffered a genetic predisposition for it, Iris would never know, but she would do what she could to help.

When they arrived in Cadgwith, she directed him through the town, looking at the familiar shops and houses along the roads.

"Call if you need anything," he said. He glanced up from the road and the look he gave her took her by surprise. "I feel responsible for you."

"That's my fault," Iris replied, looking away. It wouldn't do to get any more involved with him than she already was. "I've imposed on you too much."

"Forget it."

They went silent as he navigated his way through the town. It was a quiet day, with few people out in the cold.

"Turn left at the corner," she said.

He followed her directions and pulled into the house at the end of the road. Shutting off the engine, he turned to her. "I meant it when I said to call me."

"Thanks for the lift," she replied, trying to keep her voice even. She got out of the car and heaved her duffle over her shoulder, raising a hand before walking up to the door. She stood and watched him until the car was out of sight, feeling an odd chill at his leaving that she hadn't expected.

Iris stood there for a moment before steeling herself to go inside. The handle turned easily, and she stepped into the house.

"I see you came back," her mother said. She didn't get up from where she lay against the arm of the sofa.

"Why isn't the door locked?" Iris asked. "Anyone could come in."

"Who would drive out here, anyway?"

"Have you had a cuppa today, Mum?" Iris was still thinking about McIntyre. It had been harder to get out of that car than she had ever imagined.

"No," her mother answered.

"I'll make one for you."

Iris dropped her coat onto a chair and went into the kitchen. She filled the kettle, deciding to sort out the kitchen while the water was heating. A dead geranium in a plastic pot sat on the counter. How long it had been there, she wasn't certain. She lifted it with two fingers and tossed it into the bin. Most of the dishes had been sitting so long the food was dried on. She filled the sink to let them soak. It was either that or toss out every dish in the house. It had once been a sunny room, with yellow wallpaper that her parents had put up when she was nine or ten. She remembered her mother saying it reminded her of Claude Monet and the kitchen in his little pink house in France. She wasn't certain how her mother knew of Monet's house; a book, perhaps. Helen Martin had never been out of Cornwall. Iris stacked the bills and papers that were lying here and there and put them on top of another stack on the poky little desk with cubbyholes in the corner. Tomorrow she would go through it and see if the bills had been paid. For now, she washed two mugs and set out the tea.

"When's he coming back for you?" her mother asked when she returned with a tray.

"Who?" Iris's first thought had been of Nick, but of course he wasn't coming to Cadgwith any time soon.

"Your policeman."

"He's not my policeman."

"He's at your beck and call, isn't he? What else would you call it?"

"He's doing his job, or at least trying to."

"Well? Is he coming back?"

"No, he's not."

Helen's dark eyes searched hers. "Had enough of you, has he?"

"Yeah, Mum. He's had enough of me. Hasn't everyone?" She took a cup from the tray. "My husband's had enough of me, you've had enough of me, and probably even my children have had enough of me. I can't expect more of a police detective than I can from my own family." She brushed her hair out of her eyes. "Well? Don't you have anything to say?"

Helen closed her eyes for a moment and then opened them again. "I'm not feeling so well. I'd like to get in bed."

Iris went over to help her up. She led her into the bedroom and then brought the tray and set it on a table. When she returned, her mother opened her eyes.

"I'm sorry I shouted at you," Iris said, handing her a cup. "Do you need to go to see the doctor?"

"I probably need to be in a care home," her mother answered. "I hate to admit it, but I can't manage anymore."

"You don't need a care home," Iris told her. "I'm here now."

"You don't mean it."

"I do," Iris insisted. "I haven't been the best daughter, and I doubt I'll be a great one now. But I'm here, for what that's worth."

Helen didn't answer. She struggled to sit up and then took the cup of tea. After taking a single sip, she put it down and lay back, as if she hadn't even the strength to take another. Iris dropped into the chair beside her and finished her cup of tea.

TWENTY-THREE

CADGWITH, LIKE MOST OF this part of Cornwall, didn't get much snow, no more than ten or so days per year, but what it lacked in freezing precipitation it made up for in wind. Gales blew with a force that rattled windows and shook houses and pummeled boats on the shore. Iris was all too familiar with the blistering January wind, thinking back on her father's long hours spent huddled by the fire looking at seed catalogues. No wonder he immersed himself in them, she thought. Dark winter days left little else to do. For lack of a more meaningful job, she continued sorting the kitchen, which as far as she could tell, hadn't been done often in the ten years she'd been gone. There were cracked dishes and broken pots everywhere, and she decided for her mother's sake that she would truly clean it up. It was something to do.

Her mother seemed to sleep around the clock, waking for the odd cup of tea or bowl of soup and to take medications for pain. A nurse came twice a week to make certain there was nothing more she needed. Jonathan paid the bills, and Sarah sent flowers and ordered packets of foods to be delivered from London. Iris was glad to do her part.

The house seemed fixed in time, at least twenty years earlier. She'd spent half her childhood sprawled on the floor, drawing horses, wishing for one of her own. She missed ordinary days, when a walk around the village could provide an afternoon of delight, or a trip to the beach was the highlight of the summer. She missed scampering in and out of the house with her friend Jenny at all hours to get biscuits and a thermos of milk, and she would never forget afternoons spent on the hill, where they could watch the skiffs bobbing in the harbor, like toy boats on a pond. The coolness between her parents hadn't mattered as much then. She wondered when that had changed. When she was young, all she'd needed was food and a roof over her head, and the freedom to come and go as she pleased.

She wished a life like that for Charlotte and India, not that she had any control over what sort of childhood they might one day have. At the moment, she had to concentrate on one hour at a time, disposing of broken crockery and trying to figure out how to remove splatters of grease that clung to the kitchen wallpaper. She decided to strip it from the entire room, though she would have to wait until it was warmer to repaint the dull yellow walls behind it. It was at least some improvement. She tried to remember when it had been a proper, if small, kitchen, where there had been hot meals of cabbage and roast on Sunday and sometimes a bit of cake. Her father, as she recalled, had been fond of her mother's cakes, with their sweet, fruity taste and a layer of frosting as tough as a wedge of plastic. She sat in a chair and closed her eyes, trying to recall the smell. Perhaps she would cook some sort of proper food for her mother. It would do them both good. She made a list so that she could go into town, but before she could finish, she heard a knock at the door. It was

Tuesday, and the nurse, a pleasant older woman, was expected at any minute.

She unlatched the door and frowned at the man standing there. He was around her age, and although he looked familiar, she couldn't remember where she'd seen him before. In the last couple of weeks she'd met a number of policemen, but she didn't think he was one of them. He smiled at her as though he were expected.

A sudden feeling of panic came over Iris and she tried to shut the door, but he stuck his foot in the doorway and pushed back.

"Hold on there a second," he said. "I thought we could talk."

Iris shook her head, her heart suddenly thumping. This was no police officer. "What do you want?"

"Come on, let me in," he coaxed. "It's blowing a storm out here."

He shoved the door open, pushing her against the wall. As she tried to regain her balance, he shut the door behind him. Iris looked at her mobile on the table, but he was closer. Her first instinct was to bolt out the door, but if she did, there was little hope of outrunning him, and there was always the chance that he would hurt her mother instead.

Her hands balled into fists, but she knew she was no match for him.

"Watch it there, Iris," he said, smirking. "You don't want to start something you can't finish."

He knew her name. Her nails cut into her palms as she debated what to do.

"Sit down. I just want to talk to you."

If she made a scene, her mother would hear and come in, and she couldn't possibly defend them both from someone like this. Iris sat, perched on the edge of the chair, and watched as he drew off his gloves slowly, one finger at a time. She'd never felt as afraid as she did at that moment. He pulled off his coat, never taking his eyes off her.

"What do you want?" she asked, dreading the answer.

208

"Like I said, I'm here to talk to you. But from what I can see, you need to lighten up, have a little fun."

"You were in Truro," she said, realizing suddenly that he was the man who had given her the lift to her brother's house.

"Very good," he answered. "I wondered if you could keep all of your men straight."

She'd had an uneasy feeling in the car, but it was nothing compared to what she felt now. "Who are you?"

"Do you remember my name?"

She shook her head, trying to remember. "Stephen? Simon?"

"See, that's the reason you don't give your real name. Someone is going to remember it, especially when it's not convenient. By the way, you never thanked me for giving you a lift."

"Thank you," she managed, desperately wondering what to do.

"That's better."

She wondered if he'd followed McIntyre's car, but that didn't make sense. There was no reason for anyone to want her. She had nothing but the clothes on her back. With difficulty, she tried to swallow and found that she couldn't.

"How do you know my name?" Iris asked. "Have you been following me?"

"You had a wonderful photo on the front page of *The Times*," he remarked. "Did you see it? It was quite sympathetic. I wondered if the killer saw it, too, and how it must have made her feel, knowing she'd taken your child away from you and killed her. She wasn't emotional about it at the time."

"What do you mean, at the time?" Iris asked, shocked.

"Wrong question," he said. "We're not thinking about then, we're thinking about now."

She pulled herself up and tried to get off the sofa, but he took both hands and shoved her back down.

"Poor Iris," he said. "Bad things always seem to happen to you."

"Please, don't," she pleaded.

"Don't worry," he said. "I'm not going to hurt you."

"Stop it. Please."

He sat down next to her and put his hands at the base of her neck, using his thumb to caress the bare skin under her shirt. She wanted to scream, but she didn't want to wake her mother.

"We're just talking."

"I'm not going to talk to you," she answered. "Get out of my house."

He reached out and batted at her head, the slap catching her on the face. The pain caught her by surprise, rattling her teeth. She reached a hand to her cheek and drew it back, seeing a red smear of blood.

Suddenly she heard a sound from the direction of her mother's room, and her mother called out to her. "Iris, what's going on?"

The man froze for a second and then walked down the hall to see who was there. Iris jumped from the sofa and ran into the kitchen, grabbing the first thing she could find, a heavy metal skillet. Drops of grease sloshed onto the floor as she carted it down the hall. He'd opened the door to her mother's room and was standing a few feet inside. She lifted the skillet just as he started to turn around, but managed to slam it down on his skull in time. There was a dull metallic sound and then he collapsed forward on top of her, knocking her down. Iris wriggled out from under him as he lay in a silent heap on the floor.

"God, Mum," she said, jerking herself to her feet. "Are you all right?"

Her mother nodded. For a moment, neither of them moved, and then she took her assailant by the feet and dragged him into the hall, locking the bedroom door behind her.

"Iris," her mother said again.

She was holding her chest and Iris put a chair under the door-knob as an extra precaution. "Are you all right?"

When her mother didn't answer, she grabbed the telephone from the bedside table and dialed 999, barely able to get the words out.

"Hello, this is the ambulance."

"I have an emergency, please," Iris shouted. "There's an unconscious man in my mother's house. He tried to attack me."

"What happened?" the operator asked. "Is he still breathing?"

"I don't know. We've locked ourselves in the bedroom. He attacked me, and I knocked him unconscious."

"Is anyone else hurt?"

She looked at her mother, who was slumped over in the bed. She started to panic.

"I think my mother's having a heart attack."

Suddenly, there was a banging on the door and Iris screamed. "He's trying to get in! Get the police!"

He threw his weight against the door, but it didn't budge. Iris dropped the phone and threw her weight onto the chair, but everything went quiet. When nothing happened for a minute, she picked up the phone.

"Are you still there?" Iris asked.

"Yes," the operator answered. "Is your mother conscious?"

"Yes, but she's in distress. Help us, please."

"What are her symptoms?"

"Heavy breathing. She's holding her chest. Can you send an ambulance?"

"What is the address?"

"We're in Helena Close, at the end of the road."

"Does your mother need CPR?"

"I don't know."

"Is she breathing normally?"

"A little fast. Please send someone."

"The ambulance is already on its way. Stay calm and tell me your name."

"Iris. Iris Flynn."

"All right, Iris, tell me about your mother's progress."

"Her breathing is a little slower now. It was frightening."

"Of course it was. Do you know the intruder?"

"It was a stranger who gave me a lift in Truro the day before yesterday," she answered. "I don't know how he found me here."

"How is your mother doing?"

"She's breathing a little steadier now. How long will it take for the ambulance to arrive?"

"Not long. They're en route now."

After that, it was a blur, a jumble of memories she would never retain. The ambulance arrived and the paramedics came inside to see her mother. Iris didn't recall how she'd even gone through the house to open the door. Three men came into the bedroom and assessed her mother's condition, putting her on oxygen and lifting her onto a stretcher. It was unnerving to watch them fasten the straps over her body and cover her with a blanket before they took her outside and loaded her into the ambulance. When they pulled away from the house, the constable who'd been taking notes turned and looked at her.

"You'll need to get that looked at," he said, pointing to her bruised face.

"It's my mother I'm worried about," she answered. "What happened to him? The intruder?"

"We've got men looking for him."

"I've got to follow the ambulance."

"I'll take you 'round. You don't need to be driving."

212

Iris didn't argue. She grabbed her coat as a dozen questions swirled around her tired brain. How had the man followed her? Why did he care who she was? Perhaps more important, why had he mentioned Karen? Did he know her, or have any idea where she was?

She pulled her mobile from her pocket as she held a cloth to her face. With one hand, she dialed McIntyre's number. He didn't answer. Disappointed, she left a message and tucked the phone back into her pocket.

At the hospital, there was a flurry of activity. Her mother was examined in one room while she was examined in another. After what seemed an interminable wait, Iris was given a Valium and Helen was admitted for observation overnight. Iris sat, drowsy, in her mother's hospital room, a thin, institutional blanket pulled over her.

Sometime later the door opened, and, to her utter relief, Robert McIntyre came walking in.

TWENTY-FOUR

FOR FORTY YEARS OF his life, Rob McIntyre had felt little responsibility toward another human being. Before Alison, no girlfriend or acquaintance had inspired much sense of duty, and Alison herself had been nothing if not self-contained. Perhaps that was one of the things he'd liked about her, that she was capable of taking care of herself without demanding much from him. As he looked back on it now, he realized that was another sign their relationship had never been strong enough to make it. They had been two people who were together for lack of something better to do. Now, however, he would never forget the sight of Iris Flynn sitting at her mother's side in a hard hospital chair. She'd taken a blow to the face in the attack, and it was bruised and swelling. She'd been given a couple of stitches, and the welt would be black by the following day.

The sight of it roused in him more anger than he'd ever felt in his life, though he wasn't sure why. Possibly because she was a victim, once again, innocent of any wrongdoing, simply a person who happened to be in the wrong place at the wrong time. The world, which

214

one wanted to believe was a good place, full of kindness and decency, was full of people like the man now in the room upstairs, a criminal and opportunist who would do as he wished at the expense of others. If there was one thing McIntyre could do to prevent anyone from hurting her again, he would do it, and he wouldn't mind by starting on the man who'd done this to her.

"How are you?" he asked in a low voice as he walked into the room.

"Fine," Iris said, looking at her mother. "But I'm worried about her."

According to the nurse, Helen Martin had also been sedated and would not wake for hours. She hadn't been injured, but the episode had been a stress on her heart. She looked small in the hospital bed, needles jammed into her veins and an IV taped around her upper arm.

"She's had a shock."

"So have you," he said. "You need some tea."

"I shouldn't leave her."

"They told me she won't wake until morning," he said. "And there's not much you can do for her here."

"I can't go back there alone."

"You don't have to."

"Did they find him?" Iris asked, pulling the blanket from her shoulders. She sat up and ran her hands through her hair.

McIntyre nodded. "He ran his car off the road. He's got a concussion. We've got him here under police supervision."

"Who is he? What did he want?"

"There will be a complete investigation. The thing to remember right now is that you're safe."

Iris rubbed her neck. "I'm getting sore sitting here like this."

"Come on, then."

She stood, stretching her shoulders, and let him lead her downstairs to the café. He got a tray and poured tea into two small white mugs. On a whim, he took two egg sandwiches and put them on the tray, too, and then they found a table by the window. The afternoon light was fading and it would soon be dark.

She sighed and took a drink of the tea. "I'm getting an awful headache."

"Did they give you something for it?"

"Yes. Not that it will make that much difference."

"You know I'm not going to let you spend the night here, sitting in that chair, don't you?" he asked.

"I really shouldn't leave her."

"We'll be back early. There's nothing else you can do tonight. She needs rest as much as you do."

"I suppose you're right," she answered.

He lifted his cup to his lips and nodded. She'd had to be tough and self-sacrificing. It was the only way she'd gotten through the last ten years. After they talked, he would walk her back to her mother's room while he went to check on the assailant, who was conscious and being monitored. A constable was posted at the man's door to make certain he didn't escape, not that he would be able to after such a walloping blow to the skull.

"Do you feel like telling me what happened?"

"It was my fault," Iris said. "The other day, when I was walking to Jonathan's house, that man pulled up next to me and offered me a ride."

"You didn't."

"I got in, but I felt uncomfortable getting in the car with a stranger. He dropped me a few streets from Jonathan's house. I didn't let him see where my brother lived."

"When did you see him next?"

"Not until he showed up today. I answered the door because I thought it was the nurse. She was due any time."

"So he knew where you were."

"He must have thought I was alone. And I'm lucky I wasn't."

"You certainly are."

He didn't ask anything else. Iris had suffered enough for one day. He'd gotten a complete report from the officer on duty when he was driving back to Cadgwith. A disturbing fact had been mentioned in the notes: the attacker had clearly known who Iris was and had even alluded to Sophie Flynn's killer. McIntyre planned to get to the bottom of it as soon as possible.

A quarter hour later, he took Iris back to her mother's room and then went upstairs to see the man who had attacked her. According to hospital records, his name was Sean Campbell. He was thirty-eight years old and a resident of Falmouth, a short drive from Truro. He'd been employed as an accountant for more than four years. On paper, he was ordinary, but in person, he wasn't what McIntyre expected.

"Is he awake?" McIntyre asked the constable on duty.

"Yeah. We've had someone in already to question him in the last hour."

"Well, he's going to have to go through it again," McIntyre muttered.

He pushed open the door and walked up to the edge of the hospital bed. The man in it looked remarkably well, unlike Iris Flynn, whose face would bear the marks from his fist for days.

"Sean Campbell," he said. "I'm DCI Rob McIntyre from the Truro station."

"I've already talked to the police."

"I have a few questions for you." He took the photo of Karen Peterson from his pocket. "Do you know this woman?"

Campbell looked at the photo briefly. "I met her last year."

"When? Can you be more precise?"

"December, it was."

217

"December 17th, in fact."

"That's right."

"Tell me everything you know about her," McIntyre said, taking out his notepad.

"She wanted a ride, that's all I know. I didn't know she was involved in a kidnapping until I saw the newspapers later."

"Where did you pick her up?"

"On St. George's Road."

"And you had never seen her before?"

"Never."

"What about Sophie Flynn?"

"Never saw the child apart from that one time."

"So, the child was with Miss Peterson when you picked her up?" McIntyre felt a sudden tightness in his chest.

"Yes."

"Had you ever seen Iris Flynn before?"

"Saw her photo in the news. After."

McIntyre leaned forward. "After you picked up Karen Peterson and Sophie Flynn, tell me specifically where you went and what you did. And I'm fucking warning you, I want the whole truth. It's in your interest to cooperate as much as possible."

Campbell sighed. "She asked me to take her to the river. I had no idea why. She had the kid by the arm and dragged her into the car and then slammed the door. I thought we were dropping her off with her dad or something, and I had the feeling we'd have a bit of fun after. She had that attitude, you know?"

"And then?"

"I drove south on Trelander Highway, down past the Old Vicarage, as close to the water as I could. I felt suspicious, then, because I expected someone to meet us there."

"And it was dark?"

"Pitch dark. She got out of the car, and a minute later, I heard the kid cry. She slapped her. Then I heard the sound of a struggle, and a splash, and blimey, that was it. She got back into the car and I swear to God I was shaking, myself. Then she wanted a good shagging. I obliged, and then she asked me to take her back into town. I did, and that's that."

"Sophie Flynn died of a broken neck. You knew she hurt the girl, and you did nothing about it?"

"I didn't want to be in the middle of anything. I had no part in it."

"Oh, but you had a huge part in it. You could have saved the child's life."

"I had no idea what she was doing down there. It never occurred to me that she was going to kill her. And when I realized it, well, what's done was done, if you know what I mean. There was nothing I could do about it."

"Apart from shagging the woman and hiding the crime from the police, which allowed her to get away."

"Crazy bitch, she was. I was glad to be rid of her."

"What happened next?"

"I dropped her off in town. That's all I know."

"Did you have any contact with her afterward? Did you get her mobile number?"

"No. It was just the one time. Nothing more."

McIntyre turned and walked to the window. "You were following Iris Flynn. Tell me about that."

"I'd forgotten the whole thing, and then she came back to Cornwall. Her face was taunting me from the cover of every newspaper. I couldn't stand it. I wanted to see her up close, like her kid. I wanted to get a sense of her pain. Some people are victims. They always will be. I wanted to feel it. Share it. I wasn't going to hurt her."

Sick bugger, McIntyre thought. "How many times did you see her?"

"Five or six. I only spoke to her twice. She didn't see me the other times."

"Did you know she wasn't alone in the house?"

"No. I didn't know anyone else was there or I wouldn't have gone in. She was the only one coming and going."

"What were you planning to do?" McIntyre asked.

"I was messing with her. Just going to have a little fun, that's all."

Sean Campbell coughed, and as he did, McIntyre could see the pain the man was in from the blow to the head. He wasn't the least bit sorry for him.

"You've got one thing wrong, though," Campbell said when he stopped coughing.

"And what's that?"

"Her name. It isn't Karen Peterson."

McIntyre stared at him for a second before he could respond. "Then what is it?"

"Madeline Roy."

He blinked and looked up from his notepad. "Repeat that for me."

"Madeline Roy."

"Is that what she told you?"

"Yes, that's what she said. I saw that she went by another name as far as the police were concerned, but that's the name she gave me."

"Where is she from? What else do you know about her?"

"We weren't getting to know one another, Inspector. We had your basic, average fuck. I don't know her cousins or grandparents or what she did for a living."

Taking a pen from his pocket, McIntyre jotted the name on a piece of paper. "That's it for now, but I'll be back."

Outside in the hall, he nodded to the constable. "There will be round-the-clock supervision, won't there?"

"Yes, sir."

He went back downstairs to Helen Martin's room, where he found Iris dozing in a chair. He reached out and touched her on the shoulder.

"Let's get you home," he said.

It was dark as they left to find his car. He found his way to the Martin house without much difficulty. Iris leaned back in the seat with her eyes closed. When he parked in front of the house, she sat up and took the keys from her bag with a shaky hand. She unlocked the door and he followed her as she turned on the lights in the front room and went into the kitchen.

"What's been happening in here?" he asked, looking at the kitchen in its stripped-down state.

"I tore down the wallpaper," Iris said, shrugging. "It was filthy. It had been there forever."

"Needs a couple of coats of paint."

"I was planning to."

"You'll need a primer, too, and some tape and coverings to protect the cupboards."

"I never took you for the DIY sort."

"Oh, I have a lot of talents you don't know about." McIntyre stopped himself. He hadn't meant to say anything quite so personal.

She rescued him. "Would you like some tea?"

"Not as much as I'd like a Scotch."

"I'm afraid there isn't anything in the house. Mum's an alcoholic."

"Tea's fine." He rubbed his brow. "Then we ought to get some sleep."

"There's a guest room."

"No, thanks. I'm sleeping on the couch. The danger is over, but I'd feel better staying near the door, anyway."

They made tea and then sat down by the dark fireplace. It was too late at night to start a fire. She brought blankets and a pillow from the other room.

"Thank you for staying," she said.

"My pleasure," he said, hating the words even as he said them. It sounded stiff, when he simply wanted to fold her in his arms and not let anything hurt her again.

"I've been nothing but trouble for you."

"You're not trouble," he said. "And in case you're still blaming yourself, what happened was not your fault."

"Thank you for saying that, even if it's not true."

He listened as she went into the other room and got into bed. Her husband should have been there, getting ice for the bruises on her face and taking her back and forth to see her mother in hospital. Her children should have been sleeping in the next room. Instead, she went to bed cold and alone, without anyone in the world to care.

TWENTY-FIVE

IF ASKED, ALISON KENDALL would have stated that she did not believe in wormholes or time travel, but in spite of such obstacles, she could imagine existing in two separate dimensions at once. She had the ability to lose herself in a place where memory was almost as strong as the present, and the line between the two blurred more often than she realized. It was part of being a writer, she supposed—clinging to wisps of thoughts and images rather than being tied to a sometimes unpleasant reality. Her grandparents, at times, seemed as alive to her still as if they were in the next room, and she could imagine sitting with them at the table and listening to them talk about their day. More recently, her extracurricular thought life had centered on Rob and the cottage in Cornwall. When they were together, she'd often complained about the house's lack of insulation in the middle of winter, of drafts and mouse holes in the kitchen. She'd detested the garden, which offered no privacy, with neighbors over short walls mere feet away. There had been no room to breathe. She'd confined herself either to the front room by the fire or to the extra room upstairs, where she'd installed a writing table, a lamp, and a battered wicker chair. In spite of all its discomforts, however, the modest house and its chief occupant had begun to engage her thoughts more and more. She remembered the two of them in bed in the early morning hours, making love before he got up to make coffee and toast, or standing with him in the grocery on Charles Street, getting cheese and pasta for a quiet dinner at home. Her life with him was over, yet she still felt connected to him through some psychic or spiritual means beyond her understanding. Perhaps that was because she knew that if she asked him back, Rob would be on her doorstep as quickly as he could get to Lincolnshire, and they would pack her books into boxes and go home to Cornwall to begin again as if nothing had ever happened. In fact, she knew he would welcome the chance.

She was sitting in the doctor's office on Norfolk Street, having dressed in haste the way one hates to do, with a nurse on the other side of the door. She'd chosen a female doctor, hoping that the unfortunate intimacy of an invasive medical exam, however common, would be easier to bear with a physician of one's own sex. That did not prove to be the case. The doctor, a woman in her fifties with gray hair pulled into a loose, disorganized knot, knocked at the door and entered, looking at her file.

"How are you today, Ms. Kendall?" she asked.

Alison pulled at her jacket, as if she could cover herself more than she already was. "Fine, thank you."

"Any special concerns today, or is this a routine examination?"

"Routine," she replied.

She waited, thinking. She had to admit it was exhilarating to have an affair when one had no chance of getting pregnant. The first year or two they were together, she and Rob had talked about having a baby, but his lack of enthusiasm, combined with her own, had changed her mind. Getting pregnant, she'd decided, would take away every chance she had of making something of herself. One couldn't write while changing nappies and existing on four hours of sleep. And the cottage was cramped enough with only the two of them. It couldn't support a third person, much less the pushchairs and cots one would have to provide for a newborn. He hadn't argued when she told him her decision, though she'd begun to wonder if that had been the cause of some of the coolness between them later.

"Let's have a look at you," the doctor said, shining a light into first her left eye, then her right.

Alison hated doctors, but she'd been feeling tired lately. The doctor came around to stand at her side and lifted her hair back with a finger to shine the light in her ear. She suffered through the end of the brief interview and was at last allowed to go out into the lobby. She nodded at the receptionist and dug in her handbag for her wallet to extract her ID, which was lodged somewhere in its dark recesses. She pulled out her gloves and her appointment book before finding it and then gave the receptionist her card. She noticed an old copy of *The Times* lying on the counter next to her, and while she waited, opened the folded paper. She gasped when she saw Madeline's face staring up at her.

On the front page was a police sketch, and the subject was Madeline, without a doubt. Her round, lovely face, punctuated by solemn eyes and full lips, so shocked Alison that she dropped the paper. She picked it up again as if it were laced with poison. The headline read, Person of Interest Sought in Child Murder Case.

"Miss?" the girl behind the counter said, tapping her nails on the counter.

Alison mumbled her thanks, put her card in her wallet, and stuffed the newspaper into her bag as she rushed from the office. What did it mean? she wondered. What could Madeline possibly have to do with the Flynn murder in Truro? To her knowledge, a nanny had taken the child. She tried to remember what she'd heard about the case, but from what she could recall, no one of Madeline's education and sophistication had been involved, which meant there had to be some kind of mistake.

Alison had heard of doppelgangers, and in fact had once seen a girl who had borne such an uncanny resemblance to Kate Winslet that she wondered if the actress had come to their village to seek anonymity from the pressures of stardom. The girl, who'd called herself Annette Carson, had rented a cottage for six months, never taking a job or venturing to the church or to any event during the duration of her stay. Alison had never gotten the opportunity to hear her speak, and she still wondered from time to time if she'd been right. If not, it was an amazing likeness, the sort that would have been brought to the girl's attention often. And if Kate Winslet could have a look-alike, why not Madeline Roy?

There were other possibilities for the doppelganger phenomenon. Perhaps twins who had been separated at birth, or even siblings who closely resembled one another. And she'd once read of something called "bilocation," the belief that a person can willingly project their own double—known in parapsychological circles as a "wraith"—to a remote location, where it can interact with an entirely different group of people. Generally, wraiths were mischief-makers blamed for all sorts of wrongdoing and fear-mongering among the general population, and murder was a very dark sort of mischief, indeed.

The literary world had its share of doppelgangers as well, she knew. Percy Bysshe Shelley claimed that on a trip to Italy, he met his doppelganger, who, after gaining his attention, gestured out toward the Mediterranean Sea. A short while later, Shelley drowned in that very spot. John Donne believed that he encountered his wife's doppelganger while in Paris, where a woman of her exact likeness held out a child to him. When he returned home, he learned that his own wife had lost a child at birth in his absence. They were far from alone in their claims. Many other famous people alleged similar experiences. Even now, the *Daily Mail* boasted celebrity look-alikes; quite frequently, in fact.

Alison shook herself. Her imagination was getting the better of her. Far more likely an explanation than one of paranormal origins was that the person who'd provided the description for the sketch was flawed, either in memory or in ability to convey precisely the facial features he or she had seen.

Rob had once told her about the process of police sketching, something she'd used in her first novel. The process was fascinating. An eyewitness, generally the victim of a crime, was often traumatized and less coherent than he might otherwise be under normal conditions. The interviewer had to proceed slowly, trying to jog bits of memory and detail that were buried under the rubble of fear and confusion that accompanied most crimes. They made unreliable witnesses, though occasionally a likeness could be rendered that helped the police solve a crime. Alison knew Rob wouldn't have circulated a sketch unless he'd no other means of getting at the person responsible; in this case, Sophie Flynn's murderer. Still, it was disconcerting to see Madeline's face staring at her defiantly from the page.

The snow, which had begun a couple of hours earlier, was turning into sleet. Ice pellets hit the windscreen and she turned on the wipers to clear it while she backed out of her parking space. She shivered and reached over to turn up the heat. In her haste to leave the doctor's office, she hadn't put on her coat, instead carrying it to the car and throwing it across the passenger seat. She pulled onto the main road. Traffic this time of afternoon was light, and she reached into her bag with her left hand for her gloves. She only came up with one. At the traffic light, she dug through again and realized the other glove was likely sitting on the counter at the doctor's office. She would have to call and ask the clerk to hold it for her. They were her favorites, cashmere-lined leather ones she'd gotten at Harrods a few weeks earlier, and she would hate to lose one.

The light turned green and she turned onto Tawney Street, heading toward the A16. Normally, she wouldn't go that way in weather like this, but she was in a hurry to show the sketch to Madeline, to find out if she knew anything about it.

Alison turned on the headlamps against the darkening sky, thinking about her new assistant. She had found herself doing things she would never have dreamed of only a few weeks earlier. Becoming involved with another person so quickly, and a woman at that, had both startled and thrilled her in a way she hadn't thought possible. She wasn't ready to go public with the relationship, which Madeline wanted her to do, because it was still new, and, in her eyes, an experimental phase. Alison didn't know how she would feel about it in a month or a year. She wasn't even certain how she felt about it now. But she knew she was enjoying it, at least for the moment. Time would tell how the relationship would evolve, if at all. In the meantime, she wanted only to abandon herself to the ecstasy of it, with someone young and fiery like Madeline.

Her tires skidded as she rounded a corner and she slowed the car, trying to keep it on the road. She'd begun to perspire in spite of the freezing air. As she turned off the heater and steered with one hand, she hit a patch of black ice that sent the car sliding into the curb.

The car jerked to a stop. For a moment, the only sound was the tapping of chunks of ice on the glass. Alison had been jolted into the steering wheel so hard it knocked her breath from her. She would have welts on her chest where she'd been struck.

Opening the door, she got out to inspect the damage. There was a sizeable dent and a scratch along the side, but her car was drivable. Shaken, she got back inside and tried to calm herself.

After a few minutes, she restarted the engine, heading at a furious pace toward her house. She needed a stiff drink, a hot meal, and a very strong reassurance that Madeline had nothing at all to do with the murder of an innocent child in Cornwall.

TWENTY-SIX

THERE IS A VIEW from the hills to the north of Cairns, Queensland, where one can get a dazzling look at the port city and Trinity Inlet, which can take one's breath away. Nick Flynn had hiked a couple of hours from the city in order to see it at night. The moon wasn't full, but close enough that the entire city would be on display. He sometimes wondered what kept people indoors, watching vulgar programs on tiny little boxes, when they could experience some of the greatest things known to man. It had rained in the last forty-eight hours, but he was prepared. He had a pack on his back with a couple of water bottles, a few sandwiches, and a length of plastic sheeting to spread on the ground. This was what he loved best: lying outdoors in the great wilderness of the world, watching and listening for whatever might come his way.

The storm had blown out to sea, and there were no clouds to obscure the fiery stars against the sky. The lights of the houses and buildings in the town far below were beautiful in their own way, but he tried to imagine Cairns before even Captain Cook mapped out the site, when the ocean alone reflected the moonlight and stars. From the beach, one couldn't really understand the vastness of the sea beyond, but perched on a hilltop, away from society, one could watch in awe the swell of the water strike against the stiff neck of land, a fierce battle of wills between earth's two most powerful entities.

He'd begun fishing, as he'd told Iris he would, but it wasn't a fortnight before the stinking smell of flounder and crab had made him sick of the entire business. He'd always been too poor to be particular about what food he ate, but he knew one thing: he would never eat another squid as long as he lived. The boat, *Laura's Holiday*, had gone up the east coast to Brisbane, and he'd jumped ship there and caught a bus north to Cairns. It was a long and bumpy ride, but worth it, he thought, to see a part of his homeland that he'd never seen before. It was a life goal of his, to see as much of the world as he could—particularly Australia's six states, including the territories, at least the inhabited ones. If he figured it correctly, he was sixteen hundred miles from Sydney, there in the far north, and he could spend the next few months working his way south, looking at some of the country's greatest sights along the way. He had hoped to go north to Papua New Guinea, of which he'd heard much from his father after some of his many sailing adventures, but the boat he'd been working on wasn't headed that far north, and he'd decided on Cairns instead.

Staying away from Sydney was the wisest move at the moment, anyway. A few months would be long enough for his father to cool off about him leaving yet another job. His mother wouldn't care, of course. She knew how it felt to get the itch under her skin and the need to leave. Iris was different. She was usually angry for a while, but he knew how to put that to rights. He smiled thinking about it. He missed her, even though it had only been a few weeks, but that was one of the good things about striking out on his own from time to time. He was always happy to see her after a few months of roaming. In his opinion, their relationship was stronger because they spent enough time apart to yearn for each other again.

Nick loved the children, too, although he couldn't help feeling they were a nuisance most of the time. It was difficult to stop every bleeding minute to see to one of their needs. He was more than happy to cede responsibility for them to Iris. As his father would have said, it was woman's work, anyway. He knew there were more modern ideas for child-rearing, but he wasn't interested. If he hadn't loved his wife, he wouldn't have bothered having children at all.

A sprinkle of rain pattered on his head, but he hardly took notice of it. He'd lived through worse. This was the middle of the wet season, and one had to take one's chances. He lay back on the plastic sheeting and stretched his arms under his head. As much as he wanted to, he wouldn't sleep out in the open on the hilltop. Snakes were apt to come out at night, and he couldn't build a fire when the ground was so drenched. But for now, he relaxed, listening to the sound of his own breathing and the whip of wind rustling the grass.

Suddenly, Sophie's face swam before his eyes and he felt his heart constrict. He missed her, when he allowed himself to think about it. Most of the time he kept his mind on the present, trying as hard as he could not to conjure the day she was killed, when he and Iris had been in a blind panic and Charlotte and India were frightened to death, wondering if the worst would come. It didn't do any good thinking about it now, anyway. Nothing could bring her back. No weeping or gnashing of teeth could stir her cold, dead bones. Ashes to ashes, he thought; dust to dust. Her mortal coil had long since faded, and, he hoped, swept into the air and sky, traveling the vast atmosphere with wings of joy. She deserved no less, his girl.

It was almost as difficult to think about Charlotte and India. Both of them were so like their mother. He'd suspected that Sophie, full of life, might have been a wanderer like him. The other two were tied to their mother's apron strings, and likely always would be. Charlotte was already a homebody. She wanted to take care of them, all of them, even him. Perhaps she sensed that no one else had taken on that responsibility, but he didn't let the thought trouble him too much. He preferred to think that what the Universe brought into being, it would also take care of. Things had a way of working themselves out.

In the meantime, he would enjoy his life. He would have to work as he journeyed his way south again. In this part of the country, organic farms were a booming business, and backpackers, usually posh university students from overseas, were hired by the dozens to bring in crops. He was a few years older, but he could still pick potatoes or avocados or bananas just as well as anyone. And if there was no work in the fields, which he was good at, he could do any of a dozen things he'd picked up in some of his other travels. The key to a serious walkabout was to be flexible, if nothing else.

After a couple of hours' staring up at the stars, mulling problems and then deciding there was nothing to be done about any of them, Nick ate a couple of the sandwiches and then packed his backpack, hoisting it over his shoulder for the long walk back into town. He was glad for his rubber boots as he sloshed across the open hillside, hiking back toward the lights of the city. Iris would like it here, he decided. She'd been game for every adventure he'd suggested and never once complained. She hadn't liked South Africa as much as he had, but eventually the heat had worn him down, too. One thing about Iris, she adjusted to almost anything, and he liked that in a life companion. Not every man was so lucky.

Back in Cairns, he found a pub in Bunda Street and crossed the road to get out of the rain. It was dim inside, and it took a few seconds to adjust his eyes to see what was around him. The pub was nearly empty, with only a couple of codgers sitting at a table in the corner having an earnest discussion about football. The barman didn't even look up when he came in. He was cleaning glasses and placing them in neat rows on the shelf behind him. Nick went over and sat down at the bar.

"What brings you in on this cold, wet night?" the man asked, tossing his towel over his shoulder.

Nick shrugged. "Just passing through."

"Nothing much to do in the wet season but get drunk and look for women," the barman said, laughing. When Nick didn't answer, he stopped drying dishes. "So, what's your story, mate?"

"My story?" Nick asked, pulling off his gloves. "How about a nice lager and I'll tell you all about it."

"You got money on you?" the man asked. "You look a little worse for the wear, if you don't mind me saying."

Nick dug a few bills out of his pocket and set them on the bar.

"There. That good enough for you?"

Instead of answering, the man turned and pulled a pint and set it in front of him, wiping the counter to mop the spill of foam.

Nick closed his eyes and tipped back the glass. He took a long pull and then set it down again. "Now that's what I call a good way to end the day."

"You're not from around here, are you?"

"Sydney."

"Sydney?" the barman rumbled. "You are a long way from home, aren't you?"

"I was fishing near Brisbane, and decided to come and see what you have to offer up here."

"No family?"

Nick paused, taking another gulp of the cold beer. "Everyone's got a family, mate."

"I meant the 'strain and strife.' Most men have one."

"Mine's in England at the moment."

"Blimey. Long leash on that one."

"She's from there. Seeing family." The last thing he was going to do was tell a complete stranger about his dead child and the ongoing investigation into her killing. He couldn't even stand to think of it himself.

"How long's she been gone?"

"Dunno. Three weeks, thereabouts."

"I'd like to ship my wife off to England for three weeks," the man said, laughing. "Longer if they'd have her."

"Fucking 'ell."

"What's the matter?"

"I need to ring her."

Nick stood and took his drink to the farthest corner of the pub and sat down at the table by the window. Pulling out his phone, he turned on the power. He didn't keep it on all the time because he was never certain when he would be near electricity to recharge it. Iris had called six times. Bugger it, he thought. He'd missed their last couple of Saturday night calls. Sometimes he was better at remembering than others.

"What time is it?" he called out to the barman.

"Just after eleven thirty."

He wasn't certain what time it was in Cornwall, but it had to be daytime. He punched in her number and waited for her to pick up on the other end.

"Nick," she said, when she answered the phone. He sighed, relieved that he'd gotten through. It was good to hear her voice. "Where are you?" she asked.

"You tried to call," he said, buying time before he had to tell her he wasn't fishing anymore.

"My mother's been in hospital. She has cancer."

"That's rough," he said. "How's she doing?"

"She's refusing treatment, actually."

"How are you?"

"I moved in with her, for the time being."

He grunted, surprised. He wasn't as intimidated by Iris's mother as she was, but still, she would be a difficult woman to live with, especially when she was sick.

"That's going to be hard," he said.

"How's the fishing?" Iris asked. He could hear the tone in her voice.

"It was fine," he answered. "For a while."

"Nick, you didn't."

"Listen, you wouldn't want to be in the cold water hauling squid and whatnot all day, either."

"Where are you now?"

"North Queensland," he said after a pause. "I'm going to work my way back down to Sydney. If you're tied up there, I may even beat you home."

There was silence on the other end of the line.

"Iris?" He knew that silence as well as he knew his own thoughts. She was probably thinking they didn't have a home, or something ridiculous like that. As far as he was concerned, as long as they had a place on his parents' farm to come home to, they didn't have anything to worry about.

"Did you sleep with Karen Peterson?" she asked suddenly.

"Shit," he said, looking around at the nearly empty bar. He sighed and took a drink of his beer.

"So, that's a yes," she said. "And how many others besides her?"

He paused, rubbing his eyes. "I don't want to talk about this now."

"You do if you want to fucking stay married to me."

"Not many," he admitted. "And none of them meant anything at all, Iris, I swear. End of story."

"None of them meant anything!" she said. "That's easy for you to say. One of those meaningless fucks cost me my daughter."

He sighed. "We both lost her, you know. You're not the only one. You have to pull yourself together, Iris, and stop being a goddamn victim. Rotten things happen. We have no control over anything. We have to hold it together the best that we can."

"I am holding it together."

"You're not with the girls."

"I will be, soon enough. And neither, may I remind you, are you."

"What's happening with the case?"

He could hear her sigh from ten thousand miles away. "We finally got an image of Karen from CCTV to show 'round. We're hoping that someone will recognize it and notify the police."

"We who?"

"The detective working on the case."

"It's not likely that they'll find her after all this time, is it?"

"You don't know that. Cases are solved all the time."

"Not cold cases," he argued. "Cases with no leads."

"We have a photo now, and even though she's using an alias, or even more than one, we have a lead. Stop being so pessimistic."

"I don't see how dredging it all up again is going to help anyone. Not you, not me, and certainly not Sophie."

"I'm doing this for Sophie, Nick."

"Where does this leave us now?" he asked.

She went silent on the other end of the line. "In the same place we've always been, I suppose."

"What the hell does that mean?" he asked. "I love you, Iris. I always have. You're the only person who has ever meant anything to me."

He could hear her start to break down on the other end of the line.

"I love you, too," she said in a low voice.

"You sound tired. I'll ring you on Saturday, then."

"Saturday," she repeated.

He rang off and lifted his glass. Instead of raising it to his lips to drink the last of it, he smashed it down onto the floor. The barman looked up and raised a brow.

"That'll cost you, mate."

"Everything costs me," Nick replied. "You wouldn't believe how it costs me."

He threw a couple extra bills on the counter and then slammed out the door.

TWENTY-SEVEN

Two days later, McIntyre was back in his office in Truro, staring at a message from Superintendent Patrick Quinn: *I want an update NOW* it read. He rubbed his forehead where it had begun to throb and then reached over with his foot and kicked the waste bin across the floor just as Dugan walked in.

"Well, sir," his sergeant said, eyeing the bin. "I can get you a new one, if you like, but it's going to bear a marked resemblance to this one."

"Quinn wants an update," McIntyre replied.

"Anything I can do?"

They both knew the superintendent's patience had run thin as far as the Flynn case was concerned. Quinn felt they were wasting valuable time and assets on an unsolvable case, but the mere thought that the case was unsolvable made McIntyre furious.

"In fact, there is," he told Dugan. "Get me a list of every woman in London by the name of Madeline Roy."

"Any special spelling on the first name?"

"I have no idea." McIntyre barked. "Try everything. I'm going to London later today to check out this lead."

"The Super might have other ideas."

"If he objects, then I'm simply at my brother's for a brief visit. What are you doing this weekend?"

"I did have plans to go to Seaton."

"What's in Seaton?"

"Well, sir … " Dugan looked uncomfortable for a moment. "Ena's parents."

McIntyre's eyes widened. "You're already at the 'meet the parents' stage?"

His sergeant shrugged. "I'll go another weekend. It's no problem."

"It would be helpful if you could get to information quickly, if I need it."

He turned and walked down the hall to Quinn's office. His boss had his back to the door, looking at a book he'd pulled from a shelf. The charged atmosphere in the room felt to McIntyre somewhat like a crime in progress, that moment before a suspect pulled a weapon and he had to use deadly force. There was always the hope that someone would drop the weapon and surrender, but of course, one could never know for certain.

"Sir?" he said in a loud, confident voice.

Quinn turned and tossed the book onto a chair. "I see you're back. What happened with the Flynn woman this time?"

"She was attacked by a man who was with her daughter's murderer on the night of the crime."

This roused Quinn's interest. "The murderer, you say?"

"Yes, sir," McIntyre answered. "He picked up Karen Peterson and the child and took them on her instructions to the river, where the child was killed before he drove Peterson back to Truro."

240

"Did he see the actual murder?"

"No, he was in the car, but he heard suspicious behavior."

Quinn tapped a file on his desk. "And he thought nothing of the woman getting back into the car without the child?"

"He was interested in one thing only, if you take my meaning."

"Why did he attack Iris Flynn?"

"He was obsessed with her," McIntyre said. "He'd been following her since she came back to Truro. Her face was in the papers and attracted his attention."

"We'll need to question him further."

"He's in hospital with a head injury," McIntyre said. "He was struck during the attack by Mrs. Flynn."

"Is she still hospitalized?"

"Just her mother, sir. Flynn had superficial cuts and bruises to the face."

"I want to be present during that interview. How long until he's released?"

"I wasn't given a definite time frame." McIntyre cleared his throat. "He did impart one particular piece of information when I spoke with him."

"Which is?" Quinn asked as he rounded his desk and sat down behind it.

"The suspect gave him a different name when he picked her up. She called herself Madeline Roy."

"She probably made it up on the spot," the superintendent said, lacing his fingers together on the table.

"It's a very specific name for a random choice," McIntyre argued. "I've got Dugan looking into it now."

"What's the man's name?"

"Sean Campbell. And I'll haul him down here the moment he's released."

"I still don't know that this is a reliable lead. It feels like we're wasting our time again."

"I think we're close. I have a gut feeling about it."

Quinn snorted. "You've been right a few times, I'll give you that, but I don't believe in gut feelings, particularly when you've gotten too involved in a case."

McIntyre resisted raising an eyebrow, wondering instead who might have said something to Quinn about him and Iris Flynn. "I'm only as involved as I need to be to get to Karen Peterson," he said. "No more."

"We'll talk on Monday," Quinn said. "But if you don't have anything solid, we're going to shut this down."

McIntyre gave a brief nod and walked out the door. It was all he could do not to slam it. He went downstairs in search of Dugan, who he found sitting behind his desk, concentrating on his computer screen. The computers were looking dated, he noticed. The police station, of all places, needed the most up-to-date equipment, but budgetary restraints had hit them hard over the past couple of years.

"Boss," Dugan said, looking up. "I've got it."

"Already?" McIntyre asked. "How many?"

"There are four Madeline Roys in London. Two are elderly. One is ninety-four and in a care home. The other is seventy-six years old and lives with her son in Paddington. The two viable leads are twenty-nine and thirty-four years old."

"Addresses?"

"Here," Dugan said. "Already wrote them down for you."

"Thanks," he answered, taking the paper. "I'm leaving now. Let me know if you get any other details."

"Are you taking the train?"

"No, I'm driving. I want to be mobile once I get there," McIntyre said. "What areas of London are we talking about?"

"The thirty-four-year-old lives in Islington. If you can't find her at home, she works at the British Museum."

"The museum?" McIntyre asked. "Doing what?"

"She's a clerk in the Reading Room, helping patrons with book requests and things like that."

"What about the younger woman?"

"She lives in Clerkenwell. I haven't got information about a work record yet."

"Good work, Alex."

It wasn't even nine-thirty yet when he was on the A390 and heading east. The sky was dark, threatening rain, but if it held off, he would make it to London by two or two thirty. He turned on the radio to listen to the news to take his mind off the case for a short while, if that were even possible now. There had been an outbreak of Ebola in Spain after nationals had returned from Africa without declaring that they had come from an Ebola zone. Bloody imbeciles, he thought; jeopardizing the health of an entire continent with one thoughtless deed. The next story was about another school shooting in the United States, this time in Michigan. On the list of heinous crimes, this ranked near the top in his mind. He couldn't imagine what would possess someone to turn their wrath on large groups of unsuspecting children. Seven had been killed, four others injured. Often, it seemed, the shooter was an adolescent male, isolated, stockpiling either guns or chemicals and reading manifestos on how to kill on the Internet. Sometimes they even wrote their own.

Before taking the Flynn child, Karen Peterson hadn't shown any latent sociopathic tendencies that he knew about, but her story unsettled him all the same. The way she'd calmly asked Sean Campbell to drive down near the river and then had him wait in the car while she broke the child's neck and disposed of her body in the river was horrific. And it seemed she'd killed the child only to engage in sexual relations with a complete stranger within a half hour of meeting him. One minute, a child was safe in her own home, and the next, taken by a woman who was insane or evil or both. He would leave the psychology to the experts, but in his view, she knew what she was doing and would have to be found and held responsible for Sophie Flynn's murder. Almost as infuriating was the knowledge that Superintendent Quinn would make good on his threat to shut down the case if he didn't have more evidence by the end of the weekend. He didn't think he could face Iris if that happened.

Once he'd arrived in Clerkenwell, he checked the address again and put the paper in his pocket. He lucked into a parking space and managed to park with only a minor bump against the car behind his. London parking was the worst. He locked the car and walked up to the door. The rain had held off until a few minutes before he reached the city, and he dodged between drops to ring the bell. A young man of approximately thirty years opened the door. He wore a pair of black glasses and held a glass of wine in his hand.

"You're not Simpson," the young man said. "I was expecting Simpson."

"Chief Inspector McIntyre," he said, holding up his badge.

"Inspector?" he asked.

"Your name, please?"

"Adam Roy."

"Mr. Roy, may I come in and ask a few questions?"

Roy stepped back to allow him inside and set his glass of wine on the top of a low bookshelf. The room was inviting, with Kilim rugs and a vintage Chesterfield sofa that was scuffed to perfection. After the long drive, McIntyre wouldn't have minded sitting down on it and having a glass of wine, himself.

"May I ask why you're here?" Roy asked.

"I'm looking for a woman named Madeline Roy."

"Madeline?" the man repeated, surprised. "What on earth could you want with Madeline?"

"Is she here? I'd like to talk to her."

"Well, she's here..." he said, glancing at the staircase.

McIntyre frowned, watching the young man's obvious reticence. "Would you ask her to come down, please?"

Roy shrugged and walked up the stairs, which groaned with every step, and after a minute he came back downstairs, followed by an attractive young woman with long auburn hair. McIntyre took a step toward them and nodded.

"Mrs. Roy, I'm Chief Inspector Robert McIntyre. I need to ask you a few questions."

Adam Roy turned toward her and started moving his hands about in odd gestures that McIntyre dimly recognized. His wife was watching him intently.

"What are you doing?" he asked.

"Signing," the man answered. "My wife is deaf. She can lip read, but since this appears to be a serious inquiry, I want to make sure she fully understands. For that matter, I'd like to know what's going on myself."

Rob McIntyre sighed. This Madeline Roy bore no resemblance to either the artist's sketch or the CCTV image of Karen Peterson. He would ask a few questions to be certain and then he would go.

"Has either of you been in Cornwall in the past two years?"

Adam signed his question to his wife. She looked at McIntyre and shook her head.

"No," Roy answered. He added, "Our family is in Norfolk. When we get a mini-break, we like to go and see our parents. Madeline's father is the vicar in a village on the coast, and we like to stay at the vicarage where she grew up."

Great, McIntyre thought. Not only was she deaf, but devoted to her father the vicar. This was not a person who could have murdered a young child.

"I'm happy to say you're not the Madeline Roy I'm looking for," he said, addressing the young woman. "I'm investigating a murder that occurred last year in Cornwall, and you don't match the description of the person I'm looking for."

"Well, that's a relief," Roy said. He signed the information to his wife. "Do you have any further questions for us?"

"No. Thank you."

McIntyre moved past them and walked to the door. He opened it and turned up his collar against the wind and rain. Consulting the Internet on his mobile, he saw it would take ten minutes to reach Islington. He started the car and watched for an opening before pulling out into the rain. As he drove, he punched in the number for the British Museum and asked for Mrs. Harrington. It was a long minute before he was put through.

"Patricia Harrington," said a voice on the other end of the line. "How may I help you?" It was the smooth voice of someone who scolded pupils or tried to explain the intricacies of how to raise orchids to a complete moron.

"This is Chief Inspector Robert McIntyre, of the Devon and Cornwall Constabulary, and I want to ask you a couple of questions about a woman in your employ by the name of Madeline Roy."

"*Was* in my employ, Inspector. She no longer works here."

"When did she leave, if you can recall?"

"Just a couple of weeks ago. She'd been rather promising, with a good work ethic, but unfortunately she was interested in a rather more prestigious sort of employment than what she could find in a stuffy museum library."

"What sort of employment?" McIntyre asked.

"Something in the book business, I think, but I rather doubt it will help her in any academic career in which she might have once been interested."

"Do you know anything about her personal life?"

"We aren't here to pursue friendships or to make social contacts, Inspector," Mrs. Harrington replied. "I had one interest in her, and one only: that she treat the opportunity she was given here with respect and conduct herself in a dignified manner. Not every applicant is suited to employment in the British Museum."

He could just imagine. "Can you give me a physical description of Miss Roy?"

"She's in her late twenties, I believe, possibly older, with dark hair and a pale complexion. She's an attractive enough person, I'm sure most would say."

"Thank you for your help, Mrs. Harrington."

"Of course," she said in a clipped tone. "One is always ready to be of service to the police."

"I appreciate the cooperation," he replied. "I'll be in touch if I have any further questions."

The rain had driven most people into the cafés and shops. McIntyre took a left off Barnsbury Road onto Copenhagen Street and squinted at the numbers on the buildings. Madeline Roy's flat was in a drab little brown building that shrunk back from the road as though it were hiding, an image that made him think of Karen Peterson. He rounded the street twice before finding a place to park around the corner. He knew that his quarry was likely at work and he would be forced to come back knocking over the course of the evening, or even the weekend. However, when he rapped on the door with his knuckles, it opened right away.

A young woman stood in front of him, the door ajar. She had short, dark hair and a pair of tortoiseshell glasses. She frowned, obviously wondering why there was a policeman at her door.

"DCI McIntyre," he said, holding up his badge. He peered over her shoulder. "I'm here to speak to Madeline Roy."

The girl's face did not change expression. "She's not here."

"May I come in?"

She hesitated before opening the door and allowed him to step inside. Attired in a battered track suit with crumbs on the front, it looked as though she'd been eating in front of the telly. The room was quite small, with only a settee, a chair, and a couple of tables in the main room. A pink scarf had been draped over a lampshade, and there were books stacked in the corners. McIntyre noticed she carried a cane, on which she leaned heavily when she walked. Her limp was pronounced, and he felt a twinge of guilt at having made her get up quickly to come to the door.

"May I have your name?" he asked.

"Brooke Turner."

"Miss Turner, is this the flat that belongs to Madeline Roy?"

"Yes, but she's not here now."

"When will she be back?"

"I'm not sure," she replied. She wavered slightly and went to sit down, tucking her cane in the corner beside her. "She's taken a job out of town."

"Where, precisely, if you don't mind?"

"Norfolk," she replied. "Lincolnshire, or Norfolk, something like that."

"Norfolk," he repeated. Just like the last woman he'd spoken to. Was it possible they were related? "Do you have a number for her?" he asked.

"I'm afraid she didn't leave one," the girl said. She sat back on the sofa, elevating her leg as she did so.

"But she let you stay in her flat?"

"Our mothers are friends," she answered by way of explanation. "I'm taking care of the place until she comes back."

"And what do you do?" he asked.

The woman shrugged and lifted the cane for him to see, as if he hadn't noticed it right off.

"I'm looking for a job, but I'm dealing with debilitating arthritis. It's all I can do to get meals and give the place a good dusting."

He stood there, looking at her. "Do you know Miss Roy well?"

"No, not well. My mother fixed it for me to come and stay. Madeline wasn't especially friendly or anything. I got the feeling she resented having me here. I'm rather glad she's gone, if you want to know the truth."

McIntyre scratched his chin, trying to decide what to do. Brooke Turner seemed uncomfortable having him in the flat, and he was not going to get anything useful out of her. He pulled his card from his pocket and handed it to her.

"Do you have a photo of Miss Roy?"

"No," she answered. "And now that you mention it, I haven't seen one of her in the entire flat."

"I very much want to talk to her. If she calls or returns, please have her get in touch with me at once."

She took the card without reply and set it on the table.

"I'll see myself out," he said.

On the street, he paused and looked back up at the window. Stupid case, he thought. Nothing was going right. He decided to call David and let him know he was in town. Susan would insist he stay with them while he was in the city, but before he went to the house, he wanted to meet his brother for a quick pint. He dialed David's number and his brother picked up on the first ring.

"It's me," McIntyre said. "I'm in London for the weekend."

"Great," David replied. "Come over to the house."

"Could we meet for a drink first, if you don't mind? I want to talk to you."

"Sure. Where are you?"

"In Inslington. There's a pub 'round the corner on Market Road, The Boar's Head."

"I know it, actually. Went there once with a friend. I can be there in about twenty minutes."

"Great. I'll be one drink ahead of you."

McIntyre pocketed his mobile and went to order a pint. The pub was only half full, with a sleepy afternoon crowd murmuring over drinks. Women had packages from a day of shopping, and a group of German students in the corner were drawing maps on napkins, planning their next excursion. In a minute, he had his drink and took it to a table by the window. The table, an ancient oak, withstood the weight of his elbows as he hunched over his pint in thought.

He frowned, thinking about the wasted day and the pressure from Quinn to prove he had a solid lead. They had gotten too close to give up now. Kevin Hughes and Sean Campbell had actually had personal interaction with Karen Peterson or Madeline Roy, whatever she wanted to call herself. In spite of the fact that none of the leads had so far led to Peterson, he was certain that Madeline Roy was not a random name. Still, two pensioners, one deaf girl, and a librarian added up to nothing in his book. It was just his luck to hit another brick wall. Why couldn't things go right? he wondered. How had Karen Peterson been able to elude the police for so long? It should have been an open-and-shut case: nanny takes child, hooks up with a random stranger, and flees to London after her crime. Thousands of people had seen her, in one way or another. If only someone would come forward with information.

McIntyre looked at his watch. It was only four o'clock. He pulled out his mobile and punched in the number for the museum.

"May I speak to Patricia Harrington, please?" he asked the operator. In a moment, he was connected.

"This is Patricia Harrington."

"Mrs. Harrington, this is Inspector McIntyre again. I spoke to you earlier today about Miss Roy."

"I'm afraid I've told you everything I know. Were you able to locate her?"

"I went to her residence, where a friend is letting her flat. You mentioned she was working in the book business. Do you have any specific information about that? I can try to locate her from that angle."

"She actually went to work for an author who's just published her first novel. Not my sort of book, if you know what I mean."

"Her name?" McIntyre prompted, reaching for his pint. "Can you tell me the author's name?"

"Alison Kendall."

He nearly dropped the glass, sloshing ale all over the table.

"Alison Kendall?" he choked out. "Are you sure?"

"Completely. She never stopped talking about the woman."

"Thank you for your time," he said.

He stood, brushing off a few dots of ale that had found their way onto his trousers, and hurried to the door just as his brother was walking in.

"You're going the wrong way," David said. His smile faded when he got a look at his brother's face.

"I may have just gotten a break in the case, David," McIntyre said, shaking his head. "I'm afraid I'll have to see you later."

"But, wait—"

"Sorry," he called out over his shoulder. "I can't talk now. Duty calls."

TWENTY-EIGHT

ALISON PARKED HER CAR in the front of the house. There were no lights on in the front rooms, but she could see a faint light shining from the kitchen. Madeline had forgotten to turn on the lights, as usual. They hadn't been together long, but already she'd seen that Madeline could be thoughtless at times. Alison always turned on the lights as a matter of habit, but particularly if someone was expected. They shouldn't have to walk up a dark gravel path to an even darker doorway. She sat in her car for a few minutes, trying to decide what to do with the newspaper in her hands. Should she hand it to Madeline without a word and watch the shock on her face? Or demand to know why the police wanted to question her about the Flynn murder? She was mystified as to why the police had any reason to suspect someone like Madeline anyway. How could the girl, who until very recently spent the bulk of her days cataloguing books at the British Museum, have anything to do with murder? It was as preposterous as if she herself could kill another human being. The only possible explanation was that the witness describing the killer had made a mistake. It happened all the time.

Shaking herself, she got out of the car and went to the door, which was locked. It was ironic, the thought of a murderer locked safely inside the confines of her house away from normal, ordinary citizens; people who'd never killed or ever even thought of killing another living being. She was fortunate that Madeline had nothing to do with the Flynn case, or otherwise she would be heading straight into danger.

"Is that you?" Madeline called from the kitchen as she opened the door.

"It's me," she answered.

Alison walked into the kitchen and took off her coat, placing it in a chair in the corner. Madeline was cooking, and it smelled wonderful. She hadn't even realized she was hungry until now.

"I've been reading the book," Madeline said, stirring a pot of soup. The smell of chopped rosemary filled the room. The house was less empty with Madeline there. Alison liked having someone to talk to after Luisa had gone home.

"What book?" she asked.

"Your new book. The one you're writing."

Alison stiffened. "You were on my computer?"

"I didn't think you'd mind," Madeline said, wiping her hands on a towel. "I just wanted to read a little. The book I'm reading is really boring."

"George Eliot is boring?" Perhaps Madeline wasn't the intellectual she purported herself to be.

"I don't happen to have a thing for weak female lead characters who are so pathetically eager to marry they end up with an old git who slurps his soup."

"Regardless, you can't just take over my computer whenever you want," Alison answered, trying to control her temper. No one had ever read her writing before it was sent to her agent but Rob, and then only when asked. She'd stopped showing things to him after a while because he rarely had anything to say about it. In any case, the jumble of thoughts that make up a first draft were, if not perfect, then full of the potential the book might one day have, but not something everyone could see. "My work is private, and certainly not ready to be read."

"Especially chapter seven. I think you've gone after that section entirely the wrong way. I jotted down a few ideas for you."

"Ideas?" Alison sputtered, putting her hands on the counter to steady herself. "You've come up with ideas for my book?"

"Why are you angry?" Madeline asked. She stopped stirring and put the spoon on the counter. "I was trying to help. And in case you didn't notice, I'm standing here, making Nigella Lawson's Italian roast chicken and French onion soup for you, worrying over the mess you made with the murder in chapter seven. You should be thanking me, not starting a fight over nothing."

"I wouldn't exactly say I'm upset over nothing."

"Every book can stand some criticism, particularly if you're trying to write it too quickly. That chapter sounds rushed."

"I don't want to talk about this now," Alison murmured, backing out of the room.

As angry as she was, this wasn't the time to sort out when Madeline could read her book. Later tonight she would change her password and deal with that situation, but for now she went upstairs to her study and opened her laptop. Once she was connected to the Internet, she googled Rob's name, hoping it was the quickest way to read about the Flynn case. Most of the articles on the first page were recent ones about the child's disappearance and murder last December, as she'd suspected. She hovered the arrow over the first one and then clicked on it.

Iris Flynn's photo stared at her from the computer screen. She was an attractive-looking woman with dark hair and a solemn face. Her deep brown eyes had the most haunting look Alison had ever seen. She stared at the photo, wondering how it must feel to have one's life and sorrows dredged up by the local newspapers for all the world to see. After a minute, she tore her eyes away from Iris Flynn's face and began to read:

Truro Police have reopened an investigation into the 2014 abduction and murder of three-year-old Sophie Flynn, whose death captured national attention. The child was the daughter of Nick and Iris Flynn, who had recently moved back to the UK from the United States. The suspect, twenty-six-year-old Karen Peterson, an American who had accompanied the Flynns to Cornwall as an au pair, left the house with their three children on the evening of 17 December. Sophie Flynn's sisters, now ages six and two, were found by their mother on the banks of the Truro River that night, but Peterson was never located. Sources say it is likely she fled to London and could have returned to the States or even gone into hiding in Africa or Europe. The child's body was discovered on the banks of the Tresillian River in Penhale Wood the morning after her abduction. Official cause of death was drowning. Detective Chief Inspector Robert McIntyre of the Devon and Cornwall Constabulary said that the child had suffered a broken neck prior to being thrown in the river. No witnesses have come forward, and no motive has been identified in the case.

Alongside the article was another, smaller inset photo of the child. She was a beautiful, miniature version of her mother. It sickened

Alison that a stunning creature like this had been beaten until her neck snapped and thrown into the icy Tresillian to drown. It was a monstrous act, and only a sociopath could have done it.

There were other articles, some even newer, but she didn't bother with them. None of the headlines changed: Police Continue to Track Child Murderer. No New Clues in Child Murder Case. Will Iris Flynn Find Justice for Sophie? She couldn't bear to read another word.

She grabbed the newspaper from the doctor's office and looked at the article once again. The artist had captured Madeline's likeness perfectly, from her dark hair swept behind her shoulder to the small, almost imperceptible lines at the corner of her eyes. The left side of her mouth had a slight droop that Alison had never noticed before, but which she now realized was more than familiar. A chill ran down her spine. She had misjudged the situation. She'd misjudged everything.

She didn't entirely regret the affair, but she knew she'd been flirting with danger. Rob had been right. Something horrific could happen when you chose to live with a stranger. She could have been killed. She'd trusted Madeline, if not completely, then certainly enough to lay bare every vulnerability she possessed.

Plenty of people took false names and committed crimes. The question was, how had Madeline gone from the United States to Truro with the Flynns but covered her latest tracks so thoroughly? She knew Madeline had worked at the British Museum for only a short time, but although she'd been given a full CV, Alison hadn't made any calls to verify the rest of the girl's employment record. Now she knew it was fabricated. Whatever Madeline had done before didn't matter anyway. It was obliterated by the fact that she'd gallivanted across the ocean attached to an innocent couple, and then murdered one of their innocent children.

Alison stood and walked down the stairs, shaking. It was true. She was alone in the house with a murderer. What person in her right mind could ignore the fear of a child, someone so small and vulnerable? By the time she reached the bottom of the stairs, Alison was leaning against the rail for support, hardly able to breathe. What did this say about her ability to judge character? It was her own fault for getting involved with a stranger, no matter how attractive she was.

She stepped into the kitchen, pausing in the doorway. Madeline was chopping onions, a cookbook open in front of her. Alison watched as she pushed her hair behind her ear and studied the recipe with an intense look. She would have found it erotic had she not now known the truth. Watching Madeline wield the large, recently sharpened knife, Alison was not certain how to begin. Madeline suddenly noticed she was standing there and tried to smile.

"We shouldn't argue, you know," Madeline said, then paused. "I'm sorry. I only want to help you. You know how much I think of you."

"I already wrote one book entirely without your help, if you can imagine it," she said, as if her writing mattered at a time like this.

Madeline flinched. "What are you saying, exactly? That you don't want my help, or you don't want me here?"

"I think I'm saying we don't really know each other that well," Alison replied, clutching the newspaper in her hand. It was folded to conceal the sketch of Madeline's likeness. "Where did you work before the British Museum?"

"Seriously? I thought I was more to you than a mere employee. It certainly felt that way in bed last night." Madeline raised a brow at Alison's obvious discomfort. "Does it bother you to talk about it? Are you so repressed you can't say, 'I fucked a woman last night, just like the night before'?"

Alison colored. "I don't like to talk about it, no."

"You need a little help with that, too."

Suddenly her mobile rang, and Alison lifted it to see Rob's name on the screen. Relief coursed through her veins. He would know what to do. She started to answer it, and then realized she couldn't talk in front of Madeline. The phone continued to ring.

"Well?" Madeline asked, staring at her, the knife still in her hand. "Aren't you going to get it?"

Alison pushed a button and lifted the phone to her ear. "Yes?"

"Alison!" he barked into the phone. "Where are you?"

Stung by the tone in his voice, she took a deep breath. "I'm at home. How are you?"

"I need to talk to you. Are you alone?"

"Well, no." She avoided looking at Madeline.

"Where's your assistant?" he asked.

"Why do you want to know?" she asked, trying to sound casual. "Is something going on?"

"I can't say it with complete certainty, but I have reason to believe you could be in danger."

"What do you mean?" She turned away from Madeline's intent gaze and went over to thumb through a cookbook.

"Do you remember the Flynn case from last year?" he asked. "The child murder case, the one whose body was found washed up on the shore of Penhale Wood?"

"Yes, I remember."

"Your assistant's name is Madeline Roy."

"That's right."

Her mind began to race, full of questions. If Madeline had killed that child, had she also been following Alison all along, plotting some way to get close to her, push her way into her life because she'd lived with Rob McIntyre and had a distant connection to the case? But that didn't make sense. It was several months after she'd left Rob that her profile as an author began to rise and her photo began to appear in newspapers. And she'd never mentioned him in any interviews.

"Tell me—" she began.

"Is she there with you now?" he asked, interrupting her.

"Yes."

"I'm not certain yet how she's involved, but I don't want to take any chances. You need to get out of the house. Go anywhere. A church, a shop, a fucking pizza restaurant until I sort this out. And then I want you to ring me." She could hear a scratching sound on the other end of the line. "Let me know the minute you get somewhere safe. I'm on my way."

Her mouth flew open as the line went dead. She wanted to call him back but realized it wouldn't do any good. She walked back over to her handbag and put her mobile inside.

"Who was that?" Madeline asked.

"A friend."

"It didn't sound like a friend. It sounded serious."

Alison turned and looked at her, her heart beating too fast. Madeline still hadn't put down that sodding knife. Rob had told her to get out, but she couldn't leave yet. She had to know for certain what Madeline's involvement was with Sophie Flynn.

"Just out of curiosity," she said, "how do you feel about children?"

"Children?" Madeline asked, surprised. "They're nuisances, of course. Can you imagine letting one of them into your life? They'd ruin everything, wouldn't they?" Then she stopped and looked up at her. "Oh, no."

"What?" Alison asked. She was both triumphant that she'd tricked Madeline into a confession and terrified at the same time.

"You're going through a midlife crisis, aren't you? You suddenly crave the smell of infant flesh."

"No, I'm not," Alison snapped, thinking of Sophie Flynn. She was standing mere feet away from a woman who had broken a child's neck without even blinking an eye. "Don't be ridiculous."

"If it's true, you should rethink the idea," Madeline said, scraping the onions from the chopping board into the soup. "Your life would no longer be your own. And to what end? To become slaves of little people who will grow up resenting you and draining your resources and accusing you in the end of terrible parenting? I'd rather die than go through it."

Alison held up the newspaper for her to see. It was a stupid thing to do, but she couldn't stop herself. "Is that why you did it?" she asked.

Madeline stopped chopping and stared at the sketch that Alison held in her hands. A deep line appeared in her forehead and she looked up at Alison.

"What is that?" she asked. Her hand gripped the knife even harder than before.

"A police sketch. Haven't you seen it? You're being sought in a high-profile murder case."

"What murder case?"

Alison couldn't read the tone of her voice, but that wasn't surprising. After all, they hadn't really known each other that long.

"The murder of Sophie Flynn."

Madeline shrugged and went back to chopping. "Never heard of her. And yes, that bears a striking resemblance to me, but for God's sake, Alison, there are millions of women with dark hair."

"You killed her. I know it. And this sketch is your exact likeness."

"You're actually accusing me of murder?" Madeline demanded. "That's what you think of me, that I could ruthlessly kill someone?"

"I think you're capable of a lot of things," Alison said. "You're the most secretive person I've ever known."

"Some things are none of your damn business," Madeline said, clearly annoyed. She slammed the knife onto the counter. "It's not like you aren't guarded yourself."

"What made you contact me in the first place?" Alison demanded. "Did you read about me in the papers and realize I had a connection to the Flynn murder? Or did you just decide, 'I want a piece of that'?"

"Fuck you. You think you're so perfect."

"I'm wondering if it isn't the other way around."

"What does that mean?"

"You're pretty high and mighty for a glorified secretary."

"How dare you?" Madeline said. She reached out and slapped her.

Alison brought her hands to her face in shock. She'd never been struck in her entire life. "Get out of my house right now. And you'd better turn yourself in to the police, because I'm calling them now."

She reached for her handbag to retrieve her mobile, but Madeline lunged at Alison and in a second they were both gripping it, struggling for control. Alison tried to push her away, her heart beating so hard she thought it would burst.

"Get off me," she snapped.

Instead, Madeline leaned closer, grabbing her shoulders. "Stop it! What the hell's the matter with you?"

Instinctively, Alison reached out with both hands and shoved as hard as she could. Madeline fell back and there was a sudden ear-splitting crack as her head hit the edge of the counter. Everything went quiet for a moment. A second later, Madeline fell on top of her, blood flowing in every direction. Alison scrambled out from under her and sat up, looking at Madeline's body as it convulsed for a few seconds and then went still.

She wasn't certain how long she sat like that before staggering across the slate tiles and pulling her mobile from her bag, smearing blood across the numbers with a shaking hand. She'd heard about being in shock and knew without a doubt that she was in shock now. The only sound was the panic beating behind her ribs. Never had she seen so much blood. It was spattered on the floor, the cupboard, the walls. It was odd, she'd once thought, writing about death and dying without having any idea what the experience would be like. She'd sometimes thought it cost her something in authenticity. Well, now she knew. Why hadn't she just left the house like Rob had told her to? How had she, who through her entire life had been governed by rational thought, succumbed to panic and fear and actually killed another human being?

Rob would understand, she thought. She would tell him she'd seen the sketch and was forced into confronting the killer. At least the child-killer was dead, even if she hadn't confessed. Alison scrolled over to her saved numbers and pushed the button for his number.

"Where are you?" he growled in a low voice.

She looked down at her hands, which were covered in blood.

"Still at home," she murmured, her eyes fixed on the body that lay just feet away, contorted into a sickening sprawl across her kitchen floor. "And Rob ... I just killed Madeline Roy."

TWENTY-NINE

McINTYRE'S CAR SHOT UP the A16 at an unholy speed, siren blaring. He stopped only once to check the location of the Boston Police Station on his mobile, thankful for GPS systems and modern technology. A few minutes later he found the building on Lincoln Lane. After parking, he ran up the steps and went inside, marching up to the first officer he saw. He drew his badge from his pocket.

"DCI McIntyre, Devon and Cornwall Constabulary," he said, trying to get hold of himself. The last thing in the world he had expected was to learn that the woman he'd lived with for ten years had killed someone. He hadn't believed her capable of it. "I'm here to see a suspect you have in custody named Alison Kendall."

"Inspector," the man said, nodding. "Is that the woman they brought in tonight?"

"What's your name, sergeant?"

"Franklin, sir."

"Who's in charge this evening?"

"That would be DCI Clark."

"I'd like to talk to him, if you don't mind. It's urgent."

"Wait here, sir."

He chafed in the waiting area, looking around at the other people who were waiting on a cold, dark Friday night to take care of business of their own, reporting crimes or picking up someone who wouldn't be held overnight. For once he was on the other side of things, hoping he would be granted permission to speak to someone in custody. He wondered if any of the people in that room felt the same desperation he did at that moment, and realized that was precisely how they felt.

A minute later, the sergeant was waving him back to Clark's office. A few of the others looked up to see who was getting to go back. He almost felt guilty.

"Inspector Clark?" he said when he was shown into an office that looked like a carbon copy of his own. "DCI Robert McIntyre."

"You called about the Kendall woman," Clark stated, setting down his phone. He shuffled a couple of papers on his desk and sat back, eyeing him closely. "What brings you up to this part of the country?"

"I've been in London, looking for a person of interest in a case I'm working on named Madeline Roy."

"The woman who was killed tonight in a domestic dispute."

"That's the one. I need to speak to Alison Kendall. I know her personally."

"That's highly unusual, as I'm sure you know." Clark coughed. "It's a hell of a crime scene there. Two women got into a monster row, and one ends up dead with a cracked skull."

McIntyre frowned and stepped forward. "I didn't know the victim, but I have a few questions for Miss Kendall."

"Well, you won't get much out of her, that one. She's refusing to talk." Clark sighed, thinking it over. "Listen, I'm going to take a dinner break before I go at her again. You can talk to her in the meantime, but you only have ten minutes. Sorry, but it's all I can do. I shouldn't even let you do that."

"Thanks," Rob said, moving to the door. "I'll take it."

He was led down the hall by another sergeant, who turned a corner and pointed to the third door on the left. McIntyre nodded and opened the door. Alison sat there, looking pale and washed out, staring at the wall. Her hair was damp and she'd changed into prison clothes, clearly because her own had been seized in evidence.

"What do you want?" she asked, looking Rob in the eye. She didn't look particularly happy to see him.

"I want to talk to you," he said, sitting down across from her. The table was cold under his hands. "Are you all right?"

She pursed her lips, looking away. "I've been photographed, fingerprinted, and swabbed. Thrown in an ice-cold shower. Is this the way you treat people who've been arrested, Rob?"

The last thing he wanted to do was discuss the uglier side of police work. Sometimes, harsh measures were required, but he couldn't get into that now.

"Tell me what happened at the house, Alison."

"What's there to tell?" she murmured. "I killed a woman tonight. I killed Madeline Roy."

"Why didn't you leave the house, like I told you to?" he asked.

She sighed. "I wanted to see her face when I told her, I suppose."

"Can you remember what happened?"

She sighed. "I wish I didn't."

"I need you to tell me everything," he said. He had the sudden urge to take her hand but he didn't dare. "Start at the beginning."

Alison stared at him as though she'd been drugged. "What do you want to know?" she asked.

"How long ago did you hire Miss Roy to work for you?"

"Just after Christmas."

"And did she exhibit any alarming behavior during the time you knew her?"

Alison went still and looked away. "No. I did have some reservations on occasion. She was pushy, at times, but I was never afraid of her."

"Did something change?" he asked, leaning forward in his seat.

"I was in town today and happened to see a copy of *The Times* lying around. It had a police sketch on the front page."

"The police sketch from the Flynn case." McIntyre tried, unsuccessfully, to make sense of it. The woman in the sketch was a completely different person than the one identified by Sean Campbell as Madeline Roy. In fact, they hadn't gotten a single tip involving the psychic's vision at all.

"I knew that face right away," Alison said. "I know you told me to leave, but I lost control of things and we started arguing."

He sat back and ran his fingers through his hair. "You thought she was the person we were looking for in the case."

Alison looked shocked. "You mean, she wasn't?"

"We did want the woman in the sketch for questioning, but she's not the woman who was seen with the child, who is suspected of murdering her."

"I don't understand, Rob. You said she killed that child."

"We're looking for two different women, who both call themselves Madeline Roy. One is the nanny for Sophie Flynn. The other is the woman who matches the sketch, who happened to be the woman at your house."

"I almost told you," she said, looking at her hands.

"What do you mean, you almost told me?"

267

"When we first talked on the phone, I wanted to tell you I was seeing someone. I don't know if I wanted to shock you or prove to myself that what you thought didn't matter anymore. I realized later that what you think does matter to me a great deal. But by then, it was too late."

It took a few seconds for the information to sink into his brain.

"Wait—you mean you were seeing Madeline Roy?" he repeated. "She was more than an assistant to you?"

Alison leveled a look at him. "We had an instant attraction. It might be inadvisable to mix business and pleasure, but she was more than efficient, as far as the work goes, and it's been a long time—a very long time—since I felt for anyone what I did for her. Perhaps I never had."

McIntyre took a huge breath and leaned back in his chair, looking at Alison as though she were a complete stranger and not the woman he'd been with for the last decade.

"What happened tonight, Alison?" he asked. "I need to know exactly what occurred when you walked in that house."

"She was cooking," Alison said, a miserable look on her face. "Nigella Lawson's roast chicken. She was making it specially for me. Do you know what that's like, having someone do something just for you? Someone you didn't have to pay to do it? Of course you do. You're a man. But I never have. I've been the doer, the giver, the one who always makes for someone else. For people like you, I might add. And here was someone who wanted to please me. To cook something with the hope that it would make me happy."

His mobile buzzed in his pocket and he lifted it out to see if it was important. Iris had texted, *Rob, my mother's doing worse. Ring me when you can.*

268

He hoped her brother was with her, because he wasn't going to be able to leave in the middle of this conversation. Tucking the phone into his pocket, he looked again at Alison, who was watching him. It was difficult listening to her recount her relationship with Madeline Roy, but he had to know the truth.

"I'm sorry for the interruption," he said. "Go ahead."

"She was intelligent and charming, and she organized everything so that I could focus on my work. It was a dream situation."

With a few perks, he wanted to add. Instead, he cleared his throat. "Were you in love with her?"

The room seemed airless, the gray institutional walls closing in. He suddenly wanted fresh air.

"You don't have to be sarcastic."

"I'm not," he protested. "I really want to know."

"No," she finally answered. "We knew each other for less than two weeks."

He didn't ask her to elaborate. It wasn't any of his business, when it came down to it. "You saw the sketch. Take it from there."

"I got in my car and drove home. She was cooking, so I went upstairs to my study and looked you up online. I wanted to know about the case."

"And then?"

"There are lots of articles about it. I saw photos of Iris Flynn and of her daughter. The crime was gruesome. I'd seen the sketch, and that was it. I realized I was trapped in the house with the woman who had killed that child. I panicked, Rob. There was always something a little aggressive about her." Alison folded her pale, thin hands on top of the table. "I accused her, wrongly it seems, and she slapped me. Before I knew it, she was dead."

"There may be an argument for self-defense. Talk to your solicitor about it."

"I killed her. What more do you need to know?"

"Did you go into that kitchen specifically to kill her?"

"I went to confront her. To get her to turn herself in to the police."

"How did it happen?"

"She came at me, trying to grab my mobile. I pushed her." Alison looked away. "The sound of her skull cracking was the most horrible thing I've ever heard. I'll never forget it."

McIntyre stood, hoping for her sake that one day she could. "Don't talk to anyone else until you've seen a solicitor. Do you understand me?"

"Stop telling me what to do. It's too late, anyway."

"Don't be stupid. We may not be together anymore, but I still care about you. I don't want you to be convicted for murder if it was an accident."

"I want to know something," Alison said. The wispy ends of her wet hair had begun to dry and frizz, just as he remembered. She would hate it. She'd always been particular about her appearance. He looked down to see her hands trembling on the table before him.

"What?" he asked. What could he possibly tell her to make everything better?

"Just precisely how was Madeline connected to the case, if she wasn't the one who murdered that little girl?"

That was what he wanted to know, too. The only link between Madeline Roy and Sophie Flynn was a sketch drawn from a psychic's vision. He looked up at the clock. He only had a couple of minutes before Inspector Clark came in and put an end to their discussion. Something was missing. He just didn't know what it was.

"Did Madeline ever mention Cornwall to you?" he asked, changing the subject. "Any family there, or connections of any kind?"

"No, she didn't. We didn't talk about family, really. I never thought to ask. Sometimes I assume everyone's like me, alone in the world."

Nothing she could have said could have wrenched his gut more. "You're not alone," he said, trying to convince himself.

"Oh, you're wrong, Rob," she said, wringing her hands in front of her on the table. They were delicate hands, not the hands of someone who could commit murder. The blood had drained from her skin and left her as pale as a ghost. "I've never been more alone in my entire life."

There was nothing he could say to her to prove it wasn't true.

THIRTY

AFTER BEING INVITED BY Inspector Clark to leave the station, Mc-Intyre walked out into the cold night, hands shoved in his pockets. Wind stung his ears. The moon, a sterile, almost silver blue, was useless behind the thick, dark clouds. He went out to the car park and got into his car, turning on the engine and rubbing his hands together while waiting for the heat to kick in. It was almost midnight. His choices were to call Iris, which would wake her, and explain the delay returning her message; call David, which would wake him, to ask if he could spend the night after ditching him at the pub; or get a hotel. He was bone tired after a day of trying to find Madeline Roy and then rushing to see Alison, so he decided to drive to London and text David when he got there. It was the most forgiving of the three options.

In spite of what he'd said to Alison, he didn't believe she had a strong case for self-defense. She'd provoked what proved to be a deadly confrontation. There was no way to know for certain if she'd pushed Madeline Roy to stop an attack, as she claimed, although he was sure she'd told him the truth. In spite of what had happened between them, he didn't want to see her serve time in prison. A coroner, however, might not be so easily convinced.

He cursed when a patter of icy rain began to fall and turned on his windscreen wipers. With each passing minute, another problem arose. An inquest would be held soon, and it was possible that he himself could be called as a witness. He had, without meaning to, misrepresented Madeline's situation to Alison during their brief phone call. If the call was brought up, they would want to know why he had wanted to see Alison so soon after she was taken into custody. They might suspect him of colluding with her or attempting to give her an alibi. He tried to get hold of himself. He was tired, stressed. His thoughts didn't run rampant like this on a normal day. Of course, this hadn't been a normal day at all.

He drove into London, the traffic picking up somewhat as he crossed the city, heading for Holland Park. When he reached his brother's house, he had to circle around the road three times before he found somewhere to park. He pulled out his mobile and texted David: *I'm back in London. Can I impose on you and spend the night?*

The answer was immediate: *Of course. How soon can you get here?*

McIntyre got out of his car and walked up to the door. *I'm here now.*

After a few moments, David swung open the door. "Are you all right? I was worried when you left the pub so abruptly."

"I'm not sure I am."

David stepped aside and let him in. McIntyre had no idea how tired he was until he sat down, his senses reeling. He was too tired to even take off his coat. He wanted to lie down right there and fall asleep and forget the past twenty-four hours. Everything was a disaster. Alison had killed an innocent woman, and he was no closer to finding Karen Peterson than he'd been a year ago.

"What can I get you?" David asked. "A drink? A hot shower? You look all in."

"Alison killed someone tonight."

"What?" There was only one lamp on in the sitting room, but he could see the shock register on his brother's face.

"She saw an artist's sketch of someone I was trying to locate and mistook the woman for a killer. I'd called and told her to leave the house because the person was related to a case I'm working on, but that reinforced her idea that the woman was dangerous. She panicked and killed her during an argument."

"Christ."

"I can't talk about it anymore right now, but I wanted you to know why I'm wrecked."

"I'll get you some blankets. You need sleep."

He closed his eyes, waiting for David.

When he opened them, he was sprawled across the sofa and someone had tucked a blanket in around him. He wiped the drool from the corner of his mouth and looked at his watch. It was half past three. He sat up and rubbed his face. Reaching for his phone, he realized he'd still never answered Iris's text. Now it would have to wait until morning. If she was at the hospital, as he suspected, he didn't want to wake her.

His thoughts turned dark, as they only can in the dead of night. Iris, who had lost Sophie and then been stalked and then attacked, was now dealing with another crisis and he hadn't even responded to her. Although how could he have, when he was dealing with his ex, who had murdered someone? He wanted to wind back the clock to over a year ago, before any of it had happened. To the day before Sophie had died. If only he could have arrested Karen for some minor charge, something that would have altered the course of one three-year-old girl's life. But of course it was impossible. Murders happened. Crimes went unsolved. His brother was right. He was too close to this case to have any objectivity left.

For the rest of the night, he tossed and turned, staring out the window and into the darkened room, the one place on earth where there appeared to be any sense of normalcy. Around dawn, he fell asleep. He awoke a couple of hours later to the sound of Susan's voice.

"Want some coffee?" she asked.

His eyes fluttered open and he saw a vision before him. After a second, he realized she was holding a cup out to him.

"Yeah," he said, sitting up. Every bone in his body was tired. He needed a week of sleep. Taking the coffee from her, he took a gulp. "Thanks, Susan. I needed that."

She sat down next to him. "David told me what happened. We can hardly believe it. I can't imagine what you're feeling."

"I don't have time to feel anything." He looked up into her wide blue eyes. She was a beautiful, wonderful woman. He wanted to find someone exactly like her. "Where is he?"

"Getting the papers," she answered. "He knew you'd want to see them."

McIntyre heard the sound of small feet tumbling down the stairs. Susan stood and went to the doorway to the hall.

"I'll head them off and get them settled for breakfast. You don't need to deal with them yet."

He wanted to protest but didn't have it in him at the moment. Susan left, and he folded the blanket and tossed it over the arm of the sofa just as David came through the front door. His brother shut out the cold air behind him and lifted a stack of newspapers to show him.

"You didn't have to do that," he said.

"There's little else I can do for you right now," David answered.

He took the stack and spread them across the table, groaning as he read the headlines. An attractive, bestselling author turned murderer was far too much for any editorial staff to resist. He scanned the articles one by one and felt a tightening in his chest as he realized that his assessment of the difficulty of a self-defense case was correct. Alison was being tried and convicted in the press already, and this was before they found out the true nature of her relationship with Madeline Roy. When they discovered that, all hell would break loose.

He finally gave up and went to wash his face. Then he came back into the living room to say goodbye.

"I need to get back to Truro and check on Iris. Her mother took ill yesterday, but I was in the police station talking to Alison when I got the message. I never got back to her."

"Ring her," David suggested.

"I will. It was probably a false alarm. She had a big scare the other day. I really should go."

"Let me know if there's anything I can do."

"Thank Susan, and kiss the kids for me," he said. "I'll see you soon."

His brother slapped him on the back as he left. He started his car and turned down Campden Hill Road, with the sudden feeling he'd forgotten something important. A thought stirred in the back of his brain, and he pulled over to the curb for a minute to retrieve it.

Madeline Roy was dead, but even though she was clearly not the woman they had been searching for, there still might be answers to be found to some of his more difficult questions. What was this Madeline's work history before her brief stint at the British Museum and then in Alison's employ? How in the world had the psychic had such a clear vision of her, a vision so precise it had gotten her killed, when there was no evidence to connect her to Sophie Flynn's murder?

Was there anything in Madeline's flat that might tie her to Alison, or to Karen Peterson? As long as he was already in London, he figured he might as well try to find out. Narrowly avoiding another car, McIntyre turned the car back north to head to Islington.

It was a few minutes after eight. Once in front of the building, he ran upstairs to the second floor and stood in front of the flat she shared with Brooke Turner. He raised his hand to knock, hesitating only a second before letting his knuckles rap on the door. He'd feel like an idiot if he didn't get at least something out of the flatmate. No one answered, but he heard a stirring on the other side of the door and knocked again.

A few moments later, Brooke Turner opened it. Her hair was disheveled and she'd thrown a robe over her pajamas. It was obvious that she'd been asleep. He would have felt guilty if it hadn't been so important.

"It's you again," she said, studying him through the crack in the door.

"I need to ask you a few more questions," he said. "May I come in?"

She turned and let him step into the room behind her, looking at the stack of books on the floor. He started to ask if Madeline was the reader when he realized she didn't know her friend was dead.

"Could you sit down for a minute?" He indicated the closest chair. "There's something I need to tell you."

"What is it?" she asked. Her back arched like a cat in danger, or the way people sometimes did when the police were about to tell them something horrible.

"It's about Madeline. She was killed last night, at the residence where she was staying."

Brooke Turner sank into the chair, and he sat down across from her at eye level. He couldn't bring himself to tell her that Alison was the one who had killed her. She'd hear that soon enough anyway. The whole of Britain would hear about it before the day was done.

"Are you all right?" he asked.

"I can't believe it," she said, her hand flying up to her chest. "What happened?"

"Some sort of domestic disturbance. The investigation has only just begun. I need you to tell me everything you know about her."

"I didn't know much, really. She wasn't friendly. I told you she resented having me here."

"Your parents are friends, is that it?"

"Our mothers."

"And how do they know each other?"

"They grew up together. They're still friends."

"Where did they grow up?" he asked.

"British Columbia," she answered. "Her mother married a Brit and came to live in England, and my mother met my father and stayed in Canada. But they were in touch all those years."

"British Columbia is in Western Canada," he said, almost to himself.

"Is that all?" Brooke asked, obviously eager to be rid of him. "I need to get ready. I have some things to do today."

"Wait," he said. "What did Madeline know about the woman she went to work for last month? How did she hear about the job?"

"She never confided in me, Inspector. I have no idea."

"May I see her room?" he asked.

Brooke stood and went over to open one of the doors in the small flat. He followed her and stepped through. It was a tidy room. The bed had a blue coverlet and there were leopard-print cushions that matched the curtains. There was a small dresser by the bed with a lamp and several books stacked on it. He pulled out the drawers one by one. The dresser was nearly empty.

He turned to say something to Brooke, but she'd left, probably to make her morning tea. Across from Madeline's bed was a dresser, with

278

a china dish full of coins and assorted postcards spread across the top. He lifted one to examine it. It was a copy of a watercolor of a woman in a long gown, looking out a window at night. It was a poignant image. He turned it over and read the description: *Lost Love, John Everett Millais.* He put down the postcard and looked at the lot of them. There was one of a sleek, ugly Egyptian cat. Another, a still life of nuts and apples. There was no rhyme or reason to them; she must have purchased cards that caught her fancy on any given day.

Nothing else in the room proved of interest, which didn't mean anything. Either Madeline Roy had taken the bulk of her belongings to Lincolnshire, or Brooke Turner had already gone through them. He supposed, to be fair, that it was the former. He didn't have any reason to suspect Brooke for anything in particular, although there was something about her that made him wonder. He closed the bedroom door and found her in the kitchen.

"If you think of anything I should know, ring me," he said. "I don't care how unimportant you think it is. If there's any question, I want to know about it."

She nodded, the impossible girl. He wasn't going to get anything out of her.

"Well, thank you for your time."

He closed the door behind him, muttering curses all the way down the stairs. People could be so bloody stupid sometimes. It was endemic, the lack of cooperation and mistrust of the police. Some people acted like it would kill them to share even a single relevant fact.

He stormed down to his car and headed south once again. He still hadn't rung Iris back, hoping he would have something concrete to tell her. Instead, he'd wasted his time trying to get information out of Brooke Turner. He presumed she'd been living off Madeline Roy and was disappointed that she'd have to move, although he couldn't imagine wanting to share such a small space, even for free rent. If he were Brooke, he would be answering every advert he could find in search of a job. There were ample opportunities for people to work, even people like her with disabilities. She was a nutter, he thought; a lazy good-for-nothing who was probably used to living off others, trying to get out of assuming responsibility in life.

"Bollocks!" he suddenly shouted, pulling his mobile from his pocket. He rang Dugan, hoping his sergeant would answer.

"Hi, boss," Dugan said into the phone. "I knew you'd ring."

"Alex, where the fuck is Oregon? Isn't it on the west coast? Near British Columbia?"

"I think it is, but I'll double check."

He didn't have to wait ten seconds before Dugan was back on the line. "It is, sir. Three hundred miles, give or take a few."

"Make some calls. See if you can find out if a Brooke Turner entered the UK on the same day as Iris Flynn."

"Yes, sir. I'll ring you as soon as I know something."

McIntyre turned the car around again, conjuring Brooke's face. With slightly shorter and darker hair, and without her cane and the glasses, she matched the description of Karen Peterson. He'd been standing in the same room with the woman who had murdered Sophie Flynn and hadn't even realized it. He fought the traffic and ten minutes later, he was back at the building and running up the steps.

He knocked at the door. There was no answer.

"Police!" he called. "Open the door!"

There was no sound from inside. He backed up and lifted his left leg, aiming just below the knob. He made contact with his heel and felt the door give as the force of his weight fell against it.

Brooke wasn't in the front room, but there were bags on the floor. She'd been about to flee, and if she had, they would never have found her again. He rushed to the bathroom and turned the knob, which in her haste she hadn't locked. She stood there, a razor to her wrist, and he went still in the doorway.

"Don't come any closer," she said.

He lifted his hands. "I won't, Brooke. See?"

She stared at him, breathing hard, daring him to come at her. He wasn't afraid of her turning the razor on him. She was of medium height and weight, and certainly not in the shape to be of any sort of threat. His goal was to get the razor away from her before she harmed herself. He had no desire to lose her to suicide when the judicial system needed to mete out justice for Sophie's murder. Someone with a knife or sharp weapon was prone to panic, and an opponent had to get very close to them in order for them to do any harm. The longer he stood silently without speaking, the more he threw her off guard.

Then, before she could react, he suddenly shifted his weight and lunged at her, grabbing the hand that held the razor. He wrestled it out of her hand and threw it in the bathtub as she tried to lean forward and bite him. He flipped her around and pinned her arm behind her back.

"Nice try," he said.

"Fuck you," she replied, trying to jerk out of his arms.

He tightened his grip and turned her so that she could see his face. More than anything, he wanted to see her reaction as he finally said the words he'd wanted to say for over a year.

"Brooke Turner, I'm arresting you on suspicion of murder."

THIRTY-ONE

"GRACE" WAS NOT A word Rob McIntyre used a great deal. In fact, it was not even a word he'd thought of for years until that moment. He never thought that God could be involved in the solving of cases, but there had been an unmerited favor granted him that day, when he'd had that instant realization that Brooke Turner could be Karen Peterson. Later, he wouldn't remember how it had occurred to him; he was just relieved that it had.

After she was arrested and processed by the London Metropolitan Police, she had refused a solicitor. McIntyre had her brought to an interview room and watched as she sat at the table in front of him. She already seemed a different person, without a limp and a cane and having shed the glasses. Her brown hair, no longer in its crisp bob, hung to her shoulders, now dyed the lighter color. She watched him sullenly as he sat down with her file and his cup of coffee, turning him down when he offered her one, too. He had so many questions for her, it would probably take days of questioning.

"I'm turning on the recording machine. State your name."

"Brooke Turner."

"This is DCI Robert McIntyre, interviewing Brooke Turner. The date is Sunday, the 9th of January. The time is 12:40 p.m. I need to remind you that you're still under caution. You don't have to say anything unless you wish to do so, but anything you do say may be used in evidence against you. Do you understand?"

"Yes."

"Have you waived your right to a solicitor?"

"Yes."

"You have the right to terminate this discussion at any time and seek the advice of counsel. Is that understood?"

She nodded.

"Please give a verbal answer for the record."

"Yes."

"Let's begin. You've been charged with the murder of Sophie Flynn," he said. He looked her directly in the eye, and what he saw was chilling. There was no remorse there, no repentance for her monstrous crime. "Tell me why you did it. Tell me why you killed an innocent three-year-old child."

The word "innocent" was powerful, as he knew from his many previous interviews of suspects. It made the crime more heinous than it might otherwise have seemed to the suspect. She'd had a full year to get over the shock of what she'd done, but he was determined to bring it back for her in excruciating detail.

Her hands were in her lap and her eyes were fixed, as far as he could tell, on a remote dot on the far wall, the better to ignore his questioning. She had a stubborn lift to her chin that defied the situation in which she found herself. It didn't matter, he knew. He could keep her there until she cracked if he wanted.

"There's no reason to keep silent, Miss Turner. There are plenty of witnesses. Kevin Hughes, whom you were seeing, for one. He saw Sophie on the night she died when you brought her to his house. Sean Campbell, who took you to the river, is in custody now. Even six-year-old Charlotte Flynn has told the police what she knows."

At the mention of Charlotte's name, Brooke's eyes locked onto his.

"Oh, yes," he said, now that he had her attention. "You left Charlotte with an eighteen-month-old on the rocky riverbed in Truro on a frigid December night. If those two children hadn't been found by their mother, they would have died of exposure. That is, if they didn't stumble into the river first and drown. Is that what you wanted? To kill all three of them?"

"No," she snapped. She looked away and for the first time, appeared nervous. "I didn't mean for any of them to die."

"You had a funny way of showing it, endangering all of their lives and then murdering Sophie." He extracted a form from the folder before sliding it back inside, in no effort to rush the interview. In fact, the longer he dragged it out, the more information he could get out of her. "Charlotte said you handed India to her and said to hold her. Then you disappeared with Sophie. The next time we have you pegged is when you went to Hughes's house, trying to get him to take you and the girl to London. Seemed like you might have been trying to start a family the easy way, with someone else's child."

She didn't answer.

"Is that it, Brooke? You wanted a child? Statistically, most women who abduct children want infants. They're harder to identify, easier to hide. They don't scream for their mummy when they're frightened. So, that leaves us with a question. Why not India, then? Why did you want Sophie?"

"She was her father's favorite. Mine, too."

"Ah, now we're getting to the crux of the matter. Did you have an affair with Nick Flynn?"

There was a brief hesitation before she answered. "Yes."

"In America, or England, or both?"

"America."

"Why not here as well?"

"No opportunity, for one thing, and then there was the fact that … "

"He lost interest?" McIntyre asked.

It wasn't uncommon for men to begin affairs only to tire of them the minute the woman became demanding. He had seen it plenty of times through his years on the force. It was one of the many reasons for the ongoing domestic violence crisis in the country.

"If he broke it off in the States, then why follow him here?" he added.

"I thought he didn't mean it. I thought he'd leave Iris when we got here. I don't mean that he'd divorce her, but I knew he'd want to leave sooner or later, and I could follow him wherever he went."

"If you wanted him so much, why didn't you try to get pregnant with a child yourself?" he asked.

"I can't get pregnant."

He stopped and looked at her, and then flipped open the file in front of him. "You're, let's see, twenty-six years old and unmarried. How do you know you can't get pregnant?"

"I was pregnant once." She looked away from him and for a moment, a defiant look on her face.

"What happened?" he asked.

"A botched abortion. I had to do it. I was fifteen at the time."

He sighed. As much as he wanted to feel sorry for her, he couldn't.

"So, taking Sophie was a way to get to Nick? You thought if you took his favorite child, he'd come after you? You could get him back that way?"

"Iris didn't deserve him. She didn't deserve those children, either, you know. She's a terrible mother. Something was bound to happen to them sooner or later."

He didn't comment. "Tell me what happened when you left the Hughes house. Sophie left the house without her coat and you ran after her."

"I don't want to relive it again."

"You killed a child," McIntyre stated, shaking his head. "No matter what happens, you'll relive it again and again for the rest of your life. What happened when you ran after her?"

"She was down the road when I caught her. I picked her up, but she wouldn't stop crying. She was screaming for Iris. I nearly left her there, but she was starting to attract attention."

Jesus, he thought. She almost let her go. One of the Hughes' neighbors would have heard her crying and called the police, and she would have been reunited with her frantic family and none of this would have happened. He wanted to shake Brooke Turner until her head popped off.

"And then you got a ride with Sean Campbell."

"He wasn't the first person to offer me a ride," she said. "I needed someone who wanted something more than just to help a woman and child stranded by the side of the road."

"And you got lucky," he said. "How nice for you. You got to shag a stranger in the process of shedding yourself of unwanted baggage."

"I can't explain it. Everything got out of control."

His mobile buzzed and he took it from his breast pocket. It was a text from Dugan: *You were right, sir. Brooke Turner entered the country from the US on the same day. Canadian passport.*

"Let's take a break."

He snapped off the recording machine and opened the door, nodding to the custody sergeant. "I'm done for now. Is there a place I can make a call?"

"Of course. Second door on your left."

There was suddenly nothing more important than ringing Iris and telling her that not only had they located Karen Peterson, but she'd made a confession. It would make up, he certainly hoped, for not responding earlier. He closed the door behind him and sat down before punching in her number, both terrified and pleased to have something to tell her.

As he expected, Iris sounded both exhausted and angry when she answered her mobile.

"I'm sorry I didn't get back to you right away," he began.

"Right away?" she asked. "Try twenty-four hours later. A lot can happen in twenty-four hours, Rob."

"It certainly has. I have something important to tell you."

"What is it?"

"I found Karen Peterson, Iris. She's been arrested. I'm at a station interviewing her now."

"How?" she cried. "Where was she?"

"She was in London, as we suspected. And the how, well, that's difficult. Do you remember the sketch from the day with the psychic?"

"I thought that was a dead end."

"I did, too. But this weekend, I had some leads on several Madeline Roys, and when I followed them up, it led to Brooke Turner."

"Brooke Turner?"

"Karen Peterson's real name. She was Canadian, not American. She came into the country using her real passport."

"Tell me everything."

"There's too much to tell now. We need to sit down to talk. How's your mother?" he asked. He'd forgotten to ask before getting started on the story.

"She passed away this morning," Iris said. "The cancer didn't have a chance to get her. Her heart couldn't take the strain of the last few days."

"God, I'm sorry."

"It's my fault. If it hadn't been for that man's attack—"

"It's not your fault. People have their photos put in the paper every day, and most of the time they aren't targeted because of it."

"I should never have come back to England. My mum would be alive now if it weren't for me."

"You were meant to come back, Iris," he argued. "Because of you, we found the woman who killed Sophie. You're going to see justice done for your daughter at last."

THIRTY-TWO

BY LATE AFTERNOON, MCINTYRE was in his car heading home. There was nothing else he could do for Alison at the moment. He was glad to leave London behind and get back to his house, his job, and his other cases. The weather was dull and gray, but there was no rain or snow to impede his progress. A couple of times, the wind picked up and tried to push his vehicle into the other lane and he had to concentrate on the road, but the traffic was light. He was one of the few going west on a Sunday afternoon.

He reached the house a little after four and went straight to the kitchen to make a cup of tea. Apart from the boiling kettle, the house was silent; more silent than it had been a month ago before Iris Flynn had come into his life. Yet instead of being the refuge he'd hoped for, it was suddenly full of memories, none of which he wanted to remember. He wondered if he should sell the place and move on. Stability had always been important to him—the house, plain but comfortable, suited him, and Alison had been a fixture in his life for so long that he'd never imagined living without her.

Iris had changed that. He'd actually begun to care for someone else, much to his own surprise. She was unconventional but intriguing, and although he sometimes thought of her in a protective sense, he knew she'd persevered through tougher situations than he had ever suffered and was completely capable of standing on her own. If Nick Flynn had been out of the picture, he might have carried on with this train of thought, but he wasn't the sort to interfere in someone else's marriage. Irritably, McIntyre made another cup of tea he didn't want and then decided to go to bed early.

He woke before six the next morning. Having managed to banish both Iris and Alison from his thoughts, he kept Brooke Turner at the forefront of his mind. He went to the police station and sat at his desk an hour early to start the paperwork he'd long ignored, glad to have a good resolution for this case in particular. Paperwork was never any detective's favorite part of the job, but it was crucial for an airtight case.

He was deep in thought an hour later, ticking boxes and detailing events that had led to the breaking of the case, when his phone rang.

"McIntyre," he answered.

"I'd like to see you in my office," Quinn's voice boomed into the line. He probably should have gone in to see his superintendent first thing that morning, but as always, he'd put his paperwork first.

"Yes, sir."

He sat back in his chair for a moment, then dropped his pen on the desk and walked down the corridor to Quinn's office, ready to get this conversation behind him. His boss was tapping at his computer and looked up when he walked in.

"Sit down," Quinn said, nodding to a chair. An open file lay before him on his desk that was certain to be full of notes on the Sophie Flynn case. "Let's get straight to it. You arrested the suspect in London yesterday."

"Yes, sir," McIntyre said, not volunteering anything further until he could assess the superintendent's state of mind on the matter.

"How did you find her?"

"I was checking into the leads for Madeline Roy," he answered.

"There were four, I take it?" Quinn asked, leaning forward. "Dugan filled me in while you were gone."

"That's right. Two elderly women, a deaf girl in her twenties, and then the Madeline Roy who turned out to be the woman in the police sketch drawn from the psychic's memory. The woman from the Jennings case. It was luck, I'm sure."

Quinn sat back and frowned. "I hate messing about with psychics. It muddies the waters. I'm not convinced they provide any real insight into a case."

"To be honest, I wasn't chasing down Madeline Roy because of the psychic's drawing," McIntyre replied. "She became a person of interest when Sean Campbell named her as the woman he'd picked up with a child and taken to the river." He neglected to remind his superintendent that his boss had considered the name to be one the suspect had randomly chosen, while his gut had told him otherwise. "But Miss Roy was not the child's killer," he continued. "She was the flatmate of the killer, Brooke Turner."

"Then how did the psychic draw the exact image of the Roy woman?"

"Hell if I know," McIntyre admitted. "When I interviewed her, she mentioned the possibility that she was seeing through the killer's eyes. The point is, Brooke Turner gave her flatmate's name to Sean Campbell, and we were able to track her down on the strength of that information."

"You're very lucky it worked out," Quinn said, folding his arms in front of him. "I was two minutes from shutting down the whole operation."

McIntyre nodded. "It took a year, I know, and we didn't have anything to go on until now, but the truth was, I felt the whole time that I was one step away from getting to Karen Peterson."

"I understand your former girlfriend killed Miss Roy," Quinn said. There was real sympathy in the super's face. "I'm sorry to hear it."

"I knew she'd hired an assistant," McIntyre said, "but I had no idea who it was. They argued, and Madeline was accidentally killed during the struggle."

"So, you believe it was an accident?" Quinn asked.

"I have no doubt," he replied, although the truth was he felt responsible for the whole episode. If he hadn't caused Alison to panic, none of it would have happened. "Both parties were arguing and things got out of control. It was an unfortunate mistake."

"The inquest is next week," Quinn said. "Let's hope the coroner agrees with you." He stood and walked around his desk. "You took a hell of a risk, Rob. It's lucky for you that it paid off."

"Yes, sir."

"It looks good for the department, catching the woman who killed a local child. Sets everyone's mind at rest."

McIntyre nodded. That was as far as Quinn would go, not that he needed congratulations. And given that Alison had killed Madeline Roy, who in truth was unrelated to the murder, the case was a disaster in his mind anyway.

After Quinn dismissed him, McIntyre went back to his desk and finished the paperwork, checking his caseload for the most pressing matters. Tomorrow he would start fresh and put this all behind him. Yet Alison kept creeping into his thoughts. He tried not to think about it, but every time he was able to concentrate on something else, he would lose his focus entirely. By four o'clock, his mind began to shut down. There was only one thing to do about it. He went down the hall and walked up to Dugan's desk. His sergeant was sitting deep in thought. They needed to get away from there.

"Want to get pissed?"

"Sure, boss."

The two of them grabbed their coats and went downstairs. The sharp January wind hit them when they walked out the door, and his sergeant pulled a knit cap out of his pocket and pulled it over his ears. They got into McIntyre's car and went straight to their favorite pub, an older place a few miles away called the Red Fox. It had been there long before he was born, and it hadn't been modernized in any way. That was one of the reasons he liked it. They ordered a couple of stouts and went to sit at a sticky table. He didn't even bother wiping it down. If he was lucky, he wouldn't care before the hour was out.

"I can't believe Alison killed Madeline Roy," he said without preamble. "I'm the one who alarmed her about the woman. I've fucked everything up."

"You arrested the woman who killed Sophie Flynn, boss," Dugan said, taking a gulp of his beer. He wiped the foam from his upper lip. "I don't call that fucking up."

"Trust me, Alex, this whole thing is the biggest mess since Fukushima. Nobody would have been arrested at all if Iris Flynn hadn't come back and badgered us into it. And Quinn was none too happy about me working on the case at all."

"The important thing is, it's a solved case now."

"Good point," McIntyre said, pointing at him. He took a large drink of his beer and let his eyes focus on the wood grain of the table under his elbows. "But you know, Iris was attacked by Campbell, and if she hadn't been, we wouldn't have known about Madeline Roy, which led directly to Brooke Turner. That's a fucking slim thread to hang a whole case on."

"Slim threads are all we get, sometimes," Dugan said philosophically, eating a stale crisp. "What about Brooke Turner giving Campbell Madeline Roy's name? Did she do it on purpose, or was it randomly selected, like Quinn suggested?"

His sergeant was downing his beer almost as fast as McIntyre. They really would get well and truly pissed. The thought brought him some comfort.

"You mean, did she tip her hand in case we got wise to her?" McIntyre asked, then shook his head. "No. She did what anyone does. She pulled out the first name she could think of when asked. Even though she didn't go to stay with Madeline for almost a year, it was still the only connection she knew of in England."

"Did you interview her once or twice before you figured it out?"

"Twice. I talked to her on Friday, asking if she knew where Madeline was. Then again the next morning, after Alison was arrested. I remember feeling sorry for her that I had to deliver such bad news. Can you believe it?"

"What made you go back that second time?"

McIntyre wiped the lip of his glass with his finger. "I just had an odd feeling. I can't really explain it. I also hoped to find something in Madeline's things that would lead us to the killer."

"What's going to happen to the other suspects?" Dugan asked.

"Kevin Hughes was let go with a warning not to interfere in any police investigation in the future. He really didn't know anything." McIntyre leaned back in his chair. "Sean Campbell will remain in custody. He committed two crimes, abetting a criminal and assault against Iris. He's in hot water, that one."

"I'm sorry about Miss Kendall, sir. I know that's got to hurt."

The mention of Alison's name made McIntyre go tense all over again. He leaned forward and looked at his sergeant.

"The thing is, Alex, if Alison can kill someone, anyone can," he replied. "I used to think it was just your garden variety criminals and mentals, but no. Accidents happen. Anyone can lose it. Anyone can get the wrong end of the stick and lash out. Of course, that's not to excuse her."

Dugan lifted his glass to his lips. "I know, boss."

"I mean, we all have it in us, don't we? That wild, primitive need to triumph over others. Even if it means taking a life. We'll jump to our own defense every time."

"That's where we come in, sir. If it weren't for the watchdogs, everything in society would completely fall apart."

"You're right, DS Dugan." McIntyre lifted his nearly empty glass to his sergeant. "When you're right, you're right."

"You're pissed, sir, if you don't mind my saying."

"You're a little pissed, too. Ena might not like it. That said, let's have another."

Dugan smiled. He had someone to go home to, or at least to ring if they hadn't moved in together yet. They would, sooner or later. McIntyre could see it on both their faces. He was suddenly struck by how much he wanted to see Iris. It was hard to imagine that the case was over now that Sophie Flynn's killer was found. He wanted to get into his car and drive to Cadgwith to see her. Of course, if he did, he ran the risk of upsetting her more. He hadn't been there when her mother died. He had no idea if she'd been alone on the second-most difficult day of her life. Maybe her husband had come back, or perhaps she'd finally reconciled with her brother. For her sake, he hoped so. She needed someone.

In any case, Alex was wrong about him. He was just another stupid idiot, and things fell apart whether he was involved or not. But even if he were wrong, it didn't change one thing: he may have found Karen Peterson, but he hadn't even gotten to tell Iris about it face to face.

THIRTY-THREE

Iris stood in the center of London Heathrow two weeks later, shifting her weight from one foot to another and fiddling with the red scarf about her neck. She'd never managed to return it to McIntyre, although in a way, she was glad to have something of his, a reminder of the time they'd spent together. Although they had spoken on the phone a couple of times, she hadn't seen him since he'd arrested Brooke Turner for killing her daughter. He was back to work on his usual caseload, while she was handling things after her mother's death.

She stared at the flight status board, waiting to see if it would change: *07:15, BA016, Sydney, Expected 07:22, Terminal Five.* She'd taken the train to London the day before and spent the night at a hostel, not that renting a bed for the night meant she had actually slept. She'd tossed and turned all night and left for the airport at five in the morning, in order to be a couple of hours early.

Too nervous to sit, she looked up at the clock. It was a quarter past seven, and in minutes Sarah would arrive with Charlotte and

India. For now, they would go back to her parents' house until she made other arrangements.

Her mother's house was nearly empty now. She had spent the last week filling bags with clothes and personal effects and starting the tedious business of cleaning it up. It was the first time she'd lived alone in her adult life. There was a feeling of satisfaction sorting through old boxes and cupboards, going through the detritus and treasures of her parents' lives, looking for anything that sparked happy memories. She found it, finally, in a small wooden box that had belonged to her father. Whenever he had come across a franc or deutsche mark, he'd put it into this box. When she opened it, she was surprised to find her father's pipe among the coins. He'd rarely been seen without it, especially in his last years. She'd looked for it for months after he died. In fact, once she'd accused her mother of getting rid of it just to spite her. The old familiar tobacco smell was still there, as if he'd lit it only that morning, and she'd placed it on the mantle where she could look at it every day. The kitchen walls were painted, the rugs beaten, the dust and cobwebs brushed away. The house was once again the home of her preadolescence, before her mother had succumbed to alcoholism and her father to his depression.

It would probably be sold soon. Even though she planned to take up Jonathan's offer of a job, she couldn't afford to buy her siblings' shares in the house. She'd spent much of the previous day sitting at the small table in the kitchen, staring out at the garden. It would need tending in spring. She wondered who would sit at this table and look out the window as the last of the snow melted and the daffodils and rhododendrons began to bloom. She wondered if someone would go into her father's garden and see the potential that had existed there before all those years of abandonment and neglect, and if the stone birdbath would once again collect the rain for the sparrows and wrens who would come to nest in the spring. She wanted to think that it would. She didn't know where she and the girls would live, but the truth was, it didn't matter. They would be together, which was the important thing now.

She watched as 7:22 came and went, then 7:45, before passengers began to disembark from the plane. She frowned, moving closer to the cordon, trying to get a better look at the stream of people coming down the long corridor. Dozens of people passed by before she finally saw her sister with India in her arms, holding Charlotte by the hand. A lump came into her throat. The girls wore matching dresses and coats, obviously new, and had small packs on their backs, filled, Iris was certain, with well-loved toys. Sarah thought of everything. Iris ran over to greet them when they passed through the security gate.

Sarah smiled. "I brought something for my favorite sister."

Iris took India from her sister and knelt to pull Charlotte into her arms, hugging them so tightly she thought they might break. She looked up at Sarah, who was pulling a small case behind her. For once, her beautiful sister looked more than a little rumpled, her hair pulled back in a ponytail and with no makeup on her face. She'd never felt as much love for her as she did at that moment.

"I'd hug you," she said, "but my hands are full at the moment."

"I can see that," Sarah said, squeezing her arm.

After a few minutes, Iris struggled to her feet, still clutching India and holding Charlotte's hand.

"What's the plan?" Sarah asked.

"Train to Paddington, then Cornwall, unless you're too tired. I figured the girls will sleep."

"I may sleep, too."

"Are you sure you're up for it?" Iris asked.

"I'm ready to go home."

Iris was surprised at Sarah's use of the word. Her sister had lived in Australia for more than fifteen years, yet England, and specifically Cornwall, were still home. She was pleased to hear it. They collected their bags and joined a queue leading to the railway line. After an interminable wait, they finally settled into their seats on the train.

"You've had a very long trip, haven't you?" Iris said, squeezing her children's hands. "Tell me all about it!"

"India slept most of the time," Charlotte said. She rested her head on her mother's arm. "Except when she cried."

"Of course she cried," Iris answered. "She's two. But you didn't cry, did you?"

Charlotte shook her head, in danger of crying now. Iris pulled her closer and kissed her ruddy cheek. She pulled juice boxes and biscuits from her bag and gave them to the girls.

"Juice for you, too, Aunt Sarah," Iris said, holding out a bottle. "And then a nice glass of wine later."

"If I'm awake," Sarah joked.

"I know how you feel. I couldn't sleep last night. How are Tess and Charlie?"

"They're fine. Bill's mother came to stay at the house for a few days while I'm gone."

"I can't believe what you've done for me," Iris said. "Facing the funeral, finding Karen, and clearing away years of junk from the house … it's been exhausting. All I wanted was to be with the girls."

"What are you going to do?" Sarah asked. "Are you coming back to Australia?"

"No, I want to stay here."

"If it's about money … "

"It's not about money," Iris said. "It's about finding where I belong."

Sarah pulled off her coat and put it over her knees. "Does this mean you're ending your marriage?" she asked in a low voice.

Iris looked up. "Nick left me a long time ago, Sarah. You knew it, he knew it; even I knew it. I just didn't want to admit it."

"I'm sorry. I really am. Have you heard from him?"

"He finally called. He fished for a few weeks and then he left the ship to travel north. He says it's an adventure."

Sarah nodded, keeping her thoughts to herself, but Iris knew that she would see Nick again. He would come back two or three times in the next ten years, which was all right with her. She felt no bitterness about it. She'd never been able to change him. She would love him the same as she always had: enough to let him go.

"I'm sorry I missed the funeral," Sarah said. "It's such a long trip."

"It was simple, but nice."

It wasn't long before both of the girls were asleep, India in her arms and Charlotte's head lying on Sarah's lap. They didn't talk for a long while, the lull of the rocking train making them sleepy, too. Eventually, they fell asleep. Iris woke about an hour later and shifted India into the seat next to her. Her arm had gone numb.

Charlotte woke up and came to sit next to her, reaching for another biscuit.

"Have you got some books in there?" Iris asked her, nodding at her backpack.

"Yes."

"Well, let's get them out and read for a while."

All of them were tired by the time they reached Cadgwith, where they disembarked from the train and got into the car that had belonged to Helen. Iris drove to the house, unlocking the door after everyone had tumbled out of the car. It seemed a different place, with its crisp white walls, no longer reminding her of what had recently happened there.

"You did a good job with it," Sarah said, looking around.

Charlotte turned and looked at her. "Are we staying here?" she asked.

"Yes," Iris answered. She wouldn't explain to her now that the house would be sold and once again they would be on their own, without a roof over their heads. "Why don't you look around? You'll find a room with two little beds in it. That's where you'll sleep with India."

"I want to sleep with you."

"Maybe tonight."

Charlotte peered into the hallway and disappeared to explore. India pushed herself off Iris's lap and followed her sister.

"I think they'll like it here," Sarah said. "And I don't think we should put the house up for sale right now. I'm sure Jonathan will agree with me."

"But it wouldn't be right of me to stay on without paying for it."

"It's not going to fetch a huge sum, you know, a little place like this. I see no reason to put you and the girls out on the street when we can let you get on your feet first." Sarah looked around the room. "It's not big, but there's plenty of space for the three of you, as long as you want it."

"I wish you weren't so far away, not when we're just getting to know each other again," Iris said. "And I want to spend time with Tess and Charlie."

Sarah took her hand and squeezed it. "I'll come back for visits, maybe every summer. They've grown very fond of the girls and were sad to see them go."

"Can I get you anything? Something to eat?"

"No, thanks. Actually, I thought I'd drop in to see Jonathan."

"You should go to bed for the rest of the day and let me take care of you," Iris said giving her a look. "You've got to be jet-lagged."

"I think your girls would rather have you to themselves for a night or two. I'll pop 'round for lunch tomorrow and maybe even stay with you for a couple of days before I fly home."

"I can't thank you enough, Sarah," Iris said, hugging her. "I owe you everything for letting me do this."

"You owe me nothing. You'd do the same for me." She stood. "I'm going to freshen up before I go. And may I borrow the car?"

"Of course."

A quarter hour later, they were loading her suitcase into their mother's car. Sarah got in and started the engine, rolling down the window. Iris leaned in, her hands gripping the glass.

"Come back for lunch tomorrow?"

"Yes. I'll bring Jonathan, too."

Iris stepped back and waved. All of these years, she hadn't been a proper sister, and now that she knew what their relationship could be, she would never let go. Waving, she felt a lump in her throat. She stood on the front step for a minute before going back into the house where the girls were waiting.

The afternoon was spent quietly. They unpacked their suitcases, and Iris was pleased to watch the girls find shelves for their toys and games. The room she'd grown up in had two narrow beds with a table in between, with quilts her grandmother had made folded at the foot. It wasn't large, but it was comfortable, and certainly more than they'd ever had before. Iris folded their dresses and shirts in the sole cupboard, which she herself had used as a child, and put India's stuffed quoll on her bed. They ate a bowl of figs and eventually fell asleep in her arms while she read to them from a book she'd found while cleaning out the house. Sarah had read to her often when she was small, and it brought back good memories.

Her mobile rang, and she eased the girls out of her arms and walked over to the table to answer it. She raised a brow when she saw Rob McIntyre's name on the screen.

"Hey," she said, answering the phone.

She had no idea what to expect.

"I have some news," he said. "Brooke Turner pled guilty in court to killing Sophie. She'll be sentenced soon."

Iris brought her hand to her chest. It felt as if the wind had just been knocked out of her. "It's over now, isn't it? It's finally over."

"Well, essentially, yes. We solved the crime and have a confession in the books."

"You never think that letting someone into your life will tear your entire world apart, and yet that's just what happened with Brooke. I trusted the wrong person and ended up losing my child."

"No one deserves that, Iris. You have to remember that. It could have happened to anyone."

"But it didn't, and it doesn't just affect me and Nick and the girls. The consequences are far-reaching."

"Like for Alison," he murmured.

"What will happen to her?" Iris asked. She'd read a headline on a newspaper in the shops but didn't buy the paper. She knew the bare facts but hadn't been able to handle the gory details just yet.

"She's been charged with involuntary manslaughter. She didn't go back home to kill Madeline, but through reckless conduct a death occurred anyway. I hired a solicitor for her, and he feels she may be acquitted, but if she's convicted, she'll probably only serve the minimum sentence of one year."

"I'm sure that's hard for you."

"There's a lot out of our control."

"It's part of being alive, I suppose," Iris said.

"You know," he replied, "the best part of being alive is that every day we have a chance to start over."

India had woken and ran to find Iris. She wrapped her small body around Iris's legs, looking up at her expectantly.

"What are you doing tonight?" he asked, suddenly.

Iris reached out and brushed her daughter's bangs away from her face, smiling into her dark and beautiful eyes.

"Cooking for you, I think," she answered. "If you don't mind having fish fingers."

ACKNOWLEDGMENTS

There are so many wonderful people who help and inspire me when I write, and I'd like to extend my thanks to each of them.

Victoria Skurnick, my agent extraordinaire, who always encourages and guides me in the right direction.

The Midnight Ink team, a wonderful group of people dedicated to making great books: thank you to Terri Bischoff, Amy Glaser, Sandy Sullivan, Katie Mickschl, and everyone else who has been involved with *Penhale Wood*.

Some books are more intense than others to write, and I was bolstered by the dear friends who encourage me and distract me when I need it. Thank you, Lori Naufel, Leslie Purcell, and Cindy Gross, true friends all. And an extra thank you to Connie Miller, for everything.

I'd like to acknowledge the Information Department at Harrods, who came through with some specific details to add to the story. In addition, I was aided by some very kind members of the Devon and Cornwall Constabulary in Truro, England, to ensure I had my details correct. My sincere thanks to each of you.

I'm lucky to have a family who values writing and the time it takes to put a novel down in written form. In particular, my daughters, Caitlin and Heather, are talented, helpful, and encouraging. I appreciate you both.

And most importantly, I'd like to thank my husband, Will Thomas. Several years ago, we began this journey of writing books. I practiced the craft of writing while working as his assistant, and he not only encouraged me to write, but believed in me from the beginning. Thank you, always, for your love and support.

© Justin Greiman

ABOUT THE AUTHOR

Julia Thomas (Oklahoma) is a graduate of Northeastern State University and an educator. *Penhale Wood* is her second novel.